WHAT YOU WISH FOR

James Patric

COVER ART

www.getdigitalorange.com

MORE ABOUT THIS AUTHOR

WWW.JamesPatric.com

CHAPTER

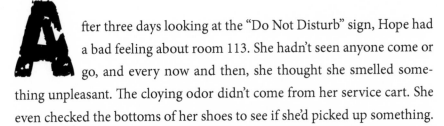

Present day.

After three days looking at the "Do Not Disturb" sign, Hope had a bad feeling about room 113. She hadn't seen anyone come or go, and every now and then, she thought she smelled something unpleasant. The cloying odor didn't come from her service cart. She even checked the bottoms of her shoes to see if she'd picked up something.

She informed Clifford, the night manager of the Lucky Lodge. He checked the registration card and found that the occupant had paid for a week, cash in advance. He found the master key and went to the room.

Cliff knocked three times without an answer. He announced himself and turned the unlocked doorknob. Swinging the door open, he was stunned by a wave of cold, putrid air. Recoiling from the stench, he saw the body lying on the bed with a length of surgical tubing connecting the tank to the plastic bag. Cliff muttered, "Second one this week."

Detective Eugene E. Perkins stretched out behind his low-bid government desk engrossed in an *Arizona Byways* magazine. An African American man in his early forties, Gene had a light-cocoa complexion, light-brown eyes to match, and a random spread of freckles. He had been a homicide detective for the Glendale Police Department for fifteen years and loved it. He was an immaculate dresser. His father had been a sharp dresser and had often told his son, "If you want to be taken seriously, you got to look sharp and be sharp."

Gene was given the nickname "Perk" before the other cops discovered that his middle name was Elvis, and from that day on, they called him "The King." He occasionally grumbled about his nickname knowing that if the other cops knew that he really liked it, they'd start calling him something else just to screw with him.

Detective Linda Garcia leaned into the office. "Ski wants to see us, now."

In her early thirties, Linda had been on the murder crew for seven years. She was Mexican American with a medium-brown complexion that flowed over features echoing her Indian heritage. Her close-cropped black hair was just turning prematurely gray. She worked rigorously at her cross-fit training for self-preservation. Linda was slim, muscular, and prone to quick, precise moves. She shopped discount clothing stores, having lost too many outfits to blood, vomit, and torn fabric. Widowed with a son, Linda was consumed by her job, physical training, and her family. Losing her husband in Afghanistan had left a chasm in her life. The other cops sometimes called her "Chica," mostly when she was out of earshot.

Gene rose from his chair, rolled down the sleeves of his sky-blue Oxford shirt, slipped into his dark olive-green suit jacket, straightened his blue-and-green striped tie, and glanced at himself in a small mirror perched on the filing cabinet. Gene's thing was to be stylishly crisp, and damn, if he didn't look good today. He followed Linda to Dave Lipinski's windowless, glass-aquarium-like office.

Lieutenant David Lipinski was stumbling into retirement age without a clue about what to do with himself when he finally left the job. He was pink from his frayed collar to the fringe of spiky gray hair that ringed his scalp. Tired, knowing eyes peered out from his fleshy face. He was a nondrinker who looked like a drunk. A vague odor of tobacco rose from his rumpled brown suit. No one in the bureau could remember when he last stood for dress inspection.

Ski sailed a piece of paper at Linda. "You and the King go check this out. Looks like another suicide at the 8 Ball Lodge. Probably a self-snuffer, but I want you to put some eyes on it."

Gene leaned in toward Ski and said in a confidential tone, "Ski, nothing personal, but I know a good dry cleaner."

Ski growled, "Get the hell out of here."

Linda drove down Glendale Avenue through heavy traffic to San Fernando Road, turning south toward Glassell Park.

Scanning the passing commercial buildings, Gene asked, "How's Jesse doing?"

Linda smiled. "He's getting to be quite a little man. He's obsessed with cars, all kinds of cars. Now he wants to go to the drag races in Pomona. What's up with you?"

"Doris got an invitation to a charity costume ball."

Linda laughed. "She got you into a costume?"

"I found a maroon double-knit leisure suit and a pair of white shoes at the thrift store. I went as my father."

The 8 Ball Lodge was located in an industrial area bordering on Los Angeles and was a constant source of police activity. Hourly rates for dealers, tweakers, hypes, and hookers. When your life finally slid down the drain it was circling, the Lodge was waiting for you.

The crime-scene van was parked askew in the parking lot, along with two Glendale black-and-whites, and a Los Angeles Police Department cruiser. Linda parked next to the LAPD black-and-white. Gene took a bottle of medical chest rub from the glove box and spread some in each nostril to mitigate the stench he knew would come from examining the body. He offered the bottle to Linda. "No thanks," she said.

"It's your funeral. You want to touch the flesh or take the notes?" Linda had no love of corpses and simply held up her notebook.

Gene recognized the L.A. cop sitting in his cruiser. "Hey Junior, what're you doing here? You don't get enough of this crap in L.A.?"

"Just divorced, thought it might cheer me up."

Gene bumped his fist and walked to room 113. He was pleased with the investigation process in place. It looked like everyone was managing the scene correctly. Cliff was talking to a uniformed sergeant when Gene broke in. "Detective Perkins, Glendale P.D. Who discovered the body?"

Cliff hesitated, changing his focus. "I'm the manager. I guess I did. I mean, Hope suspected something might be wrong. You know, the smell? So, I went to check it out. The door was unlocked."

"Unlocked? Who's Hope?"

"She's the room cleaner. I got the master key, but I didn't need it. The door was unlocked, so I just opened it. The air was going full blast on the coldest setting, and the body was just lying there hooked up to that tank." Cliff gave up a little involuntary shiver.

"Wait here." Gene stretched on his purple nitrile gloves, put some paper booties over his shoes, and turned to room 113 followed by Linda. He looked expectantly at the technicians, who nodded their assent for him to enter the scene.

"Hi, Murph. What's your take?" Tim Murphy shrugged. "Don't know, King. It's a new one for me. A hose from the tank goes under the bag. Apparently asphyxiated. I found a bottle of Bourbon whiskey on the counter. Looks like she was drinking up some courage." He handed Gene a clear plastic evidence bag. Inside was a note scrawled on a Pizzeria napkin. The message read, "Such a fool." Gene gave Murphy a skeptical look.

Gene examined the body, "I don't see any trauma or signs of violence." Next, he examined the gas contraption, noting that the brown gas cylinder was marked "Helium." Lastly, he looked for any of her possessions. "Did you find her ID, phone, or keys?"

Murphy shrugged, "Nothing. No purse either."

Gene looked around the room examining the whiskey and glass. "Only one glass?" Tim nodded yes. Gene pointed at several rings on the counter, and Tim took a picture, "Could have set the glass down a couple times."

"Could have, or maybe she had some company, and they took their glass."

Gene and Linda left the room, allowing the technicians to wind up their evidence gathering, so the coroner could take away the body. Before leaving, Linda directed more questions to Cliff. "Do you recognize the woman on the bed?"

"It's kind of hard, but I don't think I've seen her before," Cliff said.

Linda asked, "Who rented the room?"

"A woman."

"What did she look like?"

Cliff made a considerable effort to concentrate. "Nice-looking, thirties, slim, dark hair, pretty, not one of the usual skanks or crack whores. Clean-looking."

"Did you see any other strange people around, maybe coming in or out of this room?"

"Well, they're all strange, but it's just been the usual freak show. The pizza delivery guys come here a lot. Maybe one of them delivered a pie."

"Where's her car?" Linda asked.

"I looked. It's not here."

"Make?"

"A small white four-door foreign job. Don't remember the make."

"Did you ever see her after check-in, see anyone else with the car?" Gene asked.

"No. She just paid a week in advance for a single occupancy, not a big deal to me. No percentage in asking too many questions in this place."

Gene nodded his understanding. Cliff might be smarter than he looked.

"Registration card?" Gene asked.

Cliff showed them a registration card that read, "Dolly Madison."

Gene said, "I don't suppose you've read much history?"

"What?" Cliff puzzled. Gene shook his head and handed the card to Linda.

"No license number on the card."

Gene approached Henry Biggs, the sergeant supervising the uniformed cops.

"Bad news, Hank. It's a 'wobbler.' We need to canvass the whole area for at least three blocks up and down, check for witnesses, and any security videos. Better check any pizza delivery places within two miles." We'll check the local traffic violations, parking cites, and tow companies.

Biggs nodded his assent. "What're we looking for besides a guy with a sign that says, "I did it?'"

"A small white car with a nice-looking, slim, middle-aged woman, dark hair. Not much to go on."

6

"No problem. I have two new guys on probation, they'll think it's exciting."

Linda finished her notes before they left, making sure she hadn't forgotten anything.

Driving away, Gene said, "I'm getting hungry. The Bavaria Haus is close."

"You're the only cop I know who has an appetite after looking at a body."

Linda turned west on Fletcher Drive toward the Silver Lake area of Los Angeles.

"So, Doris is okay with you missing her high-school reunion and going off on some picture-taking safari?"

"I don't know if a trip to Arizona counts as a safari. She said I didn't have to go to the reunion; said I'd be a throbbing pain in the ass. She's right, as usual."

"I think it's over for you. Your wife isn't worried about you horn-dogging it with some girlfriend while she's away? You must be old and harmless."

"Stop trying to wind me up. It's called mutual trust."

Linda parked in front of the restaurant, and they walked into the dark, cool, cave-like interior. Gene took off his coat and carefully folded it, and they slid into a well-worn booth. Gene rolled up his sleeves and tucked his tie inside his shirt. Linda watched the ritual with feigned exasperation.

A middle-aged waitress dressed in a peasant outfit greeted them in a soft German accent. She placed menus, paper beer coasters, and a couple of setups on the table.

Gene ordered a cup of goulash to start, then the bratwurst plate with sauerkraut, potato salad, red cabbage, and a German draft beer.

Linda played it safe with a turkey sandwich, mustard, and a diet cola.

"You're going to explode," she said.

7

"Doris has her book club tonight. This is my dinner."

"I think I'll keep the windows down on the way back to the station. What do you think about our sleeper?"

Gene scratched his chin and said, "Well, obviously we need to find out who she is and if she was the registered occupant."

"Did she have any company?" Linda asked.

"Who cracked the gas valve? Assisted suicide?" Gene added.

"This is a new one on me. Usually it's a twelve-gauge in the garage for the guys or a bottle of pills for the gals," Linda observed.

"There was a book a while back. *Leaving Life*. It basically covered the ethics and means of suicide-on-demand. It caused lots of controversy because some people blamed the book for a jump in suicides. Then there was that guy who used to run around in his van helping people kill themselves. Anyway, the helium thing is supposed to be painless. So far no one's come back to dispute that claim."

"You know the old saying: if you want to make sure, take a bunch of sleeping pills, jump off a tall building, and blow your brains out on the way down." Linda said.

Gene examined his napkin. "The note looked like bullshit to me. What kind of a note is that? 'Such a fool,' soap opera stuff."

"Maybe she was just too far inside herself and beyond caring. Only about a third of them leave notes anyway, even Hemingway didn't leave one."

"Now, that was a serious case of writer's block," Gene chuckled.

Linda wondered, "So, why would you kill yourself in a dump like the Lodge? Why not get a decent place? Go to a nice hotel, get a rib eye, a couple martinis, eat the pillow mint, and then gas yourself? Put it on the card and stick it to the hotel?"

Gene nodded agreement. "Good question, considering she was wearing quality clothes. Her shoes cost maybe three hundred easy."

"The Lodge is a self-cleaning oven; no one notices and no one cares. Could be someone not wanting attention."

"On the ID issue, that place is full of scumbags, and the door was unlocked. Someone might have gotten in there and stolen her purse before Cliff found her.

Linda added, "Maybe it's a lame attempt to make it look like a robbery?"

"My socks are on until we get the toxicology and autopsy reports. We need to talk to any family, check insurance and medical records. If she was drugged, it might be murder," Gene said.

"Or just a guarantee that she wouldn't chicken out," Linda added.

The waitress came, deftly balancing the plates of food, placing them on the table. Gene tucked his napkin under his chin and drank deeply from the German draft.

"Man, why can't they make beer like this in the States?"

"They do." Linda sipped her diet cola. "You think it's murder, don't you?"

Smiling over his beer mug, Gene said, "Oh, yeah."

Arriving home that evening, Gene found Doris's book club meeting going full tilt in the living room. He kissed her. "Babe, what's up?" He waved to all the ladies and made a quick visual check of the Chardonnay bottles on the coffee table. He suspected the book club was really a wine-tasting club using best sellers for coasters.

"Christine's husband has the flu, so we moved the meeting over here. There's a sandwich in the kitchen."

Gene kissed her again. "You're the best. I'll get out of the way."

He changed his clothes under the supervision of Stokley, Doris's black cat. He went to the kitchen to pick up his sandwich, a can of stout from the fridge, and carried his dinner into the den.

Gene shuffled through his LP records. A Johnny Hartman album fairly jumped into his hand. He started the turntable and dropped the needle. Hartman's honey-smooth voice invaded him. "That's more like it."

He opened his briefcase and took out everything he had so far on the Sleeper death. He pinned all of it on a corkboard covering the wall. He stood looking at the pictures for a while, drinking his stout, and then toasted the woman on the bed. "I'll get 'em." Gene sat down in the chair, turned up the volume with the remote, and unwrapped his sandwich. Meatloaf.

Linda arrived home late and was jumped by her son as soon as she came through the door. Jesse was a handsome fourteen-year-old young man. His open face was framed with reddish brown hair, an inheritance from his redheaded father. "Hi, Mom, are we still going to the car show tomorrow?"

Linda kissed him. "I promised, didn't I?"

She moved to the kitchen, kissing her mother. "That smells good. Carnitas?"

Linda's mother was a diminutive woman wearing glasses, with her gray hair drawn into a bun. She wore a pink sweat suit and bright pink athletic shoes.

"Your favorite. I made tortillas."

"What a week! I'm hungry."

Her mother shot her a disapproving glance. "I know what you are doing. He's too young to have a car."

"We've been through this. He has to do things that his father would have done with him. I'm going to make sure it happens. He needs something constructive to do, and I'm going to do this with him."

Her mother mumbled something in Spanish about getting a man.

After dinner, Linda searched online looking for cars. She found several that suited her and called the indicated numbers. After a short conversation with the last seller, she hung up.

Early Saturday morning Linda gathered up Jesse and her travel coffee cup. They got into her car, and she told him, "Change of plans."

"Mom, you promised!"

"The car show will still be on tomorrow if you want to go. Today we are doing something else."

Jesse wasn't thrilled, but he resigned himself to a delayed car show visit.

Linda checked the address and drove to East L.A. She slowly cruised up and down the cracked streets lined with old frame houses, looking for an address.

Jesse was annoyed, "What're we doing here?"

"Quiet." She spotted an address and parked in front of an old well-maintained bungalow-style home with potted flowers and a comfortable-looking rocking chair on the porch.

"Come on. Watch, don't talk." They climbed the chipped concrete steps and rang the doorbell. A young Chicano opened the door. He was dressed in a clean white T-shirt, baggy shorts, and plastic sandals. In his mid-twenties, he wore a goatee. His curly hair was wet and slicked back from a recent shower.

"Omar?"

"Yeah. You're Linda?"

"Right. This is Jesse."

Omar gave Jesse a nod. "Go down the driveway. I'll meet you in back."

Linda walked down the old driveway, the kind with two concrete tracks and a grass median down the center that had long ago gone to dirt.

The driveway opened onto a concrete apron spotted with oil stains and some scattered nuts and bolts. The nose of a beautifully restored 1965 Chevy Impala was visible just inside the single-car garage. It was painted deep black with bright red upholstery. The interior of the garage was bathed in fluorescent light and stuffed with an old cluttered workbench, an engine hoist, and an air compressor. Car parts and tools hung on the walls all the way up to the rafters.

Omar opened a tall wooden gate into a backyard that was now serving as a parking lot. Five old cars were neatly parked on the dirt among the occasional patches of brown grass. Linda saw two old Chevy Impalas, a Mustang from the early seventies, a 1948 Dodge pickup truck, and a white 1971 Dodge Dart. "There it is." Omar pointed to the Dart with a black vinyl top. "My aunt died, and I picked up the car from her family. You know how it is with guys and old cars. I couldn't turn it down. Trouble is, I have too many projects now, so it has to go."

"Seventy-five thousand miles. It's a California car so the body is good; some minor surface rust but no serious rot. The interior is great. Still got the old plastic covers she put on the seats." He chuckled, pointing to the yellowed vinyl seat covers. He lifted the hood to reveal the engine. "The engine turns over but it doesn't start now. I haven't had time to mess with it. These old Slant-Sixes are bulletproof, so it's probably something minor. The trans was okay when I parked it, but I wouldn't trust the brakes without some work."

Linda looked the car over. Not as bad as she expected. She whispered to Jesse. "You like it?" He nodded his wide-eyed approval.

"How much are you asking?

"Seventeen hundred."

"Too much for Jesse. It needs a lot of work, and that engine bothers me. A rebuild would be expensive, not to mention the brakes. I can do a grand."

"No way." Omar shook his head. "This is a classic. I can get fifteen easy."

Linda looked at the car for a long moment. "I still have to pay to tow it home. It's for Jesse. We're going to restore it together. We've been watching the car channels on cable, and he's had a couple auto shop classes at school."

"That's very cool. A lot of kids don't know nothing about cars anymore, just gas 'em and crash 'em. Look, I've got a cousin who works for a towing company. I can throw in a free tow to your house."

Linda reached in her pocket and held out a fold of hundreds. "Here's thirteen. Jesse saved all the money himself. It's all we can afford. Deal?"

Omar looked physically pained. "Okay." He reluctantly shook her hand and took the money. He patted Jesse on the shoulder. "I want you to come back and show it to me when you're done fixing it up."

Jesse grinned. "Sure."

"I'll get the pink."

On the way home Jesse was excited but a little concerned. "I don't know anything about fixing cars!"

"Neither do I, but Uncle Rudy does, and he's going to help us."

"This is so cool, but you lied to him."

"Negotiating for cars is a gray area."

CHAPTER

.... *2* ....

Several months earlier.

Scott Milner slumped in his chair, his face an expressionless mask. He was resolved to endure the mind-numbing organizational training session with stoicism. Today's topic, Sexual Harassment, was particularly excruciating. He was convinced that Human Resources had chosen a warm Friday afternoon just to torture the staff. Fiona Dalton, the Human Resources Director, was inflicting the punishment with far more enthusiasm than the topic warranted.

Fiona was all business, sporting her "In charge" black pinstriped power suit and her severely coiffed silver-blond hair. New to the organization, she was rapidly developing a reputation as the "Black Widow" because of her arrogance and condescension. Fiona was a woman on a mission. She bristled with a true believer's fervor, oblivious to the daggerlike stares of some employees. The room was five degrees too warm, and people were nodding off like hypes in a shooting gallery.

Scott thought that Fiona might be losing some steam and hoped for a merciful end before happy hour had completely expired, but getting her second wind Fiona banged away. "Our employer has taken a strong stand against hostile workplace environments. There have been too many complaints in the recent past. You're mandated to practice our new code of conduct while at work. Failure to take this new policy seriously will have unpleasant consequences."

Fiona forged on. "Next week you will be directed to sign an amendment to your employment contract wherein you recognize that a violation of the new code of conduct can be good cause for immediate termination of your employment."

One young man, obviously distressed at the draconian nature of the code imposition, spoke up. "I don't think this is legal. How can you violate our first amendment rights and mandate that we accept this abridgement of our freedom of speech after employment? We already signed our employment contract before this new policy went into effect."

Fiona addressed the challenger as one might club a pup seal. "If you're going to lean on your rights, you had better understand that they're limited. In fact, some of the things you probably think are your rights are simply not. When you signed a contract to work for this company and act as its agent, the company gained the legal right to limit any activity that would be injurious to the best interests of the organization and/or other employees. To the case in point, sexual harassment is against the law, and you do not have the right to violate the law. Read your contract. There is a provision permitting either party to cancel the contract with a thirty-day notice. If you don't like the new policy, we'll accept your resignation.

"To summarize, quid pro quo sexual harassment, trading favors for sex, is strictly forbidden. Employees are not allowed to romantically fraternize in the workplace. Any employee romance issues will be resolved by the transfer or firing of one or both of the participants.

"Any behavior, including jokes, touching, comments, leering, etc., that are deemed to be offensive or distressing to another employee will be subject to disciplinary action up to and including immediate dismissal.

"There's a toll free phone number that employees may use to anonymously report violations of our new policy."

Silence fell on the room.

Scott's phone vibrated. Carol in Finance. He opened the attachment and found himself looking at a picture of her naked breasts. He looked closer. Was that whipped cream?

Scott was managing his late thirties reasonably well. He was a good-looking guy, with thinning brown hair, and a salesman's winning smile that showcased his whitened teeth. His personal fitness had taken a back seat to work and happy hours lately, so he wasn't thrilled about the thickening of his middle. Incubating love handles aside, he still thought of himself as a decent-looking guy.

Back in his office Scott nervously paced behind his desk, Fiona's warnings having cratered his motivation and elevated his anxiety. He was plagued by distressing thoughts that wouldn't stay suppressed.

Scott watched the tops of people's heads bobbing and dipping among the personal items attached to the tops of their cubicles. Everyone seemed to be in good spirits, winding up their Friday in anticipation of an emancipating weekend.

Scott closed his briefcase, turned off his computer, and checked both his mobile phones. Two more messages from Carol: "I love you," and five minutes later, "Thinking about you" and the picture of her breasts again. He had to do something about that before it bit him in the ass.

Scott grabbed his jacket, picked up his briefcase, and locked his office. Walking out, he got a text from Jeff, his longtime Army friend who had a nearby legal practice. "Chi-Chi?"

"Fifteen minutes, at The Cat," he responded.

Scott sat with Jeff Teller in a corner booth of The Catamaran Restaurant, a South Seas–themed steakhouse and tropical bar. They casually scanned the female diners.

Jeff was a successful attorney in his mid-thirties. He was darkly handsome, confident, charming, and wore an expensive suit with authority. Women in the restaurant marked his presence with furtive glances. He had been divorced for three years and was making the most of it.

Scott opened the conversation with the obligatory prompting about Jeff's latest romances. "So, how's your love life?"

Jeff glanced at his drink and smiled. "My wings have been clipped. I found a great woman. I'm looking for the fatal flaw but absolutely nothing so far. Marie's smart, funny, interesting, self-reliant, and gorgeous. She's fantastic."

"When you're tired of her, what do you think you'll use to justify the breakup?"

"That's not happening, my cynical friend. It's been three years since Bette and I split up, and I'm fed up with one-night stands and losers. I tried online dating, but the net is infested with losers and gold diggers. By the time you cull out the alcoholics, addicts, smokers, religious nuts, and the ones that are just creepy, there isn't much left but the cat lovers, and I'm allergic.

Scott tried to gin up some plausible enthusiasm. "Congratulations. How did you find her?"

"Online."

"Of course."

Jeff asked, "How's the home life?"

"Amy's doing great; she's the best thing in my life. No teenage rebellion yet, so I'm still a good guy to her. Dana and I are in a weird place."

"Meaning?"

"Well, it seems like I can't do anything right. She's always pissed off. We fight about one stupid thing after another. We don't seem to get along on anything. Our sex life went to hell. We've been together seventeen years, and our marriage is falling apart like a leper on a trampoline."

"I didn't know it was that serious."

"It gets worse."

"What else?"

Scott pulled out his phone and showed Jeff the naked picture. "Carol, in Finance."

"You're a moron."

"Yeah, I know, and she's developing into a problem. It's turned into something serious for her. She's tried to interject herself into my life away from work. I'm afraid she is going to blow it and cause me real problems."

Jeff swept his second Chi-Chi across the breadth of the restaurant, aiming his tiny umbrella at a table with three attractive women. "Look around man, dozens of women looking for romance, and you couldn't find someone in a bar or anywhere else except at work?"

"Things went fine for a while, just sex and a couple laughs."

Jeff observed. "Yeah. Well, everything's always great until somebody wants out, and then the crap hits the fan."

"She seemed okay at first, but the more you peel it back, she's really unstable. She grew to be manipulative, needy, and possessive. I wouldn't put it past her to take a shot at my marriage. I heard a rumor that once she tried to kill herself, for Christ's sake."

"You sound like the rest of my clients. They never ask my advice on the front end, then we spend lots of billable hours on the back side discussing how to get them out of their self-inflicted dilemma. Did you promise her anything in exchange for sex or pressure her?"

"God, no!"

"Have you done any fooling around at work?"

"Definitely not, always at her friend's place while she's away working."

"Does anyone else at your office know about the relationship?"

"Not from me. I cautioned her not to talk about it, but she's such a loose cannon, I guess I don't really know."

"Did you call her on your company phone or email her?"

"No way. I use a burner phone to call her. I turn it off and hide it in my car at night."

"You need to check her social media right away and see if she's planted any problems for you."

"I don't think she's into that stuff, but I'll check."

"This isn't that bad. If you're busted, you might pull off a complete denial. If you have to admit to something, your defense is that it was a consensual adult relationship away from the workplace. It's none of the company's business because there is no nexus to the company's business. Luckily, there's no supervisory relationship. Keep those photos. They could be a defense. It's hard to claim you are a victim of sexual harassment when you're emailing pictures of your tits everywhere."

"I've got to end this without a mess."

"Just try to gradually ease off. Drop hints that your marital life is straightening out, and you don't want to hurt your daughter. Invent some disease for Dana or Amy. Just moonwalk away until she gets the hint. If you are lucky, maybe she'll just attach herself to someone else. Don't confront her or aggravate her."

19

"That's kind of how I figured it. I'm not ready to pull the plug on my marriage, and I'm certainly not willingly biting off the alimony, community property, and child support for her."

Jeff ordered two more drinks. "A lot of rulebook-thumping bureaucrats are cowards when it comes to actually looking someone in the eyes and firing them. If they threaten you, don't get guilty and volunteer to resign. Force them to be the moving party, and threaten them with wrongful discharge. Come see me, and I'll write them a letter. They won't know whether to crap or check their in-baskets. You're going to need a story if you're confronted by your wife or the company. Don't be caught without a plan. Anticipate the questions and make your responses believable. Know what you want to say, but don't sound rehearsed. Trust me. I'm an attorney, and artful lying is my oeuvre. Now you can buy me another drink and a rib eye for the free advice."

CHAPTER

.... *3* ....

Scott drove home in an alcoholic fog. He pressed the remote control, but the garage door refused to open. "Damn." He sat there looking at the garage door, listening to Steely Dan's "Deacon Blues" until the battery saver shut off the radio. "Now Becker's dead."

The front door to his home opened, and Amy bounced down the steps.

"Dad, what're you doing?"

"Hi, sweetheart. Just thinking about work. It was a difficult week, and I'm fried."

"Mom's mad. She says to come in and get some dinner."

"You go inside, and I'll be in right away."

Amy tossed "Hurry" over her shoulder as she returned to the house.

Scott opened his car door and walked unsteadily back to the trunk. He felt around inside of his briefcase, cursing softly, and he finally located the burner phone in his coat pocket. He turned it off and hid it in the spare-tire well.

Once in the kitchen, Dana glared at him over a glass of wine. "Were you planning on sleeping in the car tonight?"

"Catastrophic energy failure."

"It's eight o'clock. You could have called."

"Sorry, Jeff wanted to get a drink. Time got away from us."

"So that's more important than your family?" Scott ignored the challenge.

"What's on Jeff's mind, other than women?"

"He's in love; a one-woman guy now."

"You mean this week?"

"He sounds serious and quite committed."

"Do you remember that this is my retreat weekend?"

"Uh, yeah," Scott lied, happy to be sticking close to home with Amy.

"Sounds like you forgot. You get to take care of Amy all weekend. I should be back late Sunday evening."

"What goes on at these things?"

"I pay good money to drink mediocre wine and compare husband horror stories. You're on the program."

Scott woke at ten minutes to nine on Saturday morning with a crackling headache and his mouth puckering like the inside of a vacuum dust bag. He showered, pulled on shorts and a T-shirt, and shuffled down to the kitchen.

He found Amy, a pretty girl of fifteen, engrossed in her laptop. She had long brown hair, and her blue eyes and pleasant face were complemented by incredibly beautiful skin. She was sitting at the breakfast table in her sleep clothes, intently watching the screen. "Mom left about seven."

"How about some breakfast?"

"I ate." Amy still concentrating on her laptop.

"I'm not impressed by the yogurt and fruit thing. I'm making a scramble."

Scott cracked four eggs and beat them with milk, diced up some ham, and poured it all into a pan. He tossed a couple English muffins in the toaster, sprinkled herbs and feta cheese over the eggs, started a cup of tea, and sent out a feeler. "Got anything you'd like to do this weekend that doesn't involve buying a new car?"

"I want to go to a poetry reading this afternoon. I just love the poet who's going to be reading at the Busted Mug in Pasadena."

"Really? Poetry's a new one. I don't seem to recall that from any- where." Scott quickly ran over the names of some poets in his mind in a vain attempt to establish parental relevance. Frost, Kipling, maybe Ferlinghetti or Ginsberg? He wisely abandoned that avenue of bonding.

"My English lit teacher introduced us to poetry. I really like it. There also happens to be a cute boy in class who likes the same poets that I do."

"Okay, my dad decoder ring just started glowing. I bet the cute guy is faking the poetry thing so he can put some moves on you."

"Dad! You're such a cynic. Jordan is a nice guy."

"Jordan? What is he, a missionary?"

"Stop joking. Can we go?"

"I wouldn't miss it. Come over here and eat a decent breakfast for a change."

Scott parked off of Green Street and walked with Amy to the Busted Mug. The coffeehouse was located in a large, old, renovated two-story home. Probably made in the twenties, the old dame was now an orphan among the condominiums and commercial buildings that had grown around her. A young woman greeted them at the entrance. She had long straight hair, wore a beaded headband, a long granny dress, and sandals. Scott paid the cover charges in exchange for two coffee drink tickets. They found a small table and ordered lattes from another hippie impostor. A chalkboard resting on a chair identified the three poets holding forth that evening. Scott sipped his coffee, which was quite good, and resigned himself to a culturally diverse evening, secure in the knowledge that his DVR was recording the Dodgers at home.

The first poet was a young man wearing expensive distressed jeans and a designer hoodie. He earnestly lectured the audience on the social justice issues of the day and challenged the audience to join the righteous battle against inequality. Unmoved, Scott wondered how seriously one had to take an affluent white kid with acne and dreadlocks.

Poet number two was an older guy wearing a Chargers jersey, cargo shorts, and sandals. His long gray hair was artfully disheveled. Scott liked his lighthearted ramble through his life's ironies, contradictions, and puzzlements. Scott speculated that he probably benefited from a steady income secured by a disability check. He wondered if the wise old sage persona got him an occasional night in bed with a young female admirer.

Scott stole glances at Amy. She looked so excited and engaged that he had to smile at her enthusiasm for a newfound pleasure.

Scott excused himself at the intermission for a trip to the men's room. When he returned, a young man was sitting at their table talking to Amy. He was slightly built and had a ponytail. Scott got a glimpse of some ink under the collar of his shirt. As Scott sat down, Amy introduced him as Josh, another poetry lover. Scott's parental "protector detector" pinged, and for no tangible reason, he instantly disliked Josh.

"Mom took me here a couple weeks ago, and I met Josh. We like the same poets."

Scott shook Josh's hand. "Nice to meet you. Are you a poet?"

"Ah, no. I just like poetry. I hang out here a lot."

"Are you a student? What do you do when you're not listening to poetry?"

"I'm a senior at Pasadena High School. I'm going to Cal State L.A. when I graduate this year."

"No kidding. How old are you?"

"Eighteen. Why?"

"Just curious. Did Amy tell you she's fifteen?"

Amy corrected. "Almost sixteen."

The conversation died as the last poet took the stage and the lights dimmed. This was the poet Amy had come to see. She was an angular woman in her thirties with gray eyes, and black hair with a green streak down the middle. She read from a small self-published book of her own poetry. Scott listened attentively for Amy's sake. The reading was interesting, but dwelled a little too much on her adventurous sex life to suit Scott. He rationalized that he couldn't control all of Amy's life. She was growing up and bound to hear it somewhere.

Scott carefully watched Amy and Josh during the reading. He was developing his suspicions about Josh. They seemed to be enthralled with the spoken words, and looked at each other a little too often and far too warmly for his liking. There was a pulse of feral hunger that made Scott very uncomfortable.

At the conclusion of the presentation, they drifted toward the back of the room. Amy kept looking over her shoulder at the poet holding court on stage.

"Dad, do you mind if I go meet her and get a book autographed?"

Scott fished some money out of his wallet. "Take your time. Josh and I can chat."

Josh and Scott both watched Amy join the small crowd at the stage. Scott stepped into Josh's space and looked him in the eyes. "Give me your driver's license."

"What? No! What'd you want my driver's license for?"

"I want to check your age. I want to know who's interested in my underage daughter."

"Hey, fuck you, dad. I don't have to show you shit."

Josh panicked and tried to brush past. Scott shoved him through the men's room door, grabbing his left wrist, painfully twisting his arm behind his back, and bending him over a sink.

"Hey, that hurts! What the...? Are you crazy?"

"Get out your wallet." Scott hiked up the pressure on the bent arm, causing Josh to cry out.

"Okay, okay. Stop! That hurts!" Josh managed to get his wallet out with his free hand. Scott grabbed the wallet, shaking the contents into the sink. Picking up the driver's license he read aloud. "Duane Dietz, 44352 Valley Boulevard, Alhambra. Hey, 'Josh,' your DOB says you're twenty-two years old. Empty your front pocket." Josh started to object, then changed his mind and dug deep into his pocket. He threw the contents into the sink. Scott picked up some aluminum foil-wrapped pills and ignored the condoms and a pocketknife. He held the pills in front of Josh's face, "What's this?"

No response, so Scott hiked his arm up an inch.

Josh cried in pain. "Molly! It's Molly!"

Scott picked up an employee ID card from the spilled wallet items. "This says you're a Medical Technician Assistant at Pasadena Community Hospital."

Scott pulled him away from the sink and gave him a shove with his foot that sent Josh sprawling across the floor crashing into a trash bin. "If I ever see you near my daughter again, I'll really fuck you up. Do you understand me?"

Josh sobbed, rubbing his arm, "Yeah."

"I'm as serious as cancer. If I ever see you again, you'll be pissing blood."

Scott pocketed the condoms, the knife, the identification, and the pills. He checked himself in a mirror, and walked out to meet Amy.

Amy looked around. "Where's Josh?"

"He got a bad biscotti and went home. Come on, let's get dinner."

Scott and Amy drove to Old Town and got a table at their favorite Italian restaurant.

Scott looked up from his menu. "How about sharing a Caesar salad and a large Margarita pizza?"

Amy approved. "Perfect, but no anchovy on the salad. They're disgusting."

"Done." Scott ordered, asking for anchovies on the side.

Scott looked at his daughter, thinking about how to deal with the Josh issue. He hated to spoil the evening for her, but the situation needed handling. "What do you know about Josh?"

"He seems like a nice guy."

"Someone you might want to be friends with?"

"Sure, maybe. He's cute."

Scott pulled out the driver's license and photo ID and set it on the table. "What do you think of that?"

Amy sat staring at Dietz's identification. "Is this a joke? Where did you get these?"

"I took these from 'Josh,' which obviously isn't his real name. The license says he's twenty-two. He's not a student. Near as I can tell, he empties bedpans at a hospital."

"I can't believe it. He seemed so nice and kind."

Scott put the pills on the table. "He had these in his pocket. He said it's Molly, but they could be anything."

Amy flushed. "Oh my God! What an asshole! I'm so mad that I let him get close to me."

Scott let the rectal appellation slide, not wanting to distract from the life lesson. "Amy, you're a beautiful young woman, and you're going to be admired by men all your life. Take your time and know who they are before you let them get too close. Stay away from the cool guys on the hustle. Play it for the long run. Time reveals everything. Your mother didn't sign off on this clown, did she? I'm guessing you really met him online?"

Amy blushed and nodded, yes. "We agreed to meet at the reading."

"Does he know where you live or go to school?"

"No. I didn't give him that kind of personal information."

"This guy you agreed to meet is a predator. You understand that? There are a lot of them out there. You need to be careful, guarded, and skeptical. Only takes one mistake to put you in the worst nightmare of your life."

Amy's face flushed. She nodded her understanding.

"One more thing, don't ever lie to me again." Scott noticed the waiter coming. "It looks like dinner's here."

On the way home, Amy was very quiet. Once in the house she left for her bedroom. "I need to take a shower and go to bed."

"Okay. See you in the morning. Don't kick yourself over this. Just learn, and don't do it again, okay?"

Amy came back and kissed him. "I will. Thanks, Dad."

Scott checked his watch, "I need something at the drug store. I'll be back in twenty minutes."

Scott approached the pharmacy counter at the all-night drug store on Foothill Boulevard. He asked to speak with the pharmacist. A young woman, her white coat embroidered with the name "Kathy," came to the counter.

"How may I help you?"

"Can you tell me what these pills are? There is some writing on them." He put Josh's pills on the counter.

Kathy glanced at them without picking them up. "Rohypnol."

"You're sure?"

"Yes. It's Rohypnol. Do you have a prescription?"

"Actually, no. Thank you." Scott pocketed the pills, walked through the liquor aisle, browsing until a bottle spoke to him. He picked out a bottle of single malt scotch. The label promised that the scotch whisky had been "Aged in rum casks." Sold. He checked out.

At home, Scott opened the kitchen cabinet, took out a short whisky glass, poured in two fingers of single malt, added an ice cube, and allowed it to melt a bit. He tasted the whisky. It was rich and smooth with none of the chemical taste of cheap scotch. He wandered into the den looking for the TV remote when the phone rang.

Carol sounded stressed and panicky. "Why haven't you called? I need you!"

Scott nearly crushed the glass in his hand. "Hang up. I'll call you back in two minutes."

He went to his car, retrieved the cell phone, turned it on, and dialed Carol's number. She picked up, but before she could speak, Scott angrily growled, "I told you to never call my home!"

Carol was crying. "I'm sorry, I just thought you...maybe you dumped me. I needed to talk to you."

Scott paced on the driveway. "You can't ever call my home."

"But I needed to talk to you!"

"I'm hanging up now. I'll call you tomorrow. Do not call here again. Do you understand?"

"I'm sorry, I…"

"Don't call again. I'll talk to you tomorrow. Got it?"

Carol sobbed. "Okay."

Sunday, Scott got up early and cooked some bacon. He was in the middle of making pancakes when a very subdued Amy appeared.

Scott began. "I want you to understand the seriousness of what happened yesterday. I took the pills that I got from 'Josh' to the pharmacy. They're Rohypnol, the "Date Rape" drug. 'Josh' also had some condoms and a pocketknife on him. I believe he intended to drug and rape you."

Amy struggled to speak. "I am so sorry. I didn't think anything was wrong. It seems like a bad dream now."

"I just wanted you to know how serious it was. He's probably done this before to other women. Have something to eat."

After breakfast Amy went to her room to read poetry.

Scott tried to look casual as he walked out to his car, retrieved the cell phone, and called Carol.

She sounded anxious. "I'm sorry about yesterday. I just got so lonely."

"Let's meet at the condo at noon tomorrow. Okay?"

"That's wonderful! I so need to see you."

"Tomorrow at noon."

Dana arrived home at seven o'clock. She looked tired as she dragged her overnight case into the den.

Scott rose and kissed her. "Welcome home."

"I'm beat. Quite a retreat; the drive home was miserable."

"I've got some disturbing news. You want it now or later?"

"What do you mean, disturbing? What's wrong?"

"I took Amy to a poetry reading at a coffee shop, and a young guy showed up. They had obviously had a previous relationship of some kind. Turns out they met online and agreed to meet at the coffee shop. I guess my presence was not part of the planning. I became suspicious and confronted him. He was lying about his name and age. He was much older. I also found some Rohypnol, a knife, and condoms in his pocket. I think he intended to drug and rape Amy."

"Oh, God. What happened? Is she okay?"

"No harm. Nothing happened. I smoked him out and booted his ass down the road before they got past introductions."

Dana flashed to anger, "How could she be so stupid? How many times have we warned her about Internet predators?"

"She's young, and kids have unformed judgment. I had a long conversation with her. She understands just how grave the situation was. She's been very quiet. She's quite embarrassed and feeling pretty low-down. I think it's handled. She needs some support and understanding now. She's doing a good job of beating herself up without us piling on."

"I just want to do something, but it's probably best if I let it go for now. Once she gets over the shock, I'll reinforce the lesson."

Scott went upstairs to shower, Dana plucked a bottle of Chardonnay out of the fridge and retreated to the den. She poured a glass and thought about events at the retreat.

Participants at Dana's retreat had been paired two to a room. The single-room upgrade was too expensive, by design. Dana had avoided the awkward situation of an incompatible roommate by pairing up with a known partner. She was pleased to hook up again with a trim, attractive professional woman she'd met at a previous retreat. They'd hit it off almost immediately. Their bonding was strengthened through the lectures, group exercises, and the communal meals they shared. They'd traded horror stories complaining bitterly about men.

The relaxation element of the retreat included a massage, a sauna, and of course, wine. A couple glasses of Merlot and an extended deep massage had relaxed Dana and her friend into a puttylike state. They'd gone into the sauna in a fuzzy state of relaxation.

Once inside, they found themselves alone. Dana's partner leaned over and kissed her. Dana returned a long deep kiss.

They'd retired to their room and spent the night in the same bed.

Things were going as planned.

CHAPTER

4

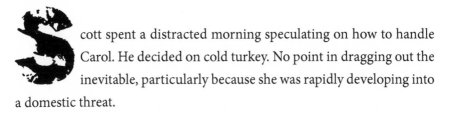cott spent a distracted morning speculating on how to handle
Carol. He decided on cold turkey. No point in dragging out the
inevitable, particularly because she was rapidly developing into
a domestic threat.

At 11:30 he left his office, went down to his car in the parking struc-
ture, and drove to an older condominium building at the north end of
Brand Blvd. Parking in his customary spot, he sat staring out the windshield, going over the possibilities, and he didn't like any of them. He took
the elevator up to the second floor and slowly walked to the apartment
that had hosted their many trysts. He stood for a moment looking at the
number on the door. Finally, he drew in a deep breath and knocked. Carol
answered almost immediately. She threw herself at Scott, clinging to him
and kissing him.

Scott separated himself and guided her into the room, closing the door. "Why did you call my home? Don't you realize the damage you could cause my marriage? What about my daughter? What'd you think you were you going to say if she answered?"

"I'm sorry, don't be mad. I just missed you so much."

Scott interrupted her, sitting her down on the sofa. "What was the agreement we made? No entanglements. No obligations. It was just going to be some fun and companionship. That was it. You remember agreeing to that?"

"But I fell in love with you. Now I can't be without you. Please don't be angry with me. I just want us to be together."

"Carol, I got involved with you because of my loneliness and a need for companionship. If I thought for a minute it would go this far, I never would have begun our relationship. My marriage was on the rocks, and I just wanted to be with someone, free of obligations and entanglements. Nothing has changed from our original agreement, except that I'm trying to save my marriage now. I have a young daughter that I want to raise. I can't abandon her. I don't love you. Love was never a part of our agreement. It still isn't."

Carol paced around the room, sobbing. She suddenly flipped to vicious and spiteful. "You son of a bitch. You tricked me into loving you, and now you want to dump me. You lying bastard, how can you be so cruel after all the affection I've shown you?"

"I never wanted to hurt you. You brought this on yourself by trying to change our relationship."

"Is that so? I think maybe your wife and kid would like to know what kind of bastard you are. How do you think they'd like that, family man?"

Scott suppressed an impulse to slap her. "Listen closely. If you come near my family or do anything to cause me trouble, you'll regret it."

Carol hissed, "I'm not afraid of you!"

Scott leaned in. "Bad things can happen to a single woman in L.A. How would you like to look over your shoulder the rest of your life? This is over. You screwed it up by interjecting yourself into my family life. You need to hear this clearly. If you become a threat to me, I'll get even with you if it takes the rest of my life. I won't be held responsible for what comes. Do you understand?"

Scott pushed Carol onto the sofa. For a moment she looked like she might come after him, but then she slumped and began to cry again. With nothing left to say, Scott left quietly, closing the door.

Scott sat in his car shaking with rage and fear. He wondered if she would believe his bluff. He stopped at a fast-food drive-in for a quick burger, took one bite, threw his lunch away, and returned to the office.

The next day, just as Scott entered his office, he was summoned to see his manager. His mind raced, wondering what was going on. Had Carol made trouble? He paused at the door, then knocked. He entered the room and found Fiona sitting with Jack Bowman, his boss. Jack was a hard-charging type, not much older than Scott. He'd been a Marine Corps officer and still had an unmistakable military bearing, including a matching close-cropped haircut. He always wore long-sleeve shirts. Scott had once seen part of a Marine Corps Devil Dog tattoo peeking out from beneath one of Jack's French cuffs. Jack apparently thought the tattoo was too unprofessional to display at work.

With Fiona there, Scott knew something was up. Jack motioned for him to take a seat. Dropping into a chair, Scott asked, "What's going on?"

Jack went right to the point. "We need to boost sales. Something big is coming up, and we need more revenue."

"What do you mean? I'm ahead of last year's sales by seven percent. Our numbers have been up every year in spite of the economy."

"Yes, yes, we know. You've been doing a good job, but we need more receivables on the books."

"I'm only one person with some clerical help. I'll try, but…"

"How about an assistant? Someone who could relieve you of the routine client maintenance and free you to hustle up some new business?"

"Yeah, okay, as long as I don't have to take a lot of time hand-holding a trainee."

Jack said, "Fiona convinced me to hire you an assistant for you just to see how it goes. If there's a positive increase in revenue, we'll make it permanent. It's worth a try."

"Sure, I could use some help. There are always potential customers that I just never have the time to pitch."

"Done. We will let you know when Fiona finds someone who can add to our bottom line. Someone sharp. A closer."

"So, what's the big deal you mentioned?"

"That's not out yet. You'll know soon enough."

"Okay. Ah…thanks."

Scott left the room puzzled. What was the big new mystery thing? Shouldn't he be in on the hiring decision? Fiona didn't know anything about sales.

Scott arrived home on time that evening. As he entered the kitchen he saw Dana drinking a glass of wine at the island in the middle of the room, a nearly empty bottle nearby.

Scott tried to spin what looked like another confrontation. "Hi. Look. I'm here on time."

Dana dripped out her sarcasm. "Great."

"What's wrong now? Where's Amy?"

"She's upstairs thinking about things."

"What do you mean?"

"I tried to talk to her about her Internet adventures, but she got snarky, so I took away her computer and phone for punishment."

"I thought we discussed this. She's thoroughly embarrassed and understands the gravity of the problem. Why did you need to further humiliate her?"

"Well, 'Captain Easy,' I'm her mother and I thought it needed reinforcement. You don't run this family. It's supposed to be a team effort. How about consulting me on something this serious?"

"Yeah, well, you were gone on your retreat. How about you consulting me? Now she'll probably stop trusting us and start hiding things. We need consistency on these problems."

"She needs to learn a lesson. I don't know how many times I've warned her about Internet predators, and then she intentionally lied and defied me."

"This isn't about you. She's young. Kids make mistakes. The point is how to make sure it won't happen again."

"She doesn't have her computer or phone, so it won't happen again."

"That's the short run. She may react in the long run."

"Don't tell me how to raise my daughter!" Dana picked up the bottle of wine and stormed off to the den.

ust as Scott got to work the next day, his phone rang.

"This is Fiona Dalton in Human Resources. Please come to my office, now."

Scott had a bad feeling and didn't like how she leaned on the word "now." He approached her office with a sense of dread, knocked, and entered without waiting for permission.

Fiona ordered, "Sit down."

"What's going on?" Silence followed as Fiona looked through some papers on her desk.

"Carol in finance has filed a workplace harassment complaint against you."

"What, me? Come on. What's she saying?"

"She claims that you sexually harassed her over a period of months and that you intimidated her into having sexual intercourse with you."

Scott quickly chose his path of defense. "Here goes nothing" flashed through his mind.

"It's a lie. I did no such thing."

"She had a list of the dates and times of your meetings."

"I don't care what she has. I didn't do it. I don't work anywhere near her. I've never contacted her at work. Hell, I've rarely even seen her outside of the company holiday party. Does she have any witnesses who back up her claims?"

"We have Carol's assertions, and she's very adamant. I find her very credible."

"So, you're picking sides? Looks like I need a lawyer," Scott challenged her. "Did you check my office and mobile phone records to see if I've ever called her?"

"We did, and there isn't any office phone record indicating that you called her. It doesn't necessarily mean you didn't contact her."

"Is that right? Well, speculation isn't proof. You didn't mention my computer because it also came up clean, didn't it?" Fiona ignored the question.

"Do you have any receipts for hotel or anything to support her story?"

"She said you met at a friend's condo."

"That's convenient."

Fiona asked, "I need to check your personal phone."

Scott feigned anger. "You're violating my privacy rights. This is nothing but a fishing expedition." Scott produced his personal phone and punched in the password. "Here." He tossed his phone onto her desk. "How about making a note in your little file that I'm cooperative, and you coerced me into giving up my private phone information?"

Fiona ignored the sarcasm. Glaring at Scott, she picked up the phone. She took her time thoroughly examining the phone and email logs looking for some evidence of contact with Carol. Scott detected a hint of desperation when her search turned up nothing.

Scott's confidence grew. "Give me the phone." Taking it from Fiona, he located the picture of Carol's bared breasts.

"Does this look like she's the innocent victim of sexual harassment? She's some victim, sending unsolicited pictures of her naked body to people in the organization? She must have a crazy fixation on me. She's the one who's been harassing me. This is what I get for being a nice guy and not filing my own complaint."

Fiona was visibly shaken. She felt embarrassed. She realized that, at best, she had failed to get an admission, and at worst, Carol may have set her up. Fiona momentarily lapsed into silence, her arguments spent.

Scott suppressed the urge to take a victory lap at her expense. "Are we done?"

"For now. I may reopen this case if any new information comes to light." She realized how weak it sounded, but too late; she'd said it.

Scott turned as he left the office. "I'm taking tomorrow off. I feel highly stressed by these false accusations. There's something you should keep in mind, sometimes women lie."

Scott got back to his office, slamming his door. He sent a text to Jeff with trembling hands. "See you at The Cat at 5:30?"

They sat in their customary booth at the back of the bar, their drinks on order. Jeff was cool and crisp after a hard day's work out-maneuvering the opposition. Scott was nervous and restless.

Jeff, picking up on his mood, asking, "What's up?"

"Shit's hit the fan. I broke up with Carol, and she filed a harassment complaint against me."

"Okay, let's hear it."

"Carol called my house over the weekend when Amy was there. Luckily, Dana was gone. I shut her down and met her Monday at the apartment. I broke it off. It got nasty. She threatened me, and I reciprocated. Then I got called on the carpet in H.R. because she'd filed a harassment complaint against me. I denied everything, showed them her naked picture, and claimed harassment myself. I think I bluffed them out. They actually had no real proof. That damned H.R. director doesn't sound like she's about to give up on this. I think I handled it well enough, but the question is whether Carol's crazy enough to call Dana."

Their drinks arrived, and Scott downed half of his Mai Tai in one gulp.

Jeff looked concerned. "Do you think she'll go that far?"

"I hope not. My marriage is probably going to fail, but for Amy's sake, I don't want it to go out ugly."

Jeff said, "You could follow up by pressing for disciplinary action against Carol if they won't let it go."

"I think I'll let sleeping dogs lie. I did some discreet snooping, and it looks like they're giving Carol a raise and transferring her to the San Francisco office to shut her up. Hopefully, that placates her, and she just moves on."

Jeff whistled. "It could have been worse."

"That's not all. Amy met up with an online predator, and I had to step in and deal with the little weasel. She's okay, but Dana blew up at her, and we had a huge fight. I feel like I'm in a batting cage, and I can't hit this stuff back fast enough."

"Anything else?"

Scott downed the rest of his drink. "It's enough."

He signaled the waitress for a refill. "I may need your services yet. I've the feeling there's more bad stuff coming my way."

They toasted each other. Jeff said, "I hope you learned something from this. I can guarantee you this much, you better stick to what you need and not what you want. Juries don't like over-the-hill pussy hounds."

Scott drank up. "I'm not over the hill."

CHAPTER

.... *6* ....

Dana paced around the house, holding the ever-present glass of wine. Amy was visiting a friend. Scott was behaving normally, but her instincts told her that something was going on, and she needed to know for sure. Her private investigator, Lance Tavidian, was coming to meet her, and she hoped to have her suspicions confirmed.

Lance was a ruggedly handsome, physically fit man in his thirties, medium height, and black hair worn in a trendy man-bun. He wore comfortable clothes, a casual sport coat and pants, and some expensive-looking leather athletic shoes. He drove a white Chrysler M300 sedan. He'd removed the SRT emblems from the car so it looked like any rental, but he did take comfort in the 475-horsepower hemi engine. He'd learned the hard way that a quick getaway could be a lifesaver in the investigating business.

Dana opened the door at his knock. He entered the house with a calm, confident air, greeting Dana, "Hello, nice to see you again."

"You look great, Lance. I've been thinking about you since our last meeting. Can I get you a drink? Wine? A beer?"

"I'll take a beer."

Dana poured him one of Scott's beers in a tall glass and set it on the coffee table.

Lance got right to the business at hand. "As you recall, my last surveillance of your husband came up empty. This time we have a different outcome."

Dana didn't appear to be shocked or even surprised. "What did you find?"

They sat on the living room sofa. Lance took a drink of the beer and began, "I slipped the lock on his car while he was at work, searched it, and found a cell phone hidden under the spare tire. I checked the call index and found that the phone had been used to call only one number. I called that number and got a woman named Carol, an employee formerly working in finance in the MacKenna office complex. I convinced her that I was an investigator working with the company and asked her a lot of questions about Scott. Carol's really angry with Scott, and she told me she'd been having an affair with him for about seven months. She had lots of negative comments about him, all boiling down to the fact that Scott had recently dumped her. She was very distressed by his callousness and consequently filed a sexual harassment complaint against him at work. The claim apparently went nowhere, and she got transferred so they would be working in different locations. That's about it. Scott covered his tracks well and escaped the whole incident without disciplinary action. Snyder sounded a bit shaky to me, so I checked out part of her story. I contacted the former friend who had let Carol and Scott use her condo for their encounters. She confirmed Carol's story. She was also angry because, apparently, Carol wasn't much for cleaning up afterwards. She was about to toss them out when they broke up."

Dana seemed to take it all in stride. "Where else does he go?"

"He sometimes meets with an attorney named Jeff Teller. Looks friendly, not business. That's about it. I put the phone back where I found it. I wrote down Carol's number on this card if you want it." Lance handed her his business card with the number penned. Dana set it on the coffee table without looking at it.

Dana was very calm and deliberate when she spoke. "Some anonymous woman, whom I assume was Carol, called me several days ago and said basically what you just told me. She sounded a bit irrational, so I wasn't sure what to believe. It looks like she was telling the truth."

Lance made sympathetic sounds. "I'm sorry, I guess you need to think about your next move. Do you want to keep up the surveillance?"

They stood up from the sofa. "I think we have a lot more work to do where my husband is concerned." She took a step into him and kissed him long and hard. "I think I'll start with some revenge sex. What about it?"

CHAPTER

.... *7* ....

he next two weeks were uneventful. Work hummed along. Scott put in some overtime and booked some good sales results. At home, he was in a frosty standoff with Dana. Amy got her computer and phone back. Scott took a lunch hour opportunity to smash his Carol phone and throw it in a dumpster.

One morning Scott got a call from Jack. "Come to the office."

What now? Scott buttoned his shirt collar and cinched up his necktie; he even put on his jacket. His episode with Fiona had made him conscious of managing his appearance in the office.

Jack's office door was open. He sat at his desk pointing at a chair. "Sit."

Scott sat where he was ordered to and sat up straight.

"Your new assistant will be here shortly."

Relieved, Scott said, "That's great. Now we can really get after some increased receivables."

Jack's eyes bored in on Scott. "What kind of business are we engaged in?"

Taken aback, Scott ventured: "You know, we make kids' educational toys, games and reading materials. Is this a trick question?"

Jack continued, "What's the image that our company strives to project to the consumer public?"

"Well, we're friendly, clean, and wholesome. We help parents educate kids. Quality American-made products and proud of it."

Jack nodded. "Exactly. We're nice. The company strives to cultivate and project that kind of clean corporate image. Our revenues and stock price rely upon the public trusting in that image and buying our products."

Scott interrupted, "Wait a minute. Is this about that bogus sexual harassment complaint that Fiona tried to tag me with? Carol's out of her mind, and that whole thing was a lot of trumped-up nonsense."

Jack said smoothly, "Relax. I know it was unproven. Here's my concern, Scott. Your new assistant isn't just another attractive woman; she's absolutely beautiful. She's the kind of woman who can charm our customers, male and female alike, and she has the potential to be a huge asset. I want your assurance that you can work with her without unduly complicating that relationship."

Scott flushed, noting that Jack had said "unproven" and not "innocent."

"Jack, come on. What kind of an idiot do you think I am?"

"As an officer in the military, and an executive in my private career, I've had to deal with some unpleasant harassment issues. Horny adolescent guys with low impulse control going off on a hormone rampage and getting themselves into professional and domestic trouble. Maybe they're tired of their wives or just out looking for some strange stuff for the hell of it. It always ends in the same goddamned mess, and I don't want our company dragged into any more of that kind of scandal."

Scott entreated, "Jack, you can count on me."

"There's too much at stake. If you go off the rails and screw up your private life outside work, that's your problem, but if you drag us into it, that's a huge problem for me personally, as well as for the entire company. If you can't handle working with this woman, and you have some kind of problem keeping it in your pants, I need to know that now."

Scott scrambled. There was obviously some doubt in Jack's mind about the Carol incident, and he needed to shore up his credibility.

"Normally, I'd be insulted, but I understand you are just doing your job. I get it. I'm not a problem, Jack. I can do what you expect of me, and you have no cause for concern."

Jack took his measure in a long pause. "Okay, but if you screw this up, the entire weight and power of this company will be brought to bear against you. We'll make sure that your career is permanently extinguished. Screw us, and you'll find yourself in a ten-year-old pickup truck loaded with gardening tools, on your way to your next lawn edging. Are we clear?"

"Got it. You've nothing to worry about."

Jack dismissed Scott with, "I'll call you when she's done in H.R."

Scott retreated to his office and closed the door. He was highly stressed and paced the floor like a caged animal. Jack's apparent mistrust had shaken him. He thought the Carol issue had subsided and he'd gotten off clean, but clearly it was back to haunt him.

Carol's complaint had metastasized, and there was nothing to be done about it except keep his nose clean to prove them wrong. Scott simply could not come up with a viable survival plan other than to hunker down and stay out of trouble. Don't give them cause to act on their suspicions, and hope to hell that Carol had disappeared off the face of the earth.

Two hours later he was still ruminating on his meeting when his phone rang. It was Jack.

"Your new assistant is in my office. Please come."

Scott entered Jack's office. His new assistant rose from her chair to shake his hand. "Hi, Julie Wilson. I'm pleased to meet you."

Damn! There was nothing wrong with Jack's assessment. She was beautiful. No, not just beautiful; she was incredible. She stood almost six feet tall in her heels. Jack could sense a trim athletic body moving under her business suit. Looking at her classically sculpted face with high cheekbones and almond-shaped blue-green eyes, he wondered "Russian, Slavic? Who cares?" Maybe a reflection of some actress he couldn't quite put his finger on? Sharon Stone, was that it?

Scott tried to shift his attention away from her charismatic presence and stick to business. "Welcome. I'm very pleased that you're joining us. We could use some help. I suppose Jack has been filling you in on what we have planned?"

"Yes, and it sounds exciting. I did some research on the company, and I'm completely impressed with your corporate philosophy and your amazing educational products. Representing such an impressive line of products that are so important to parents and the development of children makes me feel that my job is very special. It promises to be much more rewarding than simply selling other less-impactful consumer products."

Scott said, "Your enthusiasm is infectious. I almost want to buy something from you myself. I know we will make a great team." Scott thought he saw Jack squint his eyes firing a nonverbal warning at him.

Jack said, "Tell you what, it's almost closing time. Why don't we get some dinner and strategize how to maximize our sales initiative?" With that invitation they retired to the Catamaran for some drinks and dinner.

Drinks arrived, and a toast was made to the future success of their endeavor.

Meals were ordered, and shoptalk consumed the evening.

Later, about seven p.m., Jeff came into the restaurant for drinks with Marie, his new girlfriend. Spotting Scott and Julie at their table, his eyes popped. He openly stared at her. A text soon followed.

"Keep it zipped."

Scott got to the office early to kick off the training of his new assistant. To his surprise, she was already in her space, buried in promotional materials. Scott parked his briefcase, took off his jacket, got a cup of coffee, and checked on her.

"Who are you trying to impress?"

"This is a great opportunity for me, so I'm sucking up. I hope that's okay with you?"

"Jack's taught me that ring-kissing is a highly undervalued quality in an employee. I think it would be good for you to learn the product catalog first. If you're going to sell the soap, you'll need to know what you are talking about."

Julie flashed a big smile that sent a tingle to Scott's groin. "I've already studied the catalog, the advertising, and the literature. Fiona downloaded it onto my computer several days ago when we got serious about the job. There are some very exciting things here."

"Not that I don't trust you, but let's go through the products, and you pitch them to me. I'll chime in with any missing information and maybe some selling points."

"I'd love to."

That smile flashed again. Did he read something in her eyes?

They spent until noon going over all the information. She was a quick study, and Scott was impressed with her knowledge and enthusiasm. The only thing left was to road test her on some clients and see if she was a closer.

"How about some lunch?"

"I'm starving."

Scott and Julie sat at a table in Casa de Ramirez, a family-owned Mexican restaurant that had somehow survived the current wave of small-business property demolitions, all sacrificed for high-rise apartments and condominiums. Scott ordered a margarita, and Julie was enjoying a cold glass of iced tea. She hungrily attacked the chips and salsa.

Scott took the small-talk initiative. "So, tell me about yourself."

"I come from a small family, and my parents are deceased. I have a brother who works for an oil company in Alaska, so that leaves only me here locally. I had one marriage right after college that lasted almost three years. There were no children to complicate the divorce, and we had nothing of value, so we just split. He was killed in a motorcycle accident a few years later. How about you?"

"Easy. Married out of college. We have a wonderful daughter. I make a living and pay the mortgage. I like classic rock, the Dodgers, and single malt scotch."

"No other activities or hobbies?"

"Not really. There are things I could do if I was retired and had time on my hands, but I don't have rich relatives waiting to leave me a bundle. I'm happy with what I have."

"What about your wife? What's she like?"

"Smart, pretty. She keeps in shape. Volunteers for different charities, and she works part-time for the school district teaching French. My daughter is fifteen. She's very pretty and way too smart. She gets good grades and is basically good-hearted. She's an incredible gift."

"It sounds like a nice family."

"Yup. The Brady Bunch has nothing on us."

Scott changed the subject. Getting down to business. "What do you say we check you out on some customers after lunch?"

"I can't wait. That's the real test, isn't it?"

Scott and Julie enjoyed their meal. Scott had a difficult time taking his eyes off her, stealing looks and trying not to seem obvious. He was totally captivated. She was smart, poised, and charming. For such a beautiful woman, she seemed to be completely unaffected and genuine. Her visceral sex appeal had invaded him from the moment they met. Scott didn't believe in love at first sight, but he couldn't deny lust when it sank its talons into his libido.

Fear of imploding his career and losing his family was the only thing holding him back from being a total fool for this woman. It drove him crazy when she would occasionally touch him. A brush of her hand, a slight passing of bodies in a doorway was enough to send a lightning bolt between his legs. Only some last vestige of self-respect kept him from running to the men's room and relieving himself. Was he going to survive this woman, or would he fly his life into a mountain?

Back in the office, they called up Ivan on FaceTime. Ivan was a loyal but case-hardened customer. He was a legendary tough sale and had a history of being impervious to Scott's sales pitches and new product introductions. Scott almost felt guilty for inflicting him upon Julie.

Ivan's thinning gray hair exposed more and more of his forehead every time Scott called him. Now, sitting too close to his computer screen, his nose looked enormous.

"Hi, Ivan. I thought I'd check in to see if you needed anything. I also want to introduce my new partner, Julie Wilson. She'll be your account manager in the future." Scott turned the screen to show Julie to Ivan.

Ivan stumbled for a second. "I'm pleased to meet you, young lady. You have my condolences if you're working with Scott." Scott shook his head, same old Ivan.

"Hello Ivan. I am glad to meet you. Scott has told me all about your business. I want to help you be even more successful, if you'll let me."

Ivan beamed, "See, already she has a better attitude. I'm sure we'll get along fine."

Julie saw a picture on the credenza behind Ivan. "Ivan, may I ask about that picture behind you?"

"Huh? Oh, that's my daughter and her kids at Disneyland."

"You must be proud to have such a beautiful family. Life's not all about business, is it?"

Ivan was silent for a beat and said, "No, certainly not. The least of it."

Scott sat back and watched Julie work over Ivan, selling him some restock items and convincing him to order some of the new offerings. When Ivan had hung up, Scott looked at Julie with unmitigated admiration.

"You're a natural. Ivan's as tough as a cheap steak, and you got him to place the biggest order that I can remember. Congratulations. Great job."

"Nice guy. I just helped him get some things that he didn't know he needed."

"You definitely did that." Scott thought, this new arrangement was going to work out just fine.

Over the rest of the week, Scott and Julie dialed up his entire book of customers. Julie was smooth, charming, and genuine. People just wanted to please her. Scott had total confidence that he could leave the client relations in Julie's hands, and he could go after new accounts.

That's the way it worked out. Julie took care of the existing book of business, and Scott put his efforts into new accounts. They put a lot of black ink on the board, and Jack was happy that everything was going like clockwork.

One Monday Jack called them both into his office.

"Congratulations are in order for you two. Our quarterly sales figures are impressive. Top management has taken notice, and believe it or not, I took no credit for your work. You two are the big movers, and for that, I have a surprise. There's a trade show in Denver next week. We were going to skip it, but I changed my mind and had my staff sign us up for a double-vendor space. You two are going. I hope there are no problems with that?"

Scott and Julie looked at each other. "No," they said almost in unison.

"The display has been ordered. It's a roll-along, so you'll take it with you on the plane. Get ready because you're flying out Thursday. The show runs Friday through Sunday at the convention center. You're staying in an adjacent hotel. My staff has handled everything you'll need."

They returned to Scott's office. Julie could hardly contain herself.

She suddenly turned, threw her arms around Scott, and kissed him on the cheek. Scott smiled but quickly disengaged while he still had control of himself.

Julie was thrilled. "I'm so excited. It feels like such a huge opportunity. We get to go meet buyers from all over the country, maybe the world. It seems so exotic!"

Scott smiled. "Well, it's not that exciting, and it's a lot of work. We're going to have to set up our space, staff it for three days, and pack it all up when we go home. It'll be exhausting."

"I don't care. I can't wait to go!"

.... *8* ....

Scott and Julie landed in Denver after what seemed like a surprisingly short flight. They picked up their luggage, the commercial display materials in two large rolling containers, and caught a cab. They checked into the hotel, dropped their luggage at the desk, and walked to the convention center.

They registered for the show, got their laminated badges, and headed for their display space. Jack had done well; it was a double-wide space near the entrance, where people entering the room couldn't miss them. Shortly, the convention staff delivered more shipped containers loaded with their display products.

Scott and Julie spent the rest of the day setting up their display area, arranging the products, and walking around checking out the other vendors. Scott knew some of the people from previous trade shows and introduced them to Julie. She was a big hit. Scott had the feeling she could have picked up a half-dozen job offers and at least one marriage proposal on the spot.

Once the setup was finally done, there was nothing left to do but show up at the opening bell and meet and greet the customers.

Scott and Julie retired to the hotel restaurant and bar to relax and recharge their energy. He ordered drinks and started a tab. An appletini came for Julie and a shot of single malt with a drop of water for Scott. They clicked glasses and drank. Tasting his drink, Scott let out a sigh of relief. "Hmm. That's nice. The Scots call their single malt whisky 'The water of life.' They spell whisky without an added 'e,' while Americans spell whiskey with the 'e.' It's also a country where public drunkenness isn't necessarily frowned upon. Maybe it's because the weather gets so bad."

"You sound like an expert."

"I read up a bit on Scotch whisky history. It's one of those bucket-list things. I'd like to go to Scotland, travel the whisky trail, and taste my way from Edinburgh to the Shetlands. Every distillery has a distinct character based on the local water source, the peat used in distillation, and probably a lot more things known only to the distillers. By the way, the company doesn't like to see liquor on the business expense account unless you're paying for a client, so run a separate tab and pay for your own booze. It keeps the bean counters out of your hair. Are you okay with eating here?" Julie nodded yes. "I'm not sure we want to move too far from the adult beverages."

"Good thinking." Scott waved at a server. "Can we get a couple refills and some menus?"

The server said, "Of course," laid down two menus and a wine list, and quickly returned with two more drinks.

They ordered dinner and a California Syrah. The excitement of their new adventure had captivated Julie, and her enthusiasm in turn had infected Scott. The fatigue and alcohol had their inevitable effect, reducing them into near exhaustion.

Julie drank the last of the wine. "You know, this almost seems like a date."

"I don't think I'd know how to do that anymore."

"Oh, come on. You are a charming, good-looking guy, don't tell me you've given up on yourself?"

Scott thought about it. "Well, married with kids, it's a different life. You make tradeoffs. You can't be a player and stay in a relationship."

"You talk a lot about Amy, but not much about your wife. Is that all okay?"

"Not so much. I think she's tired of me. I don't know what she wants, but apparently, I'm no longer it."

"I can't believe that. There must be something you can do. You both love Amy."

"I keep looking for the right notes to hit, but I don't think they exist. Enough talk about my life. What about you? I can't believe you are not married. There must be a lot of guys pursuing you."

"My husband wasn't a reliable partner. He was consumed by his appetites, and he didn't have enough left to give for the two of us. I got pregnant, lost the baby, and now I can't have children. I'm a trap, a good-looking woman offering no future for a family."

Scott was concerned for her. "Don't give up. There is always someone out there. Lots of options for a family now, like adoption and surrogate mothers. You just need patience and the right guy, not everyone wants to have kids."

Julie said, "I hope you're right. I guess I'm greedy. I want it all, career, romance, and a family. I'm not sure how that'll all work out."

"Let's go to upstairs. Tomorrow will come early, and we'll need to be on our game. Jack's expecting us to show big for this trip."

Back at their adjoining rooms, Julie stepped close to Scott and gave him a long affectionate hug. "You're a great guy, and you've taught me so much; I owe my new career to you. Thank you with all my heart." She finished her speech with a sensuous kiss on the lips.

Scott was speechless for a moment. "Sure. I mean, you deserve it. I think we should call it a night." They went to their separate rooms.

The next morning Julie was early again, beating Scott to the display booth. She looked amazing. Scott noticed she had on an outfit that would reveal a little of her breasts when she bent over to show buyers various items. Scott smiled to himself, thinking, "All's fair in corporate sales."

"Hi, Scott. I thought I'd get a jump on things. Sure enough, I snagged some early birds that cruised by."

"Good going. The heavy drinkers, that is, most of the buyers, will be by later."

"I got some muffins and a coffee for you. I figured you might need to blow out the fog."

"Right again." Scott smiled and ate a quick breakfast so he could be in some kind of shape for the heavy traffic yet to come.

The rest of the day went very well. They attracted many potential buyers. He had no doubt that Julie was the cause of quite a few male visitors and some of the women as well.

As things wound down, they closed up the display and went to dinner. This time they took an elevator to the rooftop restaurant. Scott tipped the receptionist for a window table.

They sat looking out on the night lights of Denver. Scott nursed some eighteen-year-old whisky, and Julie made do with a dirty martini. For a while they were silent, mesmerized by the city lights spread out at their feet. Julie was enjoying the atmosphere. "This is so beautiful. Thanks for arranging a lovely end to a great day. We make a fantastic team."

Scott toasted, and they clicked glasses. "We do. This is going to be great for both our careers. I'm so glad you came to us, and I mean that personally and professionally."

Dinner passed very pleasantly. All too soon they had exhausted the food, liquor, and conversation, and then drifted back to their rooms. Pausing at her door, Scott got a pat on the cheek. "Thanks for a lovely evening." Julie disappeared behind her door.

Scott stood in the hall for a couple seconds, disappointed that no kiss was forthcoming. He shrugged, laughed at himself for his juvenile expectations, and went to his room. He took a shower and moved around his room getting organized for the big day to come on Saturday. He answered emails, contacted Jack with a progress report, and turned on the TV. He got an email from Julie almost immediately.

"Scott, I've got a great new idea for us to improve marketing. Can you come over and look? It's on my computer."

Scott responded, "Now?"

She came back, "I'm sorry, but I just can't wait. I'm so excited!"

Scott gave in. "Okay. Unlock your side." He checked himself. Pajama tops and bottoms covered with a hotel robe. Decent enough, he guessed.

Scott unlocked his side of the pass-through door and found Julie's door already unlocked.

He stepped into her room. She stood in the center of the room in her bare feet wearing the hotel robe.

"I have a great idea." She slowly untied the robe and let it fall to the floor, revealing her naked body.

Scott stood frozen as she approached him. "What's the matter? Cat got your tongue?" She playfully pushed him onto her bed, ripped off his pajama bottoms and put him in her mouth.

Scott tried to protest. His mind screamed, "No! Stop. No, no, no!" The trouble was, those words never escaped his lips. In a few minutes he experienced an explosive orgasm that nearly lifted him off of the bed.

Julie retrieved a pill from the bed stand. "Here, take this."

Scott, suspicious, said, "What's that?"

"You've had a bit to drink. It's a little something to keep you present and at attention, because this party is just starting. I want reciprocity."

The following morning, Scott again found Julie at the vendor display early. She was alert, engaged, and already chatting with prospective buyers. It would take Scott a while to resurrect himself, so he took a stroll to the coffee vendor and bought a couple of Americanos and yogurt.

Julie turned from her customer and caught him in mid-coffee sip with a smile and a wink. Scott was thoroughly confused. In one respect he was as happy as he'd ever been. On the other hand, he had just massively screwed up.

Eventually, he joined Julie to help field questions. During a pause in traffic, he said, "We really need to talk tonight." She just smiled again and nodded.

After the exhibit hall closed, they found themselves back in a far corner of the hotel bar with their drinks and picked over bowl of salted nuts.

Scott began. "We can't do that again. It's a huge screwup for me, and I just can't afford to go through another affair." He briefly told her about the Carol disaster.

Julie interrupted him. "Hang on. Let's think this through. To start with, I'm not Carol. I'm not some needy charity case, and I don't want a commitment. I simply like you. I think you're a genuinely good guy, and I'm attracted to you. I like your commitment to your family. I really like the love and care you have for your daughter. I don't know what's wrong with your wife, but she's apparently willing to drive away a very good guy."

She continued, "I'm not asking for anything but honesty. I'm content with a close physical friendship. I've read the damned company policy. I'm a fully formed adult, and I know what I want and need. I take complete responsibility for that."

She put her hand on Scott's. "I knew you wanted to sleep with me from the minute you laid eyes on me. Most of the straight men I've ever met want the same thing. Good-looking women find out early and quickly about men. I have no illusions about love, but I do want to lead a full life. Right now, that includes you, and you have nothing to fear as long as you are willing to have an honest relationship on the same basis."

Scott looked at her, weighing the situation. "I don't know what to say. I…"

Julie moved her hand to his knee. "Then don't say anything. Let's enjoy the ride. We'll figure out where we're going later."

That evening Scott and Julie met in his room.

"How's little Scotty holding up?"

"Exhausted, but happy."

She fed him another pill. She then held up a piece of chocolate. "Take this."

"What's that?"

"Weed is legal in Colorado. It's an edible piece of cannabis."

"I'm not sure I want that."

"You're naked in a hotel room with a woman who's not your wife. Are you really picking this moment to take the high road?"

Julie popped a piece in her mouth and followed it with a flute of champagne.

"It's just some weed," Julie said, "Open wide," talking to Scott like he was a five-year-old kid taking a pill.

Scott swallowed the drug, chasing it down with his glass of champagne.

Julie giggled. "That's a good boy. Better leave the honor bar unlocked. I have the feeling we're going to need it later." She kissed him, and they fell into bed in a passionate embrace.

The rest of the show went well. On Sunday afternoon, they packed up the displays and decided to let the show organizers ship them home along with everything else. They checked out of the hotel and took a cab to the airport.

Soon after the plane took off Julie fell asleep on Scott's shoulder. He looked at her for a long time, his mind racked with guilt, apprehension, and unmitigated joy.

An old saying popped into his mind. "Experience lets you to recognize a mistake, when you make it again."

$$9$$

Scott arrived home late Sunday evening. Dana was already in bed. Amy was watching a concert on TV.

Surprised, Scott asked. "How come you're still up?"

"I was waiting for you. How was your trip?"

Scott came to her chair and kissed her. "It was amazing. We got lots of new clients. I think Jack might have a stroke. If everyone plays fair, Julie and I should pull down big bonuses. Where's Mom?"

"She went to bed early. Under the weather."

Scott read the comment. "Too much wine?"

"She had some." Uncomfortable, Amy changed the subject.

"I turn sixteen next week, and I do have my learner's permit. You paid for the driver's education class at school, remember? I want to drive our car."

Scott jumped at the chance. "I bet you do. I'll come home early tomorrow, and we'll do it after school. We definitely need to get you flight-checked on the family car. Let me look up my life insurance policy first."

"Not funny."

Julie and Scott sat in Jack's office while he looked over the sales results from the trade show. Jack was more excited than they had ever seen him, which is to say, barely detectable to normal humans.

Jack looked up. "Congratulations to you both. This is outstanding work. Just so you can appreciate how much it means, I'll let you in on the secret. I'm going to tell you some information that is not to be shared with the other employees. It's highly confidential, so treat it accordingly." Jack indulged in his most convincing dramatic pause. "We're about to get bought by another large corporation."

Scott's jaw dropped. "Who?"

Jack gave him a conspiratorial look. "A South Korean company is seriously looking to buy us out. They want to retain the company organization in the States as it now exists and make the products in Korea to increase profitability. Fortunately for us here, the only part of the company adversely impacted will obviously be the manufacturing facilities. The Koreans will still need our administration, sales, and distribution staff to make it work."

Scott gathered himself. "Are you sure our jobs are okay?"

"I was worried for a while, but there's no threat to our jobs nor to the rest of the employees here in Glendale."

Scott and Julie relaxed a little. Scott ventured, "So the extra sales push makes us more desirable, and you can negotiate a better price based on projected revenue, right?"

"Exactly. You and Julie just bought us a big chip to play in negotiations. We proved our worth to the Koreans as revenue generators.

Congratulations. I have some more good news. The home office is working on a bonus for us. I'll repeat one last warning. You two are the only people who know this outside of top management. You must keep it absolutely confidential. We don't want to start the rumor mill and an exodus of critical people."

Julie said, "You can count on us to keep this confidential."

Back in Scott's office, they sat down and looked at each other. Julie spoke first. "Did you buy it?"

"Yeah, I think so. What are the Koreans going to do, come in here and function in our jobs? Not likely."

Julie still looked concerned. "I've been through this before. I hope they don't turn loose some cost-cutters trying to save a few dollars in staff overhead. It's all going to depend on whether they want to squeeze us for every last dollar."

"God, I hope not. I've got a mortgage, a pissed-off wife, and a kid who is going to college in a couple of years. I don't need to go job shopping at my age."

Julie looked concerned. "I finally have a new career in something I love. I'm going to do some snooping."

"Be careful."

When Scott arrived home that afternoon, Amy was dressed comfortably for her student-driver outing. Scott put on a pair of old Levi's and a flannel shirt.

He drove to a gas station and showed Amy how to gas up the car, then out to a large vacant parking lot in an industrial area of Glendale. Amy took the wheel with Scott observing. She put on her seat belt, checked her mirrors, fired up the car, and toured the lot. Scott was impressed. She was very coordinated on her acceleration and braking.

"Nice work. Now we need to do some street driving." Amy drove to an adjacent residential neighborhood, and they cruised up and down the quiet streets. Amy was conscientious, courteous, and alert. They turned onto a larger street. Again, Amy was sure of herself and handled the car well. They drove straight into Griffith Park, past the zoo, the golf courses, Travel Town, Forest Lawn, and out the Burbank end, driving back to Glendale on surface streets.

Scott looked at Amy. "Did your class cover freeway driving?"

"Once, briefly."

"It's rush hour. Do you think you can handle a short hop?"

"I've got to do it sometime."

"The good thing is, rush hour around here is really just stop and go. Getting on should be easy. By the way, it's not a bad idea to stay away from cars with body damage. There might be a good reason for it, like a bad driver."

Amy got on the 134 freeway at San Fernando Road. Scott coached. "Don't dawdle. Check to your left. You want to accelerate up to traffic speed so you can slip into the stream. Watch for people coming into your lane trying to get off."

Amy capably handled the merge. She stayed in the right-hand lanes approaching the transition road north. She drove smartly up the transition road, arching onto the 2 freeway. They exited in Montrose. Her last test was parking the car at a coffee shop. They celebrated her triumphant motoring adventure over a couple of frothy coffee drinks and brownies.

Scott eyed her. "Are you sure you haven't been doing this without me?"

"Of course not. I did get an A in my driving class. Now I can steal the car when you're not looking."

"That shouldn't be too hard. For now, you don't ride with your friends in the car. It's too easy to get distracted. Wait until operating a car becomes second nature, and you won't have to concentrate so hard."

Scott mined Amy for information. "What happened while I was away?"

"Not much. I stayed over at Britney's house on Saturday night."

"Oh, a sleepover?"

"Yeah. I think I'm getting a little old for that. Mom had an event to go to."

"An event? Did she say what kind of an event?"

"Some kind of women's thing."

"Really? Did she say anything about it?"

"Personal Development, she said."

"Well, that's interesting."

"There's another one this weekend."

That evening after everyone had gone to bed, Scott searched the family credit card bills and Dana's emails. He found the name and location of the spa hosting her retreats. He searched the net for the retreat organization and found their website. He learned enough to raise a strong suspicion about Dana. He then checked the archive for the home high-tech security system he had installed earlier in the year. Last logout on the system set the alarm at 5:44 p.m. The next log-in turning the system on was at 6:32 a.m. "Looks like Amy's not the only one who had a sleepover."

Scott left early for work. He stopped for a coffee at a drive-through stand and sat in his car thinking. He had to do something. His life was getting out of control. His wife was doing who knows what away from home. His continued employment might be tenuous. The trouble was, what to do about it? Maybe make things worse? Do nothing and ride it out? How do you ignore infidelity? Then he felt like a hypocrite, considering his own infidelities.

Throughout the morning Scott and Julie finalized all their paperwork and clarified any ambiguity in their sales contacts from the show. All the follow-up clients were more than happy to hear from Julie again.

Scott got an email from Jack. "I talked to corporate again on the bonus. It's going to be a while before the check gets cut. They are closing out the books for a review by the people I mentioned. Hang in there."

Scott sent a text to Jeff. "Urgent, can we meet for lunch?" Jeff immediately responded for them to meet at a local Italian restaurant.

Scott watched the clock all morning and left early for his meeting with Jeff.

Sitting with an iced tea, he saw Jeff enter the restaurant and waved him over.

Jeff looked interested. "What's so important?"

"Do you have any snoopers working for you?"

"I have someone when I need surveillance, or if I need to discreetly run down something. What's up?"

"Something is going on with my wife, and I want to know what it is. She's been spending a lot of time away from home on some supposed 'retreats' for women. She also disappeared for a night while I was in Colorado. She's scheduled to go for another retreat this weekend, and I'd like to have someone follow her. Here's the name of the place she's been going." Scott gave Jeff a piece of paper with a copy of the website home page.

"A woman's spa. My investigator is a woman, that may come in handy. I'll tell her to take video on anything interesting and find out who's who, if there is a 'who.' This is where you will be spending some money."

"Don't worry about that. I just need to find out what's going on."

"Speaking of interesting things, is that amazing-looking woman I saw the other night your new assistant?"

"Yeah. She really is something. She accounted for the majority of the business we knocked down at the trade show."

"You two are not…?"

"Definitely not."

10

The week passed quickly. Dana went to her retreat on Friday afternoon. Amy and Scott were left to fill the weekend. Scott thought he had a pretty good father-and-daughter plan.

Friday night they ordered pizza and caught up on the recorded programs, bingeing on old movies and mini-series.

Saturday was a road trip day. Scott and Amy left early for a drive up the coast to Ventura. Scott stopped for gas and a windshield cleaning.

Amy asked, "When do I get to drive?" Scott took the wheel and said, "As soon as we clear the Valley." He took a CD out of his pocket and fed it into the dash player. "Paul Simon. *Graceland*, great driving music."

Amy shook her head. "I hope this won't be another long, annoying ride with classic rock."

"Three songs. If you don't like it, we're done."

"Okay. I just don't want to get stuck again in acid rock hell. Maybe next time we could shoot for something recorded in this century."

Amy took the wheel in Thousand Oaks when Scott needed a break, and she drove all the way to Ventura. They explored the city, strolled the waterfront, and ate lunch. They went north to Ojai to check out the artisan vendors and look in on the lifestyles of the former flower children now approaching the advent of their second childhood. They passed on the crystal and incense purchases, returning to Glendale through Santa Paula and Fillmore. They stopped for an antique train ride in Fillmore and bought some fresh fruit from a farm stand.

Sunday, they immersed themselves in a movie marathon at a multiscreen complex in a mall. They sat through three movies. Lunch came from the theater snack bar in between movies. They binged on nachos, hotdogs, drinks, and Scott's favorite, popcorn with mints. By the end of the day they suffered from sore backsides and incubating indigestion.

Scott drove home. "Have fun?"

"Definitely. An awesome binge."

Dana returned late Sunday evening. Scott greeted her at the door. She was civil and even a bit mellow for a change. Scott couldn't smell any alcohol.

The following morning at work, Scott got a text from Jeff. "Got something. Can you come to my office?"

Scott told the receptionist that he was going to meet with an old client and wouldn't be back until after lunch. He didn't care if they believed it or not.

Waiting in Jeff's reception area for a half hour, he realized just how successful Jeff had become. The office walls were clad in old-school oak paneling, comfortable dark-blue leather chairs, and a big matching sofa. Beautifully framed original photography graced the walls. Jeff's receptionist was an elegant woman in her mid-fifties with an understated English accent. Jeff obviously paid enough for her to wear fine clothes. She was a genuine touch of class for the office. He picked up a coffee-table book of street photography. He hadn't known about Jeff's appreciation for art photography.

Jeff blew into the room, apologizing. "I'm so sorry. I got hung up with a client who was about to do something catastrophically self-destructive. I had to talk him off the ledge."

"No problem. I was just admiring your office."

"This way." Jeff led Scott to a glassed-in conference room looking out toward Los Angeles. There was an expansive view of the gathering smog over downtown L.A. and thousands of cars crawling along the freeway.

"Please sit." There was a computer monitor set up on the conference table.

Jeff picked up a phone and dialed. "Hasmik, can you please come to the conference room and bring your information?" He rang off.

In a few minutes a completely unremarkable young woman entered. Plain features, straight brown hair, and brown eyes. She wore a nondescript pair of gray slacks and a black jacket over a white shirt.

"Scott, this is Hasmik, my investigator." They shook hands. "She has some video for you if you want to see it."

"That's why I'm here. Roll it."

Hasmik put her drive into the computer and found the right video file. She paused. "I followed your wife starting Friday afternoon. She went directly to an apartment on East Garfield Ave. The apartment building had a locked gate, so I didn't see exactly which unit she went to. She stayed there until about six p.m. She left in the company of a man, and they went to the Trattoria Napoli in Pasadena for dinner. They returned to the apartment for the rest of the night. The man drives a white Chrysler 300 sedan.

License is a black custom plate that reads, 'GR8 GUY.'" She smirked at the license plate.

Hasmik hit the play button.

The video was surprisingly clear and vivid. Scott saw Dana and a medium-tall, well-dressed man with dark hair leave the apartment and get into the Chrysler. The video skipped a beat, and then a dimmer image appeared. Dana and the same guy were sitting at a candlelit table, holding hands and drinking wine.

Hasmik stopped the video. "I took that on my phone from the restaurant bar. You get the idea."

Jeff broke in. "Do you recognize the man?"

Scott was amazingly calm and detached. "Never seen him before. Who is he?"

Jeff spoke. "We ran the plate. 'GR8 GUY' is a private investigator named Lance Tavidian. He's got a P.I. license but no office we can locate. Some kind of bottom-feeder P.I. working out of his hat."

"That's it?"

"Not exactly. Hasmik?"

She started another video, clearly showing the front of a tidy-looking town house. "Saturday, she went to this town house on North Pacific Ave. She stayed overnight. In the morning she and another woman came out, and they went to brunch." Hasmik pressed the "play" button, and the video rolled. Dana and a woman left the apartment and walked to Dana's car. They paused by the car and engaged in a passionate kiss.

Hasmik narrated. "They went to a brunch at an old hotel in Pasadena. They spent the day together going various places. Lots of obvious affection and passion was shown between these two."

Scott sat back. "That *is* rather obvious."

Jeff spoke. "Do you recognize the woman?"

"Yeah. Fiona Dalton. The H.R. director where I work."

Jeff sat up. "What?"

"You couldn't make this up. She's the one who went after me about that harassment policy violation last month."

Jeff was taken aback. "Do you want further surveillance?"

"I think it might be useful to know more about Lance, the gumshoe. Good job, Hasmik. I think I have what I want. My wife seems to be on an indiscriminate romance binge."

Jeff spoke to Hasmik. "Thanks. You're excused."

When she was gone, Jeff asked, "What are you thinking?"

"I'm thinking I'm in for a divorce, and my work life is going to get a lot stranger. Is there any other conclusion?"

"Well, the video is a great inoculation against any further work-place problems. She's in a clear conflict of interest. You don't seem upset by all this."

"Actually, I'm not. The marriage has been in trouble for a long time. I was in denial about it. That fling with Carol was just the canary in the coal mine. Now Dana's out screwing around, so she's obviously given up. I have to admit the bisexual stuff is an eye-opener. But then, we're as good as divorced, so why should I care? I'm screwed financially, but that's second-ary to what happens with Amy. If I get out of this mess with my daughter not hating me, I'll be satisfied."

Jeff was thinking. "So how does the guy figure? She hired him to check on you, and they hit it off?"

"Could be, but what in the hell is she doing with Fiona?"

Jeff leaned in on Scott. "Seriously, don't tell anyone about your wife and Fiona. You might be able to leverage that sometime in the future. Don't squander it."

"Makes sense. I've got a lot to work out."

"You're really sleeping with your assistant, aren't you?"

"Yeah. I lied."

"You know what they call clients who lie to their attorneys?"

"Losers?"

On Thursday, Scott went to Julie's apartment. They'd kept away from each other for a week, and it was driving Scott crazy. This time the sex was slow and deliberate, none of the passionate frenzy of Colorado. Scott thrilled to her touch. Her skin was flawless. He couldn't believe he was making love to her.

Julie rested with her eyes closed. Scott watched her, trying to figure out where she played into his catastrophic life. He gave up, resolving to enjoy it while it lasted.

The weekend passed with ease. Dana was in a good mood for once, and there were no arguments. On Saturday, she went shopping. Scott couldn't care less if she was out getting banged or not.

Amy came into the den where he was working and asked to go for a drive.

Scott jumped at the chance to get away from his paperwork.

They stopped by Old Red Neck's BBQ, got pulled pork sandwiches and coleslaw, and drove to Griffith Park. They found a shaded table in a cool grassy area and had lunch. It was a stunning day with dappled sunlight playing on their table, and a light breeze ruffling the trees.

Toward the end of lunch, Amy put her hand on top of Scott's, stopping him from gathering up the trash. "Are you and Mom getting a divorce?"

Scott instantly choked up. He tried to speak, but instead he wadded up their papers and walked them over to the trash can.

"You're pretty darn smart, aren't you? The answer is I don't know, but I'm not going to lie to you. We seem to be headed that way."

"I'm not sure Mom loves me anymore. If you break up, I don't want to live with her or anyone else; I want to live with you."

Scott felt his heart convulse. "Don't say that. I'm sure she loves you. I think she's going through a hard time right now. We both are. If she stops loving me and we split, that's just between us. You'll still have two parents who love you. You shouldn't be drawing catastrophic conclusions right now. People under stress don't act normally."

Amy spoke. "I saw it coming. Everything has been changing. I pretended it was okay, but things just keep getting worse and worse. You know Mom is seeing some private detective, don't you?"

Scott's emotions were raging inside. It was all he could do to keep from screaming, anything to let the pressure off.

"Well, it was going to be someone. This is a hard one to handle when you are sixteen. You're too smart, and I'm not going to pretend it's not serious. Both of us have been seeing others. It wasn't serious with me, and I don't know where your mother is on that. When love dies, people go searching somewhere else."

Amy tried not to cry, but she gave in to her sadness. Scott sat next to her and hugged her until the moment passed.

"Parents always try to shield their kids from bad things, but sometimes that's impossible. I want you to know that I'll always be there for you when you need me. We're a team, and we can survive anything."

"I know. You've always been there for me."

"How about you coming to work? I'll show you off to the office, and we'll go out to lunch."

"Okay."

Monday, Scott was checking his computer for new orders, when Julie came in the office. He immediately knew something was very wrong. She had a piece of paper in her hand, and she was crying so hard that her whole body convulsed.

Scott stood and embraced her. "What's wrong?"

Julie pushed the paper at him. "The bastards are all lying."

"What do you mean?"

"Read that."

Scott read the memo from the Chief of Operations for the company, directing Fiona to develop the succession of layoffs for a smooth transition after the company was bought out. The memo said that negotiations so far had ruled out the retention of existing Glendale staff, and except for a few key people who would be transferred elsewhere after operations were combined with the San Francisco office, the Glendale office would be shut down.

Scott looked up. "We're screwed."

CHAPTER

 *11*

cott was skeptical. "Where did you get this?"

"Fiona keeps her computer password on a sticky note in her desk."

He was still in denial. "This is for real?"

"I printed it off her email. Look at the CC to Jack. He's in on it, the lying jerk."

Scott stood and picked up his jacket. "Come on."

They passed the receptionist. "We're in the field for the rest of the day."

On the way to the car, Julie asked. "Where are we going?"

"The war room."

The Tally Ho opened in 1946. The ambience was Old English tavern. The restaurant had no windows, and the seating was red vinyl booths with red-checkered tablecloths illuminated by dim candlelight. The restaurant was an unapologetic purveyor of brown liquor, red meat, and amazing garlic-cheese bread.

They camped out in the bar, ordered drinks, and settled into the dim atmosphere.

Julie broke first. "I'm afraid I won't have enough experience to launch myself into another professional sales job."

"You are a natural. That trade show gave you enough exposure to easily nail another job."

"Maybe. I'm not ready to go back to the ground floor."

"You'll have my support whatever you do."

The familiar scotch and martini appeared.

Julie glanced at Scott. "What are you thinking?"

"I'm trying to look past this, but I'm not seeing it. Dana and I have cratered our marriage. She doesn't make much money, so I'll max out on her alimony for ten years. I'd gladly pay Amy's child support and college, but how am I going to live even if I get another well-paying job? Dana will get the equity in the house, and I'll wind up with my 401K and a single apartment, nursing along a ten-year-old car."

"There must be something we can do."

"Let me know when you figure it out, because I'm out of ideas."

They drank in silence.

Later, in Julie's apartment, they lay on the bed in their work clothes watching the afternoon light fade, struggling to imagine a promising future.

Julie brightened. "As long as we're getting fired, why don't we try to hold them up for some severance money so we keep quiet about the buyout?"

"They might give us some temporary relief money, but I can't see it making a big difference in the long run. Dana would get half of mine."

"I could sue them for sexual harassment. Wouldn't that piss off Fiona?" Julie laughed.

Scott smiled at the idea of an apoplectic Fiona. "You're joking, right?"

"You should have faith in me by now. Loyalty goes with my love."

"You never said love before."

Julie looked in his eyes. "I'm not saying crazy love, but some kind of love. I think it must be obvious how much I care for you."

Scott propped himself up on an elbow and looked at her. "I thought I was just convenient."

"Convenient is a harsh word. It cheapens what I feel for you."

Scott leaned over and kissed her, and they held each other tight.

Dana and Lance embraced on rumpled sheets in his apartment.

Lance kissed her. "I hope this is more than just revenge sex?"

"You're not done. I was working on multiple orgasms."

"I'm serious. I've always liked you. I never let myself say anything until your marriage was in question. I want a future with you."

"It's a little too soon, and things are too complicated now. Let's give it some time. I obviously like you. I need to see where this is all going. I don't want to share Amy with him. He's lost the right to be called a husband, much less a father. I want him out of my life."

Lance stared at the ceiling. "Now we're talking about money or misfortune. Do you think he'd turn loose of Amy for money?"

"To hell with him. I figure I earned everything I've got, and I'm going to keep what's mine."

"Then we're going to need a plan on how to deal with that."

The following day, Amy came to Scott's office looking radiant. He wanted to hug her, but he knew she would be embarrassed. She sat at his desk while he explained all about his job and how the company worked. He showed her some of the products they made and explained the company's mission.

He showed her around the office and introduced her to the staff. She was a nice diversion from the drudgery, and everyone welcomed her. Jack was particularly gracious and complimentary of Scott.

Just as Amy and Scott were leaving for lunch, Julie walked into the office.

"Julie, this is my daughter. Amy, my partner, Julie."

Julie shook her hand and engaged her with a winning smile. "I'm pleased to meet you. Your dad talks about you all the time; I feel I already know you. He didn't mention that you were such a beautiful young woman."

Amy blushed, stammering, "Thanks. You're new, aren't you?"

"That's right. Your dad's been educating me on the nuances of corporate sales. I'm very grateful for the chance to work with him."

Scott broke in. "Now I'm embarrassed. Why don't you join Amy and me for lunch?"

Julie smiled, "There's nothing I'd rather do."

They walked two blocks to a restaurant and were quickly seated amid the noon business crowd. Amy watched Julie and her father select their meals and order non-alcoholic drinks. Not wanting to look like a kid, she ordered an elaborate salad and iced tea in lieu of a cheeseburger and fries.

Julie carried the conversation. "So, what do you think about where we work?"

Amy was animated. "I thought the books were beautiful. I enjoy reading a lot."

"Me too. What do you like to read?"

"Lately, my English lit class has been covering poetry. I love it."

"Has anyone tried the old trick of trying to pass off some rock music lyrics for poetry?"

"Yeah. We busted him, but the teacher didn't catch on at first."

"I used to write poetry, but I wasn't very good at it."

"I tried it too. I think I have a lot to learn."

"Tell you what, maybe someday I'll read you one of my poems, and you read me one of yours. Worst poet buys lunch."

"Deal." They laughed.

Scott watched in silence. Now Julie was working her charms on Amy. Her personality sparkled like a magic wand.

Lunch arrived, and they passed an hour in small talk.

Scott called an Uber for Amy and walked Julie back to the office.

"You're amazing. You made a big hit with Amy."

"I wasn't just being nice. I like really her. She's an incredible girl. I'd congratulate you, but it would go to your head."

"Too late."

Later that evening, Julie watched Scott pace around her apartment. The accumulation of insecurities had left him constantly on edge.

"Scott, come here and sit."

"Don't feel like sitting."

"I have a plan. It's going to take a lot of nerve, and I want to see if you think you can handle it."

Scott sat across from her, his mind racing. "I'm listening."

"What would you say to a plan that would give us plenty of money for a new start? We could simply pay off Dana's alimony, give her the house, and forget her. We could disappear and start a new life. You, me, and Amy starting fresh, far away from here."

"You're serious?"

"It's risky. We would have to give up our current lives, move on, and try something entirely new. We could never return, never contact old friends, a real fresh start. It involves some unpleasantness for both of us. Do you think you can handle that and keep your eyes on the future?"

Scott focused. "Tell me about it."

That Saturday, Scott got Amy up early and told her to get ready.

"Where are we going?"

"You'll see."

"Really? We're doing surprises?"

Scott drove through light traffic to the Los Angeles Sheriff's Academy driver training facility in East L.A.

Amy was interested in all the young men and women in uniform. "What's this?"

"The Sheriff's Department runs a driving academy for young drivers. I signed you up. Today, you get to go wild on wheels."

"Awesome! This is way cool!"

They went to a nondescript building and checked in with an athletic young man with a high, tight haircut, wearing a Sheriff's Department cadet uniform. Amy gave him a warm smile.

Scott pulled her along by her arm. "No flirting."

They sat on folding chairs in a large training room. There were maybe thirty kids and their parents chatting and waiting for the program to begin. A sergeant stepped onto a low stage and welcomed everyone. She described the course of study and the hands-on driving exercises.

The sergeant's assistant, a female cadet, passed out workbooks. The instruction began in earnest with the sergeant talking about the physics of automobiles in motion. She spoke of the forces in play and how vehicles react in various emergency situations. The lecture was supplemented with good graphics and some interesting videos. At the end, questions were answered, the kids took a quiz, and they were ushered onto the tarmac.

Amy was paired with an older deputy driving instructor. She was fitted with a safety helmet and buckled into an old plain-wrap undercover car. Amy drove the big car through a tight road course lined with orange highway cones. She was encouraged to push the car faster and faster, until she lost it and plowed through the wall of cones. She got the car back onto the course and started all over again.

The exercise was repeated over and over until she traveled the course at a respectable speed without wiping out any more cones. She then drove to a large area flooded with water. She learned how to steer into a skid to keep on the road in the wet. She mastered car control with the brakes locked up, keeping the car pointed straight ahead. She participated in a braking exercise demonstrating how far a car travels from the time an emergency is seen by the driver until the car can be stopped. The instructor made her get out and walk the distance the car traveled from the time she hit the brakes until the car stopped. In the last exercise, the instructor had her texting on her phone. She immediately plowed into some cones and a dummy "pedestrian." The dangers of distracted driving were brought home.

The course of instruction lasted three hours. She got a certificate of completion and congratulations from the sergeant. Overall, she had done very well.

Leaving the academy, Amy was animated. "That was amazing! I'm pumped!"

"Better to mess up there than have a real accident. I know it was fun, but you know why we went there, right?"

"Sure. You don't want me to wreck your precious car?"

"Smart-ass. You would be doing me a favor, try again."

"You love me?"

"That's always the right answer."

"I'm hungry."

"We're going to Tito's Baja Burrito Factory."

"Where?"

"It's a storied Mexican restaurant in East L.A. It's also an LAPD hang-out now that you're uniform crazy."

Amy punched him in the arm.

12

week later, Julie came to Scott's office an hour after the close of the business day. Scott was looking out the window.

"Are you okay?"

"I'm not comfortable with this. We're taking a huge chance."

Julie tried to reassure him. "We can change our minds later if we want, but we need to get the ball rolling and make the videos now. We need to make at least three before the buyout goes through."

"I know."

Julie left to check all the offices and found them empty. Having previously looked at the janitorial schedule, she knew the cleaning service wasn't due until after midnight. Julie walked around Scott's office looking for the best place to put the camera. She placed it on top of a tall file cabinet and propped it up amongst the clutter. The angle of view worked well.

"It's time for the show. Don't say anything other than what's on our little script. We'll just make the video and walk out of the room. Do you remember what to do?"

"Yeah. Let's get it over with." Scott left the office and positioned himself outside the door.

Julie set the self-timer, and the camera began recording. Her face suddenly turned stressful and anxiety ridden, she looked into the camera and made her speech. "Scott ordered me to stay late tonight. I think he's going to want sex again. I don't want this!"

They waited about fifteen minutes to make it seem like Julie had set up the camera in advance without Scott's knowledge. Scott walked into the office, ushering Julie ahead of him. He sat in his chair, leaned back, unzipped his pants, and pulled out his penis. Julie went over to him, massaged him until he was erect, and fellated him. It wasn't romantic, it was crude and emotionally sterile. Julie appeared to be a disgusted, reluctant participant. Scott appeared self-satisfied and obviously in charge. Julie left immediately after she was done. Scott tucked himself away and left the room. They waited another hour before retrieving the camera. They watched the video together. It looked like a badly done amateur porn video.

Julie put the camera away. "That's good enough. It looks like I set it up in advance, you walked into the room not knowing you were being recorded, and then I retrieved it much later. Did you notice the neon sign in the background on the building across the street? There's no doubt that the location is your office."

"This sickens me. How many do we have to do?"

"A half-dozen should do it. We could use more, but we need to get going on the plan. The camera records the date and time so it has to be coordinated. If they announce the buyout before we pull the trigger, we will miss our leverage for the big payday."

"I feel like I need a shower."

"Maybe we should get you a tool belt and one of those little porn mustaches."

"I'm glad you think it's funny."

Two more videos were made in the next two weeks, but Julie wasn't satisfied.

She would have to bring Scott along and convince him to cooperate for the next phase. "There are two levels of compensation for sexual harassment, one amount for sex, and a lot more when you combine it with duress. We need to step up our game to get enough money to make a real difference."

Scott looked anxious. "I don't like the sound of that."

"Next time we do a video, you need to rough me up and I'll make it look painful."

"Absolutely not!"

"Come on Scottie. Don't go stupid on me now. We're up to our tits in this. I need you to man up."

"What am I supposed to do?"

"You don't really have to hurt me. We'll just make it look like you did. We just have to make sure it looks real enough."

For the next video, the location was moved to Fiona's office. With the video rolling, Scott shoved Julie into the office and bent her over Fiona's desk. He tore her pants down and entered her from behind. Scott roughly pulled her head back by her hair. Julie spent the next five minutes of violent thrusts looking at pictures of Fiona's little white dog on the credenza. He finished, shoved himself away from her, and left the room. Julie turned, pulled up her pants, leaned on the desk, and cried for the camera.

Two days later they shot another video in Scott's office. This time, Julie slapped him. He pulled a punch to her stomach and pushed her back against a bookshelf. They had sex against the wall with Scott pinning her arms.

Three days later, their last video rolled. Scott was sitting in his chair again, with his pants down around his ankles. Julie straddled him. They struggled, and she hit him. Scott punched her again, and she fought back. He slapped her and shoved her abruptly onto the floor. Scott pushed his chair back, pulled up his pants, and walked out.

Scott was distressed. "This is depraved. I won't do it anymore. You'd better go with what you have, because I'm finished."

Julie was calm and cool. "It's okay, we have enough." She approached him. He resisted her arms. She persisted and held him. He reluctantly held her tight.

"How did I let my life get so screwed up?"

"We're almost there. The rest of this is going to be my show. I'm sorry, but this is the only way it works."

Scott looked at her. "How can you do this?"

"Do you think you are the first jerk who's tried to rough me up?"

"Now I'm a jerk?"

"You know what I mean. Everything I've accomplished in my life has come to me the hard way. The only thing that came easy was pain and disappointment. I thought this job would be a new start, but here I am getting the lousy end of the deal again. I'm tired of my life being out of control. I want freedom and security, and that means money. Are you still with me?"

Scott felt ashamed of his weakness in the face of Julie's strength. "I won't let you down."

Julie spent the next few days copying the videos, writing a draft of her complaint, and buying burner phones for herself and Scott.

Scott asked Jeff for a recommendation for a good employment law attorney, evading Jeff's follow-up questions.

The next day, Julie sat in the waiting room of Howard, Swan, and Kurtz. After a brief wait, a well-dressed office assistant ushered her into Patricia Kurtz's office.

Patty Marilyn Kurtz was a soft-looking, middle-aged woman. She wore her brown hair medium length, and her makeup understated. Clothed in an unremarkable cream-colored pants suit and sensible shoes, her appearance was a trap, inviting the overconfident to underestimate her. Julie thought she looked like a divorced working mom with kids. She almost excused herself to go look for another lawyer.

Kurtz took the initiative. "Julie Wilson, I believe? I'm Patty Kurtz," offering her hand. Julie took it and returned a firm grip. "I understand from my assistant that you would like to lodge a sexual harassment complaint against your employer."

"That's correct. My supervisor coerced me into having sex with him numerous times. He told me that if I wanted to keep my job, I had to have sex with him. He said that my job was to keep him happy. I wrote a memo describing my experience." She handed a folder to Kurtz.

"What company are we talking about?"

"The MacKenna Company."

"Children's educational products, smart toys, etc.?"

"That's it."

Kurtz read the complaint and looked up at Julie.

"This is an egregious violation of law that puts MacKenna in a position of extreme liability if it can be proven."

Julie opened her purse, removed a thumb drive, and handed it to Kurtz.

Patty put the drive into her computer and opened the files. She watched each video, taking notes. At the end of the videos, she studied Julie.

"How did you get this?"

"I put small cameras hidden in the places he liked to do it. I recorded everything because I knew no one would believe me if it was just my word against his."

"That was a brave thing to do. Who is he?"

"My supervisor, Scott Milner. I was hired several months ago as his assistant. The touching and comments started almost immediately. As a new employee, I was on probation, and he used that for leverage to make his sexual demands."

"Why didn't you go to the company?"

"They've proved themselves to be a pack of liars. They don't care about their employees, and I don't trust them."

"This is incredible documentation. It puts them in a vice, and we're going to squeeze them until they scream."

"How much is it worth?" Julie watched Patty carefully.

"Everything I can get, is the stock answer to that question, but practically speaking, I'd estimate lower six figures."

"They're in the middle of an international buyout, and they don't want anything to sully the company's reputation. Bad press could seriously lower the buyout price, or kill the sale altogether. All their retirement benefits are invested in company stock. Needless to say, the stock would take a huge hit. Publicity like this could cost them fifty million or more."

"You probably just hit seven figures."

"Take a look at this." Julie gave Patty the second thumb drive.

Patty watched the videos with a frown. She looked up from the screen in disbelief, "Well, that's disturbing. Do you have any subsequent physical issues?"

"Just one."

Julie took a large envelope out of her purse and passed it across the desk. Patty read the contents. She licked her lips and beamed her most benevolent soccer-mom smile. "We're going to rip them a new asshole."

Julie was feeling better about Patty.

Later that afternoon, Julie answered a knock at her apartment door. Scott stood at her threshold rumpled and needing a shave. He looked depressed. They hadn't made love since making the videos. Julie pulled him in and embraced him.

"How'd it go with the lawyer?"

"Patty's a velvet hammer. She's going to crush them."

"I figured Jeff would come through."

"Patty's going to file my complaint with MacKenna on Monday. Things will get interesting rather quickly after that. Until this is over, we can't be seen together, and we can't use our usual means of communication."

She picked up two phones from her coffee table. "From now on, we use burners and only in an emergency. They might hire investigators, so no sense in pushing our luck."

Scott nodded. "I expect them to quickly fire me once they see the videos."

"I've been thinking about that. It's best if you act like a normal, irate, fired employee. You should work with Jeff to try and get some compensation from MacKenna. See if they'll give you a severance package for not talking. That's something you would do in the normal course of things. Just keep our goal in mind. When we finish this, we disappear out of here. The unpleasantness will fade into the past, and we can rebuild our lives."

Scott kissed her. "I hope it's worth it."

Julie turned to a bottle of wine on the kitchen counter. She poured two glasses.

"To our future."

Scott left the apartment with his new phone. Once in his car, he texted Jeff. "The Cat in an hour?"

The immediate reply, "You're on."

As Scott drove away from Julie's apartment, he noticed a white Chrysler 300 a block behind him. He drove slowly, turning several times until he was sure he was being followed. He thought he'd seen the car occasionally in the last couple weeks and had written it off as paranoia. It wasn't.

Scott drove to the parking lot behind the restaurant and walked into the rear entrance, stopping to look around for the Chrysler. Inside, his eyes slowly adjusted to the darkness. He spotted their customary booth, strode to it, slipped in, and ordered a White Russian. Quickly downing one, he gulped another. Number three was chilling his hand when Jeff appeared in front of him.

Scott looked up. "How's it going?"

"I thought I'd ask you the same thing. You look like hell."

"MacKenna's going to fire me, and I think their bloodsuckers are going to screw me out of my bonus. I'm not happy."

"That's tough. What did you want with Patty? I thought I was your lawyer."

"The referral was for a friend. Everyone is getting canned. Not everybody is willing to go quietly."

"Is that a White Russian?"

Jeff ordered one.

"Do you need any help?"

"Are we client and lawyer officially? I mean, does confidentiality apply to our conversations?"

"When you hired me to do the snooping, we signed a contract, and you gave me money. That's your bond. Anything you tell me is held in

93

absolute confidence. I can't divulge anything out of our relationship, unless I want to get disbarred."

Jeff's drink arrived. They clinked glasses. "Happy Trails."

"I want you to represent me when I get fired. I want some 'Go away' money."

"I'll be glad to wind them up and see what I get for you."

"I'm concerned that my personnel records will be made public."

"Employment matters are covered by the state's privacy laws. They can't just go around divulging that information without risking a violation of law and a subsequent privacy lawsuit. Just don't give that right away when you sign an agreement. I'll look at it."

Scott looked at the back of the room and spotted Lance at the bar.

"Son of a bitch. That private investigator in your video has been following me, and now he's got the nerve to come in here."

"Calm down. No big deal. What's he going to see?"

Scott was already moving out of the booth, picking up a bottle of pepper sauce on the fly.

Jeff reached for him and missed. "Don't go over there! SCOTT!"

Scott was moving quickly. Breaking the neck off the pepper bottle, he circled around behind Lance, pulled his head back, and threw the hot sauce in his face.

Lance screamed. His face felt like it was on fire. He tried to rub the burning sauce out of his eyes, but it just got worse.

Scott pulled Lance off his stool, turned him around, and kicked him in the testicles so hard that it seemed to lift him off the ground. Lance grabbed his crotch and fell to the floor. He was throwing up when Scott got down on his hands and knees and whispered to him.

"That's for fucking my wife. Quit following me."

Jeff hoisted Scott to his feet and frog-marched him out the back door.

Driving away from the restaurant, Jeff angrily looked at Scott, slumped against the passenger door.

"What in the hell is wrong with you? I'm not a criminal defense attorney."

"He had it coming. Anyway, nothing's going to happen. Dana's divorcing me, and he's her new squeeze. It won't go anywhere."

"You better hope. Assault and battery is a serious charge."

"I need you to negotiate my hush money."

"It's hush money now?"

"Julie and I have been having sex after work. She suckered me in and made some videos. Monday, she's going to file her harassment complaint, and I'll be fired shortly thereafter. I have some leverage because no one knows about the buyout. If I let the cat out of the bag, employees will be charging out of there before the ax falls. It's got to be worth some money to keep me quiet."

"You want to blackmail them?"

"After they fire me, I'm no longer under their control. If they want me to behave in a certain manner post-employment, that's a fee for silence."

"You sound like a lawyer."

"Can I stay at your place for a while?"

After some sober-up time and a stern lecture from Jeff, Scott made his way home to get some personal things. Still a little high, he weaved up the front stairs and launched himself into the living room. Amy was on the sofa watching the news.

"What happened to you?"

"Another rough day. Where's your mother?"

"She got a call from the ER at Community Hospital and went there to help a friend."

"That's nice of her." Scott smiled. "No dinner, I guess?"

"No, and I'm getting hungry."

"Is Italian with you, or do you want to go out?"

"Pizza's fine."

Scott pulled out his phone and dialed. "How long will a delivery order take to get here?" Scott ordered dinner and gave them the address.

Scott took out his wallet, tossed it to Amy, went to the master bathroom, shaved, and took a shower. He had just gotten dressed when the doorbell rang.

The food was hot on the breakfast table when he came down, and Amy was reaching for some salad bowls.

"Smells good." Scott got the chili pepper flakes out of a kitchen cabinet, and they dug in.

He watched Amy devour a slice. "What do you think of Julie?"

Amy wiped her mouth on a napkin and nodded her head. "I think she's very nice. She's so beautiful, it's kind of intimidating, but then she also makes you at ease. I felt very comfortable around her."

"She's quite a woman, very capable."

"So, is she your new girlfriend?"

Scott almost gagged on his salad. "What gave you that idea?"

"Come on, Dad. I've got eyes. What's going on?"

"There you go, figuring things out again. Yes, we're more than friends. There's a lot more going on, so you can't tell your mother yet. She's going to find out soon enough. Deal?"

Amy thought for a minute. "Only if you tell me what's going on."

"My company is getting bought out. They're eventually going to fire everyone after the takeover. I'll have to get a new job. The rest of the bad news is, I'll be fired early because of my relationship with Julie. Seems that

I violated a company policy. I've got a few enemies there, so no mercy for Scott."

Amy started to tear up. "What about me?"

Scott embraced her. "I love you, and I'll take care of you. Things will have to change, but I'll be with you through it all, and when you're not with me, you'll have your mom. She'll be keeping the house. I'll make sure it all works for you, and we'll keep everything going well."

Amy sobbed, "This isn't fair."

"No, it's not. Life likes to kick you around every now and then. All you can do is keep your head up, make the best of it, and move on. Would you rather live in a home with two bitter people fighting all the time? That wouldn't do anyone any good. At least this way, your mom and I can stay friendly, and life goes on. We'll make it good for you."

"I don't like the guy that Mom's been seeing."

"Drives a white Chrysler and has one of those nasty man-buns?"

Amy choked a laugh. "That's him. He thinks he's pretty special. He creeps me out."

"Watch yourself until you are sure about him. If Bun Boy does anything that bothers you, tell me immediately, okay?"

Amy nodded and held him closer. "I like that. Bun Boy."

"That's my girl."

Later, after Amy went to bed, Scott went into the den. He opened the closet, knelt down, and punched in the combination to his safe. He took out three handguns and put them on the desk, examining each one. The first gun was a hammerless Airweight Smith & Wesson .38 revolver. Five Shots. The second gun was a childhood gift from his father, an old worn .22 caliber Ruger Bearcat revolver. The last gun was a 1911 Colt .45 automatic that his father had liberated in Viet Nam. Scott disassembled and lubricated each of them, putting two guns back in the safe. He put the Smith &

Wesson in his briefcase and locked it. Then he packed up some clothes and left for Jeff's place.

CHAPTER

13

On Monday, Fiona arrived late to her office. A big-rig driver hauling a load of grapefruit turned his truck over on the freeway while trying to abvoid a meandering driver. The spreading grapefruit turned the busy roadway into a rush-hour parking lot. Fiona eventually found her way to work using a patchwork of surface streets; she was so annoyed, she had to stop for a morning cup of tea.

Fiona's assistant entered her office and dropped an overnight delivery envelope on her desk.

"This came early, signature required."

Fiona opened it and removed a smaller envelope. It was a letter from Patricia Kurtz stating that Julie Wilson was lodging a sexual harassment complaint against the MacKenna Company for egregious sexual misconduct perpetrated by her supervisor, Scott Milner. The letter further stated that Mr. Milner had created a hostile working environment, in which Ms.

Wilson's job was held hostage to Mr. Milner's demand for sexual gratification. The envelope also included a draft of a lawsuit ready to be filed in superior court. The letter further stated that the lawsuit was being held in abeyance pending negotiations with the MacKenna Company and its insurer. The letter requested that representatives of the MacKenna Company and the insurer meet in Patty Kurtz's office because Ms. Wilson was too traumatized to return to her workplace. Ms. Kurtz stated that she didn't think it wise to exacerbate the deep psychological damage already inflicted upon her client.

Fiona asked her secretary to check whether Julie and Scott were at work and found they were both absent.

She immediately went to Jack's office, entered without invitation, and waved him off the phone.

Annoyed at the intrusion, he spat, "What's so important?"

Fiona showed him the letter and draft lawsuit.

"Damn! He must be out of his mind. I warned him what would happen."

Fiona watched Jack's color rise from his collar to his ears, "This is going to be expensive if they have proof. It's classic quid pro quo sexual harassment. Luckily, they don't know about the buyout."

Jack squirmed in his chair and looked away.

"Jack, is there something you want to tell me?"

"She knows. I told them both in confidence when they blew the sales numbers out of the water at the trade show."

Fiona looked disgusted, "Well, the crap's out of the horse now. They're going to crucify us if they have proof."

"Set up a meeting this afternoon with the insurance people and someone from Legal. We need to get ahead of this. Damn! If this gets upstairs, we're done. Our jobs are hanging on by a thread the way it is now."

Fiona remained calm, "It might not come to that. Let's see what they want."

Fiona's secretary called their insurance company and the Legal office.

Later that afternoon, Fiona and Jack met with Carl Fratelli, their insurance agent, and Todd Betts Jr. from Legal.

Todd had the corporate lawyer look down pat. He was trim, well dressed, slightly balding, and sported a USC law school ring. He looked great sitting in Jack's office wearing his charcoal-gray pinstripe suit, a blinding-white shirt, and a maroon school tie with little gold embroidered Tommy Trojans. Playing with his designer pen, he seemed anxious to move the meeting along.

Carl sat opposite Todd dressed in his blue Discount Menswear suit and an unusual necktie that his wife had bought him for Christmas. He was approaching fifty, pudgy, and wore a short beard that made his face look even fatter than it already was. He was perspiring, and his eyes were darting around the room.

Carl was visibly upset, "For God's sake, how did this happen? I thought you did the training and explained the consequences to your employees. Is he nuts?"

Jack gave it a shrug. "Maybe. He's got a reputation as a drinker, but then he's in sales, so it's an occupational hazard. Maybe he's gotten into something that blew out his judgment."

Todd chimed in. "Doesn't matter, does it? We're on the hook. If there's no mitigating circumstances, the only option is to negotiate the cheapest deal we can get."

Carl shook his furry head. "You won't like dealing with Patty. We've been up against her before, and she goes for the throat. This is going to get a lot worse before it gets resolved."

Todd asked to look at Julie's employment file. He paused when he saw her photograph. "Has Milner had any previous incidents?"

The room was silent. Todd snapped his head up. "Don't tell me he has a history of this stuff, and you put him in charge of this incredible-looking woman? For Christ's sake, what were you thinking?"

Jack on the defense. "It was never proven. Someone filed a complaint, but there was no real evidence, so we had to let it go."

Fiona came to Jack's rescue. "You know how it works; no evidence, no case. It's easy for you to come in here late in the game and be the smart guy after something unforeseen happens."

Todd was getting worked up. "Unforeseen? You geniuses couldn't have hired a male assistant?"

Carl broke in. "Stop this. Let's turn this thing inside out and see if there is any mitigating evidence. Maybe we can get some kind of angle going to limit the damage."

The following morning at ten sharp, Team MacKenna huddled in Patty's waiting room. She kept them waiting for thirty minutes so they could work up a good head of steam. Only then did she come out, apologizing for the wait.

"Hi. I'm Patty Kurtz. I'm so sorry for the wait. Something came up, and I had to deal with it."

Patty shook hands all around and ushered them into her conference room. A laptop computer was set up on the conference table. A coffee maker stood on the credenza next to bagels and yogurt.

Patty played the consummate host. "Would you like coffee or tea? We have some breakfast over there." She waved in the general direction of the food.

No one was interested.

Carl poured a glass of water from the carafe on the table.

"Thank you all for coming. As you can read in my letter and the attached draft of our lawsuit, my client suffered serious psychological damage, humiliation, and degradation at the hands of your employee, Scott

Milner. Today, I hope we can come to some kind of a compensatory agreement for my client. Unfortunately, there's nothing that can remove these horrific experiences from her life. We can't castrate Mr. Milner, so monetary compensation is the only avenue open to make this right."

Todd interrupted. "Alleged sexual harassment."

"These were violent predatory sexual violations of my client. Let's not waste time on your fantasy defense." Patty turned her monitor around. She played the first three sex videos for Team MacKenna. When the last video ended, there was dead silence in the room. Carl squirmed uncomfortably in his seat and exchanged a glance with Todd that telegraphed, "We're screwed."

For the second act, Patty called her assistant via the intercom. "We're ready."

In a few moments, the door to the conference room opened, and Julie Wilson was ushered in. She was dressed in a plain gray business suit. She was beautiful, her makeup subdued.

"Ladies and gentlemen, Julie Wilson. Fiona and Jack, you all know each other. Julie, this is Carl Fratelli from the Pugh Western Insurance Company and Todd Betts from MacKenna's legal office."

Julie looked around timidly, hardly meeting their eyes as she shook hands. She looked like an abused puppy anticipating another painful blow.

"For obvious reasons, I've spared my client the pain and humiliation of watching the videos again. Julie, would you please tell these people what happened to you?"

"From the moment I came to work at MacKenna, my boss, Scott Milner, was after me. It began with leering and comments about my appearance. I mean, comments about my body, my face, how I moved, things like that. He was obsessed with my appearance. Then the touching began. He started patting me low on the back, brushing by me, resting his hand on my back and letting it slip down. Eventually he got around to hinting that it would be hard to pass probation if my boss was unhappy. In the end, I was pressured to have sex with him in order to keep my job. He said if I didn't keep him happy, he'd find another assistant who would. He initiated sex with me nine times. I just couldn't take it anymore, so I placed hidden cameras in our offices and recorded him assaulting me. I had to do it because I wanted to expose him as a predator. No one would believe me if there wasn't proof."

Todd broke the silence. "Speaking for all of us and the MacKenna Company, we are very sorry for your pain, and we regret and apologize for these terrible acts. Why didn't you go to H.R. with your complaint? You had the training and knew about MacKenna's policy against this kind of behavior."

"I have been consistently lied to by these two people," pointing to Fiona and Jack. "I earned a bonus that never came. I believe they delayed payment so I'd be fired before they had to pay me."

Jack rose to the bait, but Todd cut him off, "What made you think you were going to be fired?"

Patty gave him a copy of Fiona's layoff letter. He read it in silence.

Todd was getting anxious and trying not to show it. "Where did you get this?"

"I printed it off Fiona's computer after Jack told Scott and me about the upcoming buyout. Jack assured us we wouldn't be losing our jobs. I was suspicious and went looking for more information. That's why I don't trust them. I anticipated more bad faith on their part."

Todd was starting to redden from the collar of his custom-tailored shirt to his expanding forehead. "Can we have some privacy for a moment?"

Patty was enjoying the palpable discomfort of Team MacKenna. "Of course. Julie and I will retire to my office."

Patty and Julie had barely gotten out of the room when Todd exploded.

"What the hell kind of carnival act are you running, Jack? You and Fiona have turned a simple case of harassment into a colossal fuckup!"

Jack whined, "At the time, we had no idea this was going on. Scott and Julie came back from a trade show, and they just nailed the sales numbers. They were a part of the team. I didn't want them to hear some rumor and bail on me before we maxed out our receivables. In hindsight, it wasn't a good idea, but I had no idea this was going on."

Fiona chimed in. "Jack's telling the truth. If we'd had any idea, he wouldn't have told them about the buyout."

Todd's professional demeanor returned. "What's the limit of our liability insurance?"

Carl had visibly paled. "Three million dollars."

Todd looked at him. "It's your money. Do you want me to do the talking, or do you want to handle it?"

Carl swallowed hard. "You do it. Just remember this payout will affect your insurance."

"That's the least of our problems."

Todd looked at Fiona, "Go get them."

Patty came back into the conference room alone. "I don't want to add to Julie's distress. Well, what's the deal?"

Todd didn't answer immediately.

"Come on. Give me a number that will make Ms. Wilson feel like you mean it."

Todd spoke first. "We don't negotiate with ourselves. You're asking for the money, what do you want?"

"Try two million."

Todd rolled his eyes. "Get serious. These kinds of cases are lucky to hit six figures. Do you want your client to undergo the expense and humiliation of a court battle?"

"No, and neither do you. You can't afford to let a jury bond with my very sympathetic client. You can't afford to have the terrible publicity this case would generate mucking up your big buyout deal. You'll need to check with the powers that be at MacKenna, so we'll meet tomorrow at the same time. Maybe you'll see the reasonableness of my position. You'd better have some good news for Julie. By the way, that's a clean two million. You pay my fees and Julie's state and federal taxes."

Todd. "Yeah, right. No point in arguing now. See you tomorrow."

Team MacKenna filed out of Patty's office and retreated to the restaurant next door. Huddling in a small room off the main dining room, they ordered drinks.

Todd stared at the ceiling. "Patty's right. She has an incredible hand, and she knows it. We're totally without leverage. Carl, you better crack the piggy bank. My advice is that you let your people know just how bad this is. They need to sharpen their pencils. Don't let the chiselers get stupid. If you go to court, you'll screw yourselves and us, as well. We need to be together in handling this."

Carl took a sip of his beer. "Yeah, I've got it, but MacKenna might need to chip in considering your overall exposure. Something bothers me about this, but I can't put my finger on it."

Todd perked up. "What do you mean?"

"I've been doing this a long time, and it's just too clean. These things are usually messy as hell. This one is all buttoned up with a bow on top."

"Intuition gets us nothing."

Everyone got into their drink and wondered what the play would be tomorrow.

14

The next morning at ten a.m., a grim-looking Team MacKenna gathered in Patty's reception area. Patty's assistant ushered them into the conference room, leaving without a sound. Ten minutes later, Patty entered, sitting across the table.

"Well, what do we have today?"

Carl cleared his throat. "I'm authorized to offer one million dollars. She pays her own taxes."

Patty never stopped smiling and addressed Carl like he'd spent too much time under the ice. "That's an insulting number, Carl. It is, in fact, an invitation to a court date."

She turned her monitor around again so they could see the screen and played the second three videos of Scott assaulting Julie.

Team MacKenna visibly cringed at the videos.

"Now do you understand? What do you think will happen if a jury sees my client violently abused during a forced sex act? How many of those jurors will be women? How many jurors will have wives, sisters, daughters, and granddaughters? Indeed, how far was what you saw from rape? You need to talk to the half-wit who's screwing this up and get some real money on the table." She tossed a thumb drive to Carl. "Show that to your bosses. We're done here. I advise you not to upset me the next time you come into my office."

Patty got up and left the room without further comment.

Todd wiped his face. "For God's sake, pay them the damned money."

Carl slumped in his chair. "I told them. They don't get it."

"Well, you better make them believe it. This thing is going to hell on a bullet."

The following day, Team MacKenna met again in Patty's reception room. Carl was missing in action, and in his place Buck Preston was representing the Pugh Western Insurance Company. Buck was seventy-three years old and rail thin, with some wisps of white hair carefully arranged on his spotted scalp. He was immaculately dressed in a brown suit and expensive armadillo skin cowboy boots. His cream-colored western shirt was secured at his chicken-like neck with a string tie and a silver-dollar-size chunk of turquoise. He introduced himself to the others. Just then, they were brought into the conference room.

Patty entered, her eyes immediately falling on Buck.

"Buck dear, how nice to see you again."

Buck stood, brushing his lips on her offered hand. "Likewise, Patty. You look fantastic."

"Thank you, but that's not going to get you anything."

Buck almost smiled. "Understood."

"Okay, let's dispense with the foreplay. What's your offer?"

108

Buck sat with his spotted hands crossed on his thigh. "Two bucks, and we'll pay the taxes."

"Buck, honey, that's almost an insult, but I'll cut you some slack because you haven't been here. I presume you've seen the videos showing your client's agent having sex on the job with Julie. I presume you also heard about the disgusting videos showing Scott Milner violently attacking and sexually abusing my client. I can see that you need something else to bring you up to speed."

Patty opened a folder and distributed a medical report to everyone.

"This is a doctor's report from the Adventist Hospital Emergency Room documenting my client's recent miscarriage caused by physical abuse administered by Scott Milner."

Just as Team MacKenna was digesting the medical report, Patty passed out another report.

"Before you say something stupid, this is a DNA lab report identifying Scott Milner as the father of the fetus. If you don't believe it and want to further waste our time, get a swab from Milner and have it tested."

The room was dead quiet except for Todd, who made an involuntary noise like a small animal being strangled.

Buck put the report on the table and sat stone-faced. "Patty, could you excuse us for a minute?"

Patty nodded and left the room.

Buck turned to Team MacKenna.

"Do you people know what my job is?"

Jack refocused his eyes off the floor, "What?"

"I'm paid to spot losers, and this case is a catastrophic loser. If you cause the death of an unborn fetus, you can be tried for murder in some states. This is beyond the pale. I have daughters and granddaughters, and I can tell you where this is headed. If you let Patty get this clusterfuck of a case in front of a jury, you'll go home every day with blood in your underwear."

Buck paused for effect.

"These things aren't just about money. They're about getting even. What Ms. Wilson wants is for MacKenna Company to suffer. I'm out."

Todd panicked. "Buck, if you roll over, you'll hang us out to dry. We'll have nothing left."

"You don't have anything left, and you don't even know it. She wants MacKenna to pay. My advice is for you give her what she wants. My best guess is she wants MacKenna to match our check with another three million. I suggest you do it."

Buck went to the door and signaled Patty to return. He opened his briefcase and took out some paperwork.

"Tomorrow I'll send over a check for three million. In exchange, you need to have your client sign this release and the nondisclosure agreement. We'll put her estimated taxes in an escrow account in her name. Bill my office for your services up to the end of the week."

Buck closed his briefcase, shook Patty's hand, and walked to the door. He turned the knob, paused, and looked at Todd. "I almost forgot. In case you are in doubt, you don't have any insurance."

Patty looked directly at Todd, "You need to go back and tell your brain-dead boss that this is his last chance to get his head out of his ass. Three million, no taxes, and you pay for half of my services. Clear?"

Todd nodded his understanding while staring into the middle space between them.

"Tomorrow, same time."

Early in the morning a messenger from Pugh Western delivered a three-million-dollar check to Patty's office and collected the notarized paperwork.

Later in the day an attractive young female attorney from the MacKenna legal office came to Patty's office. She handed over a cashier's check for three million dollars made out to Julie Wilson, a release of liability, and a nondisclosure agreement. She left with the signed paperwork.

Patty sat at her desk looking at the two checks with satisfaction, and then picked up her phone.

"Are you free for lunch? I have something for you."

CHAPTER

15

Jeff and his girlfriend had booked on a two-week vacation in Hawaii, but his workload was just too heavy for him to leave. She went with a girlfriend instead, while Jeff got to babysit Scott drinking up his liquor and pacing around his condo in his underwear.

Scott was relieved to be staying with Jeff now that things were so seriously strained with Dana. He wasn't sure that Dana had even noticed that he was gone all week.

He called his daughter regularly to keep in touch. She was putting up a good front, but he could detect the underlying stress. He asked her to go to dinner.

Amy hopped in his car and kissed him. "I miss you."

Scott got a lump in his throat. "Me too."

"Mom wants to see you when we get back."

"I can imagine."

"What are we doing?"

"Back to the fifties."

"Oh."

Scott smiled at the obvious lack of enthusiasm in her voice.

"Cheer up. I think you'll like it."

Amy asked, "Are we going to have to listen to surf music are we?"

"No, but if you ask me, the best music flew into the mountain along with Stevie Ray Vaughan."

Scott drove to Bert's Big Bun restaurant in Toluca Lake. He had to park a block away because it was a busy night.

While they walked to the restaurant, Scott explained. "I got to thinking about your grandfather the other day. He used to take me here when I was a kid. You never met him, but he was a serious car guy. He used to call himself a 'gear head' and always had some old car that he was working on in the garage. He used to hang out here with his high school buddies."

"Why did he die so young?"

"Agent Orange. He died from pancreatic cancer."

Talking above the rumble of the custom cars, Scott told Amy the history. "Bert's is one of the few surviving old-fashioned Southern California drive-in restaurants still in operation. They still serve the same menu as they did fifty years ago, and they don't make any concessions to current dietary trends. It's really busy on Friday because of the car show in the parking lot."

They walked into the restaurant just as two people left their counter seats. Scott and Amy sat down on the padded stools and watched the servers hustle behind the counter.

Amy looked around. "What's next, a 'surfers vs. greasers' rumble?"

Scott gave her a menu. "How about a double cheeseburger, fries, and a cherry cola?" Amy shrugged, so Scott doubled his order. "No onions."

Amy giggled. "This is amazing." She pointed to a couple in rockabilly outfits. "What's that all about?

The guy wore threadbare button-front jeans with the cuffs rolled up, exposing white sweat sox and black high-top sneakers. He wore a sleeveless denim jacket over a stained Hank's Cams T-shirt with his cigarettes rolled up in one sleeve. His hair was jelly-rolled, and he sported Elvis-size sideburns. His girlfriend's green-tinted hair was braided in pigtails. She wore a green-and-gold letterman jacket over a poodle skirt. Her tattoos flowed from under the jacket cuff all the way to her fingertips. Red high-tops finished the fashion statement.

Scott laughed. "Rockabilly people mimic the fifties. It's over the top, sort of like the fifties viewed in a fun-house mirror. They have car clubs, drive hot rods and old cars. It's a whole retro thing back to the James Dean era. I kind of like the nostalgic feel of it going back to a simpler time."

"Not for me, but I sort of like the look. It sure sets them apart."

The food came, and Scott asked for a side of blue cheese dressing.

"If you are really cool, you don't use ketchup. You get a side of blue cheese or Thousand Island dressing for your fries."

"This might be why your friends are having heart attacks."

"I'm just catching the spirit. Would you rather have chili fries?"

After dinner, they walked out to the car show.

Amy pointed to a cut-down, rusty hot rod. "What's that?"

"A rat-rod."

"How come they're called rat-rods?"

"What else would you call something that looked like that?"

Amy liked the rainbow-colored cars and gleaming chrome. It was obvious that she preferred the restored classics. She particularly liked a copper-colored 1959 Chevy Impala with the famous cat-eye taillights. She asked the owner lots of questions about the car and got an invitation to sit in the driver's seat.

Amy looked out from behind the steering wheel and teased, "If you loved me, you'd buy me one of these."

"That car costs as much as your first year in college; you should be in focus."

"I am focused."

"I mean in a Ford Focus, about six years old. Let's go."

They left the car show when Scott sensed that Amy was getting bored. It's impossible to be nostalgic for something you never lived through.

Scott pulled into the driveway at home. "Is Bun Boy around?"

"Not when I left."

"I want you to go upstairs immediately, okay? Your mom and I might have some words, and I want you gone."

"Okay."

"I mean it. Don't snoop."

"I said I wouldn't."

They entered the house. Amy ran upstairs, and Scott faced Dana in her power center, the kitchen.

"Amy said you wanted to see me."

Dana slid a bundle of legal papers across the counter to Scott.

"It's a divorce agreement. Please look it over and sign it."

Scott scanned the documents. "I want Jeff to look them over. If there are any issues, I'll let you know. How soon can you file these, if I sign?"

"My lawyer can file as early as Wednesday."

"I'll let you know on Monday. If the papers are okay, I'll have Jeff meet your lawyer in court to make sure they are filed as promised."

Dana slightly relaxed from her battle stance.

Scott was conciliatory. "For Amy's sake, I'm not interested in turning this into a battle. The only thing I want is my legal visitation rights with Amy. Are we in agreement?"

"Agreed, if your lawyer doesn't go crazy with conditions."

"Okay, then."

"I should have Lance file charges against you for assault. He's just a private investigator I hired because I couldn't trust that you'd been telling me the truth."

"I understand he's investigating under your bedsheets. You can skip the fake indignation. I know he's your boyfriend. I don't care. Screw anyone you want, but keep him away from me from now on."

"Fine, and you keep your hands off him."

"Amy said that Bun Boy creeps her out. If anything happens between Amy and him, I'll hold you responsible. You better keep your boy on a leash."

"Get out!"

Scott picked up the papers and walked to the door. "I'll be back for some clothes tomorrow. I don't want him here."

In order to show his appreciation to Jeff, Scott bought a bottle of single malt on the way home. Back at Jeff's place, he poured three fingers, slid in an ice cube, and read the divorce documents, making a couple of notes. Overall, Scott was amazed. He had no issue with the papers, but Jeff would have to check them.

Jeff arrived home at six in the evening.

Scott greeted him with, "Dana served me with divorce papers today. They're on the kitchen table."

Jeff paused while hanging up his jacket. "Is that good or bad?"

"It's good. I'm done. I want to sign them Monday. She doesn't know that I'm going for some separation money from MacKenna, and if the papers are filed before I get the money, community property is null and void, and she doesn't get half of it."

"I can see you've been thinking. Let's not count our money just yet."

Jeff came back into the room wearing sweatpants and a Clapton tour T-shirt. He poured himself a shot of the whisky.

"Do you want to watch a movie?"

"I want to talk about Monday."

16

onday morning Fiona walked into her office and saw Scott and Jeff sitting in her visitor chairs. The first thought that came to her mind was, "What now?"

"How about calling for an appointment?"

Scott looked through her. "You'll be firing me quick enough, so I thought I'd visit while I was still on the payroll. This is my attorney, Jeff Teller. Jeff, meet Fiona Dalton."

Fiona shook Jeff's offered hand. "You just saved us a stamp." She picked up a letter from her desk and handed it to Scott. He read a short memo saying he'd been terminated for unspecified causes. The letter was only as long as it needed to be. Someone in Legal must have abridged it. The letter gave no causes for the termination, and no allegations were stated. Nothing written that a clever attorney could turn against them; just "Get out."

Scott handed the paper to Jeff, who quickly read it and put it in his briefcase.

"I want to talk to you about my severance package."

Fiona snorted a laugh. "You're really something. First you sexually abuse Julie Wilson, beat her, and now you want to get paid for it? Get out of here."

"If the other employees find out that the buyout will cost them their jobs, you'll have a stampede on your hands. If the issue of my relationship with Julie gets out, there will be more public relations problems for the company. I'm offering to keep my own counsel for a small amount of money."

Fiona was incredulous. "You're trying to blackmail us?"

"Look up the first amendment to the Constitution. I have the right to speak the truth. If you want to abridge my rights, then you need to motivate me to accept limitations on my rights. I may or may not talk about these things after I leave here. That's up to me, unless I'm motivated to stay silent."

Fiona went quiet, weighing what Scott had said. Privacy laws in California cover employment records, but someone could certainly talk about their own employment records without liability. Technically, the buyout information was covered by the confidentiality agreement that Scott had signed when he came to work for MacKenna, but if he let the cat out of the bag, the fallout could be catastrophic. What good would it do MacKenna to sue someone who didn't have anything?

Scott doubled down. "Do you think it would raise questions if the company found out the Director of Human Resources was firing the husband of the woman she's sleeping with?"

Fiona froze. She didn't trust herself to speak for a moment.

"Someone's been telling you stories."

"Cut the crap. I have video of you and my wife swapping body fluids, so let's talk money."

"What do you want?"

"Two hundred thousand. It's nonnegotiable. You need to go sell this to Jack and the rest of them. Make them believe that I'm dangerous and I'm about to bring down their house of cards. The two hundred grand is chump change to the company. I'm going to lose half in taxes, and I need to have something left over for a new start."

Fiona pointed to Jeff. "What's he here for?"

"He's keeping me from coming across that desk and beating the crap out of you with your electric stapler."

Scott and Jeff left with a promise from Fiona to call when she had something to report.

In the elevator Jeff grabbed Scott by the arm. "What's that about beating Julie?"

Scott's stomach sank. Jeff had no idea the harassment claim was a scam. He had to think fast.

"An exaggeration. Sometimes Julie likes her sex rough, so I'd slap her now and then. Look, you've seen her. I was having sex so far out of my league that I couldn't even see the ballpark. If she wanted me to slap her now and then, I did it."

Scott went to his bank, withdrew everything from their checking and savings accounts, and closed them out.

Scott parked in front of his house in the early afternoon. He opened the garage door with his remote and didn't see the Chrysler. He went inside the garage, got out a large rolling travel bag, and closed the garage door.

When he entered the house, Dana was waiting for him.

"Jeff looked over the papers. I'm agreeing to everything. There are just two changes, and then I'll sign off. Jeff is working out the language with your attorney. If all goes well, he'll meet her in superior court Wednesday to file the papers."

"What additions?"

"The first addition is that you won't charge up our credit cards or do anything to further indebt us before the papers are filed. There's also a statement to the effect that we agree to extinguish our community property rights as of the filing date. I'll be checking with a credit agency. If you add anything to our debt before Wednesday, the deal is off, and I'll have Jeff drag out the divorce for as long as he can."

"What's the second?"

"It spells out, in unequivocal terms, my joint custody rights. I want fifty-fifty. When the changes are finalized, your attorney will run them by you."

Scott opened a small zippered bag, removed two bundles of cash, and set them on the counter. Dana picked up a bundle and examined it.

"This is all the money from our checking and saving accounts, it came to $34,511.00. I split it into bundles of fifteen thousand each. Amy will need a car now that we're splitting up. I've tested her, and she's a good driver. I'm going to take the extra forty-five hundred dollars and match it out of my pocket. That gives me about nine thousand dollars that I can use to buy Amy a decent used car and her first year's insurance.

"I closed our accounts, so you need to take that $15,000 and open a new account somewhere. That money will carry you over until the alimony payments start. Are we good?"

Dana stood silent for a moment. "Yes, I think so."

"I've been fired from MacKenna, but I'll still have my personal phone and computer. If you have trouble contacting me, go through Jeff's office."

"If you are unemployed, how are you going hold up your end of the divorce agreement?"

"I saw this coming, so I've been shopping my résumé around. I've had a couple nibbles, so I anticipate that I'll be employed by the end of the month."

Scott went into the master bedroom and loaded his travel bag with clothes and toiletries. He went to the den, packed up his laptop, and took the other two guns from the safe. He returned to Dana.

"I guess that's it. I'll stop by tomorrow to take Amy car shopping. I'll make sure she gets a good one that will take her all the way through college."

"I can't believe you thought all this out."

"I'm closing out the books on a lot of things. Time to start over. One last thing, do you know what an emancipated minor is?"

"No."

"In this state, any minor child over the age of fourteen with an income of minimum wage or better can petition the court to be declared an emancipated minor. That means that they're completely free of parental control. If you try moving Amy out of the state, or hassle me about my visitation rights, I'll have Jeff put her on his payroll as an intern for minimum wage, and we'll go to court to have her declared an emancipated minor."

"I wouldn't do that."

"I wouldn't think you'd be fucking Fiona and Lance at the same time, but there it is."

Scott left the house and walked toward his car thinking, "I'm getting good at this lying thing. I may pursue a second career in law."

On the way home that night, Scott made a side trip to Jimmy's in Eagle Rock. He came through Jeff's door with double cheeseburgers and chili fries.

Jeff sniffed the air. "Jimmy's!"

"I hope you don't have to go to court tomorrow. Jimmy's chili can take one out of social contact for a while."

"No problem, I'm inoculated. I've been hitting the original Jimmy's down on Figueroa since high school."

Scott put the food in the microwave and uncapped two Belgian ales.

Scott brought Jeff up to date. "I think we're good for Wednesday. I laid it out for Dana, and she seemed to roll over. If she doesn't do something stupid like buy a new sports car tomorrow, we're done."

"I cleared my calendar on Wednesday. I talked to her lawyer, and she sounds cool, doesn't seem like a game player. Everything should go smoothly."

"Did you ever find out any more information on Bun Boy?"

"Who?"

"Dana's gumshoe."

Jeff laughed. "I'll never look at one of those buns again without thinking, 'Bun Boy.' Thanks for putting that in my head."

"Hasmik worked him up. He came from Fresno. Had a couple small legal scrapes as a kid, possession of weed, etc. Went to Afghanistan as a private contractor. Got his two-year degree in police science at Valley College. He went to some Mickey Mouse detective academy that prepped him for the state exam, and bingo, he's a private investigator. He's got a concealed-carry permit, so be careful. He could be armed at any time. There was only one thing that stood out. He was hired to shadow some guy for a client, and the guy he was shadowing just disappeared. No trace."

"You think Lance disappeared him?"

"No indication of that. Cops investigated and came up with nothing"

Later that evening, Scott called Amy. "Hi. What's up?"

"Hi, Dad. Doing my homework. Bun Boy showed up. He's sitting in the den with a freezer bag full of ice on his privates."

Scott suppressed a laugh. "I guess he was your mom's emergency the other night. I talked to her about the three of us settling into a new normal situation, and we thought you might like to have your own car."

Scott held the phone away from his ear as Amy went crazy.

"Really! You're getting me a car! I can't believe it!" Then her voice dropped. "It's not your car, is it?"

"No. Tomorrow after school, we're going to go out to Auto City. Let's see if we can find you something sensible."

"You shouldn't have told me; I won't sleep tonight."

"Okay, calm down. We're just shopping. If the right car doesn't pop up, we'll keep looking until it does. Okay?"

"Absolutely! This is so awesome!"

"Just remember, if you stack this car up, the default option is a bus pass and Uber. You can buy a lot of Uber rides for the cost of a car."

Scott drove by the house at 3:30 p.m. on Tuesday. Amy was waiting on the front steps. She ran to the car, jumped in, and buckled up. "Come on, let's go."

"I think I created a monster."

Scott laid down the ground rules while they drove to Burbank. "I know Mustangs and Camaros are cool and sexy, but you need basic transportation. We're looking for a nice, clean, low-mileage car that's within our budget, which is about ten grand. Good gas mileage is mandatory, because you are buying your own gas. Are we cool with all that?"

"Sure. Oh, I can't wait!"

They pulled into Auto City's parking lot in an industrial park near the Burbank Airport. They barely got out of the car when a salesperson with "Sofie Martinez" printed on her nametag came over to them. "Hi, can I help you?"

"Hi, Sofie, I'm Scott, and this is Amy. We're looking for a car for her. Low miles, good gas mileage, and under ten grand. No smoker cars."

"We can do that. Come on inside." Scott and Amy sat down in her cubicle while Sofie began a computer search using Scott's parameters. She printed an impressive list of cars, including thumbnail color pictures, and handed it to Scott. He borrowed her pen and crossed out the convertibles, pickup trucks, the fast cars, and anything with over 50,000 miles. He handed the list to Amy.

"See anything you like?"

"How come you scratched out the convertibles?"

"Because a lot of new drivers crash their first car, and convertibles don't have rollover protection. I don't want your next set of wheels to be a wheelchair."

Amy put on a fake pout and got working on the list, circling several cars.

She handed the list to Sofie. "Let's get going."

Scott estimated that the expansive asphalt lot held over five hundred cars. Sofie navigated them through the sea of rubber and chrome like a ship's pilot.

They looked at Corollas, Civics, and Focuses. In all, they looked at a dozen small cars. All of them were in good shape and acceptable to Scott, but they didn't appeal to Amy. They walked by a baby blue 2013 VW Beetle. It looked good, and someone had put a flower vase on the dash as homage to the old original Beetles. Amy's face lit up.

"This is so cute. I love it." She got in, adjusted the seat, and beamed out the window. "I think I found it!"

Scott looked at the sticker. The price was $10,500. It had 25,000 miles, air-conditioning, and an automatic transmission. It was late in the afternoon, and the light was fading. Scott got out a small flashlight. He opened the hood and trunk and shined his light into the far corners looking for rust or evidence of a prior accident. He looked under the car for fluid leaks and put his foot on the bumpers, pressing up and down to check the condition of the shocks. Lastly, he checked the fluid levels and the condition of the tires.

"Let's take it for a drive."

With Sofie in the back, Amy drove them all around Burbank. Scott insisted that she drive long enough to get a real feel for the car. As they drove, Scott tried every switch, button, and lever in the car to make sure everything was operational. When they pulled back into the lot, Amy was still excited.

"This is my car."

They sat in the office while Sofie drew up the paperwork. The price was fair, and the company had a one-price, no haggle policy, so there weren't any negotiations to conduct. If Amy changed her mind, Sofie said, the car could be exchanged for another within seventy-two hours. The car had a twelve-month warranty, if she brought it back to Auto City for repair. It was a done deal. Scott put down a three-thousand-dollar cash deposit, and they shook hands. Scott told her they would pick up the car on Wednesday morning. Sofie said they would detail the car and go over it again for Amy.

On the way back to the car, Amy hugged Scott. "Thanks, Dad. This is the best thing we've ever done!"

"Be sure to thank your mom, too. This is your first adult obligation. Driving is a great adventure, but it comes with some serious responsibilities. You can die at the wheel if you screw up, or worse, wind up a vegetable. You can also kill someone if you aren't careful. Driving is a joy, but one that carries a lot of weight. I think you're ready."

"When can we get my big-girl driver's license?"

"Tomorrow, about noon. I have some things to do in the morning, then we'll go to the DMV and get it done. You'd better download the DMV study guide and bone up tonight."

"What does 'boning up' mean?"

"I have no idea. It's just something people say."

17

t ten in the morning, Scott went to a new bank, opened a
checking account, deposited three thousand dollars in cash,
and purchased a nine-thousand-dollar cashier's check.

He drove to his house at eleven. Amy was ready and waiting.

They drove to the Pasadena DMV in an attempt to avoid the crowd
in Glendale. Scott had called for an appointment, and after a brief wait,
Amy passed the written test. Going outside, they met David, a thin, young,
black man, resplendent in his hipster outfit. Scott figured that he might be
on the edge with the DMV dress code, lax as it is. He cheerfully greeted
them, checked Amy's learner's permit, and they got into Scott's car. Amy
buckled herself in, and she also checked to make sure David was buckled
in. She checked her mirrors, put on her turn signal, and pulled out into
traffic.

Scott got a diet soda from a machine and paced outside, nervously awaiting their return. Twenty minutes later, Amy pulled into the parking lot and drove over to an area marked out with orange cones. She parallel parked on the first try and then pulled into a visitor parking spot. David entered some information into his laptop and looked up. "Congratulations. You passed." Amy looked at her dad with a big smile. She shook David's hand, thanked him, and took her certificate inside. She got her picture taken, passed the vision test, and got her interim license, allowing her to drive until the permanent license arrived. They proudly drove away.

The next morning Scott showed up at the house. Amy was waiting for him. He parked and locked the car. "Uber should be here in about ten minutes, then we can go get your car." The Uber driver pulled into the driveway as they spoke.

Scott and Amy walked to Sofie's office space and greeted her. Scott gave her the cashier's check for nine thousand and paid for the remaining balance in cash. Sofie called the bank to verify that the check was good and handed Amy the keys to her new VW.

Amy pulled off the lot as happy as she could be, driving very conservatively. She drove so cautiously that Scott was a bit concerned. The functional speed limit in L.A. starts at ten miles an hour over the posted limit. Anyone driving the legal speed limit is treated like a mobile speed bump and an impediment to expeditious travel.

They went to a Thai restaurant for lunch.

"Have you ever had Thai before?"

"Not really."

"You can get one of the lunch combos and sample things. I'd recommend pad Thai. It's mild and tastes good."

It was settled. They ordered two pad Thais with shrimp and two Thai iced teas.

"I guess you got me the car because you and Mom won't always be available to drive me around?"

"That's part of it. Also, you've been doing great in school, and you're handling our family situation like an adult. We're pleased that you are doing so well."

Amy blushed. "What's happening with you and Mom?"

"It looks like the divorce papers are going to be filed on Wednesday. No hassle and no drama. We're just moving on."

Amy held back her emotions as the finality of the family dissolution hit home.

The timely arrival of the food shifted her focus.

"Be sure to squeeze that slice of lime on your food. It makes a big difference."

She tentatively tasted the noodles. "This is really good."

They arrived home, and Amy immediately put her new car in the garage to protect it.

Scott smiled at her. "We're going to have a little session on maintaining your new car. Oil changes, keeping the right amount of air in the tires, that kind of stuff. You're going to love it."

"I think I'm going to give her a name."

Back at Jeff's place, Scott called Fiona.

"Where's my check?"

"They agreed to your request, and it's being processed."

"Good. I can tear up my press release. When will it be ready?"

"Tomorrow noon. You'll have to sign a mandatory nondisclosure and confidentiality agreement."

"Fine. I just want the money."

The gun shop was open until six p.m. Scott entered, and right away he liked the old-school ambience. The shop had obviously been in business a long time. The dark wood paneled walls held wall-to-wall gun racks loaded with all kinds of rifles, ranging from antiques to black rifles. There was even a moth-eaten old moose head on the wall looking a little worse for wear. Scott opened the empty cylinder on his Smith & Wesson Airweight revolver and set it on the counter. A salesman named Dean came to him.

"What do you need?"

"Ammo and a holster."

Dean read the stamping on the gun barrel.

He reached behind and pulled a small box of .38 +P ammo off the shelf. "The gun is made to take the more powerful +P ammo. These rounds have ninety-grain bullets. They're designed to provide moderate recoil and high impact from these short-barreled light revolvers." He pulled one round from the box and dropped it in Scott's hand. It looked impressive.

"Sounds good, how much?"

"About thirty-five bucks for a box of twenty-five."

"That's expensive."

"It's not for practice; it's for saving your life. With any luck, you'll never have to fire one off. I've got some reloads here that you can practice with. Fifteen bucks for a box of fifty."

"Good. I also need some .45 ACP ammo and a couple boxes of .22 long rifles. Got a compact holster?"

Dean produced a thin pocket holster. "The exterior of the holster is made with a gripping material designed to make the holster stay inside the pocket when the gun is withdrawn."

Scott put the holster in his front pocket and slipped the unloaded revolver in the holster. It was comfortable, and the average person would never know the gun was there.

"I'll take it all."

Scott was already home when Jeff arrived. Jeff walked by Scott's open briefcase and noticed the revolver.

"What's the gun for?"

"Disappearance insurance, I'm still not sure about Lance, but I'm not taking any chances."

"I doubt you'll need that."

"There was a sign in the gun shop. 'Better to have a gun and not need it than to need a gun and not have it.' I think that fits my relationship with Lance at the present time."

CHAPTER

18

ednesday morning Scott put on athletic shoes, a T-shirt, and shorts. He was determined to start fresh, and that meant getting in shape. He parked by the Rose Bowl in Pasadena and prepared to join the other joggers lapping the Bowl. It was a beautiful, cool morning, with a light misty fog rendering the adjacent golf course a little mysterious. His phone was strapped to his waist. He put his earpieces in and selected the Allman Brothers tune, "You Don't Love Me," for company. He took it easy, and while he didn't run very far, he got further than he thought he would, walking the rest of the lap. He enjoyed the feeling of doing something for his health. The rock music helped to keep his feet moving. The alcohol abatement would be more difficult.

He returned to the condo and made a scramble with eggs, ham, zucchini, and some feta cheese. He was determined to reel in his carbohydrate intake and lose some weight.

Scott roamed around the condo, tried to watch TV, but lost patience with the political talking heads. He wondered when would Jeff call and verify the filing of the divorce papers.

Jeff finally called him in the afternoon. "It's done. Papers are filed."

"Fantastic! I've been on edge all day. I didn't even trust myself to have a drink, I didn't want to be totally wasted by the time you called. Thanks, Jeff. I owe you so much. I don't know how to repay you for helping me through this mess."

"That's easy. Get a new place before my girlfriend gets back."

"You'll have it! How about a dinner and drinks on me?"

Scott sent a text to Fiona. "When can I pick up the check tomorrow?"

The reply, "Eleven in Jack's office."

Dana called Fiona. "What's happening?"

"Scott and his lawyer were in here asking for a severance package of two hundred thousand dollars. MacKenna gave it to him."

"He didn't mention that to me when he was here. I guess it doesn't matter. He signed the divorce papers, and he's out of my life. What about Julie? Where is she?"

"No contact yet. When can I see you again?"

"Soon. It'll be over soon, and then we can celebrate."

Lance stood at the kitchen island. Dana was in another foul mood.

Lance didn't say much. He was learning.

He finally tried, "What's wrong?"

"Scott was here. The divorce papers got filed, but he's being a bastard."

"So, what's wrong? I thought that's what you wanted?"

"It's Amy. He has me over a barrel. I'll still have to deal with him because of the visitation rights."

"Can you buy him off?"

"He won't do that."

"Do you think he could be scared off? I'm good at that sort of thing."

"Hold that thought. I want to see how this plays out with him getting a severance package from MacKenna. He's up to something."

"Whatever you need, I'm here."

"I want you to follow him again."

"Sure."

"He knows your car, so get rid of the pimpmobile, and get that ridiculous bun off of your head or wear a hat. It's about as subtle as having a parrot on your shoulder."

He stepped to her and kissed her deeply.

She caressed him between his legs, "Are you back in commission?"

"The spirit's willing."

Lance grabbed her ass as they went up to the bedroom.

The following morning at eleven sharp, Scott went to Jack's office. Fiona stood behind Jack.

Jack was sullen. "Look who's here for his blood money."

"What are you talking about?"

"It's not enough that you humiliated and beat Julie, you caused her miscarriage."

"Stop babbling and make some sense. What miscarriage?"

Fiona threw the hospital report at him, followed by the DNA test report. "Read it, you pig."

Scott was stunned reading the reports. He sat down. "I didn't know anything about this. She told me she couldn't get pregnant."

Jack was seething. "Liar! You knew she was pregnant and wanted to end it to protect yourself."

"I didn't know a thing about this. It's terrible!"

Fiona threw a sheaf of legal papers at him. "Sign these, and get out!"

Scott was disoriented. He signed the waivers and agreements, picked up the check, and walked out.

"Liar!" echoed down the hall, chasing him to the elevator.

When Scott got to his car, he took out the burner phone and called Julie. No answer, so he sent her a text. "Need to talk now. Call me."

CHAPTER

19

axwell Moon was a hard man. He'd been an LAPD investigator for twenty years, and his job led him to believe that
just about anyone was capable of doing just about anything.
He was naturally reserved about people until he got to know them well,
actually, very well. Five years ago, Max was working undercover, tailing a
suspect in his unmarked car, when a drunk blew through a red light doing
fifty miles per hour and T-boned his car. Max's partner was on the impact
side and died immediately. Max was seriously injured, spent a year and a
half in rehab, and was forced to take a disability retirement against his will.

From the waist up, Max was a broad-shouldered, muscular, fifty-
year-old, with close-cut salt-and-pepper hair. He had a scar on his chin, a
legacy of the car accident. He had fairly short legs and now walked with a
limp. He looked like a tough guy to knock over. He now made his living as
an insurance investigator.

Max sat in Buck Preston's office while Buck made himself a cup of tea. He wondered just how long it took to dunk a tea bag and whether Buck was going for the world record. Buck finally discarded the exhausted bag, noisily sipped his tea, and the meeting proceeded.

"We just took a huge hit on a harassment case, and I'd like you to look into it. On the surface it looks open-and-shut with good documentation, but something is off. Carl sensed it, and I agree. They had us over a barrel, and we had to shell out a lot of money for lack of a credible defense. Look at this." Buck played the videos and showed Max the lawsuit, Julie's personnel file, and the lab reports.

"That's disturbing. It's one thing to read about an allegation of violent sexual harassment and quite another to see it played out. What set you off?"

"There were some unusual elements. The company had alienated the Wilson woman by lying to her about losing her job to a layoff, and then tried to chisel her out of a bonus. I'm wondering if she might have staged a phony harassment complaint to get even and make some easy money."

"How much are we talking about?"

"We're in it for three mil and another three thrown in by the company."

Max whistled. "Serious money."

Buck frowned. "They maxed out the policy, had us pinned like a butterfly. Look into it, and see if you can shake anything loose. If we discover fraud, maybe we can claw back some of the money. MacKenna should cooperate because they also got reamed."

Max began by meeting with Todd from MacKenna Legal. Todd was cooperative, calculating that he might look good to the company if Max found out something and helped them get back their money.

Max wasn't impressed with Todd, writing him off for a spoiled frat boy. "I've read the reports and talked to Buck about the case. What's your take?"

"They had us by the short ones. The company didn't want the bad publicity, Julie had some solid proof, and the accused had a history of bad acts."

Max shifted his papers. "There are some unusual things in this mess. For example, Jack telling Julie and Scott about the buyout against company orders. He gave them the leverage they needed to really turn on the money screws. I'm also interested as to why, knowing his history, they put Scott in charge of this stunning woman. It looks like either grotesque incompetence or a setup."

Todd said, "It's not that simple; everyone has credible explanations. I think organizational pressure and the need for big sales revenue clouded their judgment."

"I'd like to see the personnel files of Jack, Julie, Fiona, and Scott."

"Strictly speaking, Julie's is the only one who waived privacy rights to her file."

"It's just you and me alone in here. Wouldn't you like to take credit for getting the money back?"

Todd paused for a beat and dug in his desk drawer. "I need a cup of coffee." He put the files on the desk and walked out, leaving Max alone with them for fifteen minutes.

Max photographed most of the documents with his phone before Todd returned. "I think I'll start with Scott Milner. I'll call you when I want to talk with the others."

Max met with Bruce in an old classic coffee shop. Tinker came in rubbernecking like a felon on the run. He worked for the NSA and had gambling issues.

"How's your luck?"

"What are you, a comedian? I was snake bit all last week."

"That's tough. Could you use some cash?"

"What do you have?"

Max slid a folder across the table with pertinent information on the four people. "I want a full package on these four people. I need names of family members, personal history, phone records, social media, credit and financial info, the works."

"That's expensive."

"I can do a grand per person."

"No way! If I get caught, it's my ass in a sling. I want three."

"Six grand all in, or I'll shop it elsewhere else."

"Make it seven. You're on an expense account. How about a little taste now?"

"Done. Here's a grand and the rest upon completion. Nothing personal, but you're a degenerate gambler, and I want to keep you focused on what I want."

Scott got a call on the burner phone and ran to answer.

"Julie?"

"Why did you call? We agreed not to do any contact until things settle down."

"You never told me you were pregnant. How could you do this? You talked about us starting over with a new family, and then you cynically made me complicit in the termination of your pregnancy? There's a line I won't cross for money, but apparently that doesn't apply to you."

"Do you remember me saying that my first husband rode a motorcycle? I was riding with him one day, and we got hit by a car. My drunken husband had a couple scrapes, and I had internal injuries. The doctors told me that I'd never conceive. While we were married I had two other miscarriages trying to prove them wrong. After that, nothing more happened; the pregnancies stopped. This one was a complete surprise to me.

You didn't cause that miscarriage. It happened spontaneously. It was just a coincidence."

Scott was incredulous. "That sounds pretty damned convenient."

"It's true. Have some faith in me. Has anything happened between us to make you think I'm some kind of monster? It was an accident."

Scott went silent listening to his angry breath hissing over the phone.

"Look, this isn't smart. I'm getting off the phone. Have faith in me. I love you."

Scott was too late, and his "Where are you?" went unanswered.

CHAPTER

.... *20* ....

Scott scanned the local papers looking for a place so he could make good on his promise to Jeff.

He found a furnished two-bedroom apartment, half a duplex. The ad said it was available for a maximum of one year. Scott called the number and got the owner's grandfather. The occupant was gone on deployment to Iraq for a year and had left it to his grandfather to rent the apartment out. Scott agreed to meet the landlord in an hour.

He knocked on the door of the appropriate unit. A short balding man wearing an old black suit with a white shirt open at the collar, maybe seventy years old, answered the door.

"Hi, I'm Scott. I guess this is the place for rent?"

"I'm Arbi. Come in. My grandson moved all his personal things out, including the kitchen utensils, but the furniture, exercise equipment, and TV are a part of the rental."

Scott took a tour around the apartment. He checked the operation of the taps, flushed the toilet, checked the locks on the windows, and lastly, the thermostat. Everything worked, but none of the furniture matched. The place was obviously furnished by a single man in the "yard sale revival" style. A big-screen TV dominated the living room, and there was some exercise equipment in one bedroom. The frayed rug was faded and sported some interesting-looking stains. The mattress slumped in the middle, and it looked like a Petri dish to Scott.

"Who did you say the owner is?"

"My grandson. He's a Marine stationed in Iraq."

"I was over there for a tour in the nineties. I hope he returns safely."

"Thank you. My wife and I worry, but he's a man, and he lives his own life and makes his own choices."

"How much is it again?"

"Twenty-five hundred a month, first and last, and a cleaning deposit. Six thousand dollars for all."

"Man, that's more than my house payment."

"If you have a house, what do you need with this place?"

"Divorce. I need a temporary arrangement to get my feet on the ground. I'm still paying for the house but not living in it."

"Bad luck. Well, this would serve you well. You can afford both?"

"I'm unemployed due to a layoff, but I have a letter from the bank certifying that I have sufficient financial resources for several years' rent, and more. I can provide personal character references, as well. I'd be glad to sign a waiver of my renter's rights, so if I cause you any trouble, or fail to pay the rent, you can immediately evict me. I'd also like to prepay a third month in a show of good faith."

The old man added up the money, thought for a minute, and held out his hand. "We have a deal."

Scott and Arbi took care of the paperwork on the kitchen table, and Arbi gave him the keys. Scott turned on the refrigerator, set the thermostat, and went to the market. He bought food, plastic glasses and utensils, paper plates, several Belgian ales, and a half-dozen frozen pizzas to stock up the kitchen. A quick trip to a discount department store and he brought home a coffee maker, a slow cooker, and some extra cooking utensils. He bought a couple of nice ceramic coffee mugs and some tall beer glasses. He walked to the bedding department and bought linen and the cheapest mattress he could find on sale, with a promised delivery later that afternoon. All that was left to do was to collect his things from Jeff's place.

Scott was gathering his clothes and packing up when the doorbell rang. He opened the door to find Max standing in the hall.

"Can I help you?"

"Max Moon. I work for the Pugh Western Insurance Company. I'd like to talk to you about your experiences at the MacKenna Company." He held out his business card.

"I've got nothing to say. I got fired, signed a nondisclosure agreement, and I am not about to get into a legal hassle by talking to an insurance investigator. Good luck and goodbye."

"I'd appreciate a little of your time. I won't ask you to disclose anything confidential. If you can help me, and it bounces back to MacKenna that you were helpful, it might do you some good someday."

Scott laughed. "Nice try, Mr. Moon. That's not even remotely believable." Max smiled. "I know, but I had to try, didn't I? Can I have a moment of your time? I promise to be brief."

Scott liked his frankness and stepped aside. "Enter. I hope you don't mind me packing while you talk, because I'm leaving here."

"No problem. I'll save us some time by telling you that I've read all the reports and seen the videos. I have a good idea of what happened."

"Not proud of that, but it's done, and I'm moving on."

"Do you know where Julie Wilson is?"

"Why would I know where she is? She filed her complaint and got me divorced and fired. I never want to see her again."

"What do you think about how the MacKenna people handled this whole thing?"

"They're a pack of lying, conniving backstabbers."

"Do you think any of them are suspicious? Maybe had another agenda?"

"I don't know, but I could believe it. You saw the DNA report. Did you think it was legitimate?"

"Yes. They matched the fetus DNA against the coffee mug from your office. Julie must have bagged it somewhere along the line."

"I was hoping that it wasn't true."

"You didn't know?"

"No." Scott zipped up his two bags. "We're done here. By the way, you might be interested to know that my wife is sleeping with Fiona Dalton, the H.R. director at MacKenna, and her private investigator boyfriend has been following me. Good day, Mr. Moon."

Scott returned to his new apartment, opened a cold ale, and poured it into a tall glass. He washed his new kitchen items, put them away, and waited for the mattress delivery.

When the mattress arrived, Scott slipped the delivery guys ten bucks apiece to get rid of the old one and saluted it going out the door. "Thanks for your service."

He called Amy, "Hi, how's it going?"

"Hi, Dad. Everything is great. I drove my Beetle to school today. I love it."

"Remember your promise. No driving your friends around until you have six months' experience. You need to concentrate on driving."

"I remember."

"Anything new around the house?"

"Bun Boy has moved in full time. What a jerk. I can't stand him. Maybe he took a good look in the mirror, because he lost the bun."

"Is he behaving himself?"

"He's not bad, but he does try to be the man of the house. It's comical. He has a new car now, a white, four-door Honda Accord sedan."

"That's interesting. I have a new place. Would you like to come by and check it out?"

"Sure!" He gave her the address. He drank his beer and considered Lance while he waited.

Scott answered Amy's knock. She came in looking all around. He showed her all the other rooms, and they made the new bed while they were in the bedroom.

Amy swallowed hard and managed to mutter, "This is nice."

Scott laughed. "You don't have to fake it. It's pretty grim, but at least it's temporary. Are you ready for your second big adult responsibility?"

"I guess. What are you talking about?"

"I think Lance is a loser, a poseur, and he's probably harmless. If I'm wrong, I have something you can use to protect yourself in case he steps over the line. It's pepper spray."

"You mean those things you can disable people with?"

"Well, it kind of disables people. Mostly it gives them something else to think about while you run away."

Scott took a Pepper Blaster gun out of his briefcase and showed it to her.

"The trouble with aerosol canned pepper spray is that it goes all over; it can even blow back on you, as well as your attacker. This little plastic squirt gun doesn't use compressed air. It works like an airless paint gun and just propels a pepper blast out in a tight little blob at high pressure. It goes onto the target without going all over. There are two loads in here. You put your finger in here and squeeze, twice if you need it."

Scott let Amy handle the Blaster, and they watched a YouTube video showing how to use it.

"Let's go out back."

They went into the back yard, and Amy fired the pepper shooter twice. She coughed a little when she got a slight whiff of pepper. Scott threw the used Blaster into the trash, and they went back inside.

"Looks like you have it managed." He handed her a new Pepper Blaster.

"This is not a toy. You don't show it to anyone, including your mother, and don't take it to school. Got it?"

"Okay." Amy put the pepper shooter in her backpack.

"You're legally not supposed to have this at your age, so if you use it and the police ask, it didn't come from me, okay? I'm running at the Rose Bowl now. Would you like to join me this weekend?"

"It's about time."

"Hey, no judgments. Are you in?"

"Absolutely. I've got to see this."

Later that evening after Amy left, Scott called his house. Lance answered.

"Yeah."

"Lance?"

"Yeah?"

"This is Scott."

Momentary silence.

Lance flashed angry, "I'm going to kick your ass."

"You had it coming, and if you come after me, more bad stuff will happen. I don't care what you do with my wife or anything else. There's only one rule. You're going to stay away from my daughter. You are not her father. Her mother and I will supervise her and handle any issues. If you ever lay a hand on her or cause her any distress, you're going to wind up in a trash bin with a cat sniffing you."

"Maybe I'll just put you in the hospital instead."

"A lot of people tried that in Iraq, and I'm still here. You might want to consider that. By the way, you might want to ask Dana how she likes sleeping with Fiona Dalton, the H.R. director at MacKenna. Maybe if you're a good boy, they'll let you watch."

That evening, Scott went to Julie's apartment and let himself in. It was empty. Not a paper clip nor a button left. Nothing. He made a quick check with the building manager, who said that she was hardly ever there and abruptly left two days past. Scott had the uneasy feeling their relationship was over, and he was in deep trouble.

CHAPTER

.... *21* ....

cott's ringing phone showed Jeff's number.

"Hey, Jeff. How's it going?"

"I see you took me seriously and packed up."

"It was time. Nothing so awkward as a fully grown adult friend overstaying his welcome."

"Are you up for that free dinner?"

"Sure. What do you have in mind?"

"Six o'clock at Mort's Steak House."

Scott and Jeff walked into the restaurant at nearly the same time and were quickly seated. Noisy chatter and laughter from the happy hour gathering made the atmosphere upbeat and cheerful.

They ordered drinks and settled in.

"Where are you staying?"

"I rented a furnished place in Montrose from an old guy while his grandson's deployed in Iraq. It's temporary, but at least I'm out of your hair."

"What's the latest?"

"I'm just figuring out what to do next. I have some startup money thanks to your help, so there is no immediate urgency."

Drinks arrived, and they toasted each other.

"When are you going to tell me what's really going on?"

"You know most of it. I'm an outcast looking for a job. My wife is living in our house with Lance the shamus. Dana's also in the bag with Fiona, although I can't quite figure out how that fits into this soap opera. Amy is doing remarkably well, considering the family dissolution. I got her a car so she can gain some independence. I figure she may need to escape the circus at home from time to time. That's about it."

"Julie?"

"Haven't seen or heard from her and don't expect to, now that she got what she needed out of me and vaporized."

"I'm looking forward to hearing the rest of the story."

"You're my oldest and dearest friend. There'll come a time after I get things figured out. That time isn't quite now."

"You can count on me as long as you don't get me disbarred."

Three days later, Max's phone buzzed. "Meet you at the coffee shop in an hour."

Max always arrived early for meetings just to see if someone else was waiting with a surprise for him. He was sipping a cup of tea when Bruce came ambling in, looking guilty as usual.

He set a thick envelope on the table. "Got it. I had some trouble with Wilson."

"What trouble?"

"Wilson isn't her birth name, and she did a lot of work in order to keep people from discovering who she really is."

"That's interesting." Max set the money, folded in a local newspaper, on the table between them. Bruce kept his eyes locked on it.

"Aren't you going to lecture me on my gambling?"

"I like you just as you are."

Later at home, Max got into comfortable clothes, put on a pot of coffee, and sat down at his kitchen table. He went through all the materials that Bruce had given him.

Four hours later, he'd finished a sandwich, and he added a little Irish whisky to his third cup of coffee. He put down the last documents and studied his yellow legal notepad.

"We'll, I'll be damned."

The next day Max met with Todd and briefed him on his findings.

Todd was nearly speechless. "I can't believe it!"

"You don't really have a choice."

Max looked at him with resolve. "Let's start with Fiona Dalton."

Todd asked her to report to the conference room, removing her out of her own territory. She appeared at the door shortly after the call. "What is it?"

Todd played the host. "Come in, Fiona. This is Maxwell Moon. He's a representative from Pugh Western."

Max rose and shook her hand. "Please take a seat."

Max was a firm believer in delivering the first punch in a fight, so he went straight at her.

"I've been looking at your personnel records, doing some background research, and you appear to be a total fraud."

Fiona was temporarily caught off guard. "You don't know what you're talking about, and how did you get my personnel record?"

"You stated on your résumé that you have a bachelor's degree in business from UCLA and a graduate degree from Pepperdine. Those schools have no record of your attendance. You graduated high school in Long Beach, so I checked Long Beach Community College. You got an AA degree in Liberal Arts from there, but I found no further evidence of higher education. You want to straighten me out on that?"

Fiona tried to dissemble. "There must be some mistake. You can see my degrees on my wall."

"I'm sure you have a piece of paper with your name on it. I also checked your alleged former employers. Contrary to the claims on your résumé, you have no human resources experience. Immediately prior to this job, you were an office manager for a temporary employment agency."

"This is outrageous. You're mistaken."

"You've been a frequent visitor at the Woman's New Life Spa for the last two years."

"I'm gay. What of it? If this is some anti-gay witch hunt, I'll have you crucified in court."

"Well, to each her own. That's not my point. It seems that Dana Milner and the person known as Julie Wilson also frequented the same spa at the same time you were there. I have credit card receipts and calls to the spa on your phone records."

"A coincidence. How did you get those records?"

"That gets us to Julie Wilson, also known as Sara Jane Townsend. It seems she had absolutely no qualifications for the position for which you hired her. Townsend's background includes two years of drama classes at Pasadena Community College, various retail sales jobs, and a brief stint as a realty sales associate. She also has an old arrest for soliciting. Do you have any explanation for hiring someone with no qualifications?"

Fiona was struggling. "My staff did the background investigation. There must be some misunderstanding."

Max said, "After she was involved with her alleged sexual harassment problem, you were a strong advocate for the large payoff, is that not true?"

Fiona kept her mouth shut. With Todd present, there was no use denying it.

"Were you not the moving party in convincing MacKenna to buy the workplace harassment insurance in the first place? What do you think this all adds up to?"

Fiona was silent.

"It adds up to insurance fraud. I think you and Julie Wilson cooked up some scheme to defraud Pugh Western and MacKenna based on a fake workplace harassment claim. What I want to know is, who else is in on the scheme? Where does Dana Milner fit into this? I know you and she have been having an affair. That's of no interest in itself, until one considers that you were instrumental in getting her husband fired while their marriage was disintegrating. I am also curious as to Ms. Milner's simultaneous affair with one Lance Tavidian, a private investigator who's apparently in her employ. Lastly, tell me; is Scott Milner in on it, or was he just a sucker?"

Fiona looked down at the floor, fidgeting with her bracelet.

"The jig is up, Fiona. This is your best chance to spill the rest of it. I want to know who else is involved, where Julie is, and who's got the money?"

Fiona glanced at the door like she was ready to bolt.

"In some ways, I admire this scam. It's pretty creative. You could have hidden things better, but then, it looked like a sure thing, right? The thing is, my client is an insurance company. They don't want to hurt you. They're all about the money. If the money comes home, you can go on your merry way. The police will be kept out of it, and you can find a new host that you can attach yourself to. If you're going to play it stupidly, there's a very unpleasant alternative waiting for you. The state runs a nice little spa called The California Correctional Facility for Women in Chowchilla."

Fiona stood. "I'm leaving."

"You have three days to cough up the money. Then we bring in the police and the District Attorney, and you'll be looking at serious jail time. Believe me; you don't want to be the prettiest woman in the cellblock on date night in Chowchilla."

Todd chimed in. "You're relieved of your duties. All your pass codes have been changed, and Security is waiting outside the door to collect your identification card and keys."

Fiona walked out of the room and into the company of two security guards.

Todd watched Max pick up his materials. "Do you think she'll roll over?"

"Depends on how smart she is. As long as she still knows something that we don't, she has some leverage. What I don't know is, where Jack, Scott, and Dana fit in. I still have to shake that tree."

CHAPTER

22

Todd asked Jack to meet him to the conference room.

Jack looked concerned as he entered and took a seat.

"Jack, this is Maxwell Moon, a representative from Pugh Western Insurance. We're helping him investigate the Wilson harassment incident. Max, this is Jack Bowman, our district manager." They shook hands.

Earnest Jack. "What can I do for you?"

"Hmm. I think you've done quite enough."

"What's that supposed to mean?"

"You fired your old H.R. director and hired Fiona Dalton for the job, did you not?"

"What of it?"

"She's proven to be a complete fraud. Her education credentials are fake, and her employment references are fictitious. Suppose you tell us how you happened to hire her for the job?"

"That's nonsense. She had all the qualifications needed, and she's done a good job here."

Max bored in. "I contacted all the universities she claimed to have attended and called all her supposed former employers, and none of them ever heard of her. Who did her background?"

"She brought all her diplomas in with her, so I didn't bother calling the schools. I did call her job references and talked to some people."

"The organizations are real enough, but the phone numbers on her résumé don't relate to the organizations and are now out of service. It seems that there was an accomplice who answered the phones and gave you the good references. You didn't check the legitimate phone numbers against those stated on her references?"

"No. I had no idea."

"You told Scott and Julie that the company was going to be bought out. Without that knowledge, she couldn't have leveraged her settlement like she did. That's on you."

"Look, I didn't know. How was I supposed to anticipate that a couple of high-performing employees would go off the rails? For Christ's sake, Scott was an excellent employee for ten years. I didn't want to lose either of them."

"What did you have to do with the hiring of Julie Wilson?"

"Fiona did the search. She narrowed it down and recommended Julie. I concurred."

"She's another fraud. Her résumé is total fiction. Wilson's not her real name."

"My God. I had no idea. She was fantastic and did a great job. What the hell is going on?"

"I suspect there was a conspiracy to bilk Pugh Western and MacKenna out of six million dollars. The question is, what was your role?"

"I had nothing to do with it. I'm a longtime, loyal employee of this organization. You can check my job performance with anyone in top management. I am a doer, and I make things happen."

"Apparently, cheating these people out of their bonuses might have partially motivated them to get revenge on the company. Was that your idea?"

"I had nothing to do with that. It was the damned bean counters in Finance. The money-grabbing bloodsuckers are never happy unless they're screwing someone."

"My job is to figure out if you're complicit, incompetent, or just have your head up your ass, and I'm going to figure it out pretty soon. If you were involved in this, there's a narrow window here for you to tell me what I want to know. When that window closes, you'll be in deep jeopardy."

"I know nothing about a fraud. We're done."

Jack rose and stormed out of the office.

Todd and Max regrouped in Todd's office.

"What do you think, Todd?"

"I have a hard time picturing Jack as a part of this. He makes a really nice salary with bonuses. Granted, there is a coincidental run of stupendously bad judgment, but still I have trouble seeing him ripping us off. He actually stood to make more money in the long run by staying out of it and doing his job."

"Maybe, but if he could keep the harassment money and his job, he'd be in even better financial shape. I need more information. Julie appears to be quite intelligent, and she's in the wind with the six million. She's been very organized and disciplined throughout this thing, so she probably had an alternate set of identification papers and a good exit plan. I doubt that the money's within easy reach, but I'll take a shot at it anyway. Next stop is to question Dana."

Fiona went home and opened a bottle of wine. She'd guzzled most of it before she had the nerve to call Dana.

She was anxious. "We need to talk. I just got fired."

"Not on the phone. I'll meet you on the top floor of the shopping center parking lot. Half-hour."

Dana drove through the parking lot and spotted Fiona's car in the far corner.

She drove up to her and motioned for Fiona to get in her car.

"What happened?"

"Some guy, Max Moon, an investigator from Pugh Western, showed up with Todd from Legal. They grilled me. They know everything! They know about my background, they know who Julie is. They know what we did!"

"What did you tell them?"

"Nothing. I tried to deny it, but they had too much information, so I just shut up. They fired me, and Security threw me out. It was humiliating. They said you had a relationship with your private detective."

"They're bluffing about Lance."

"They know about us. I mean, our relationship. They said that all they want is the money back, and no one would go to jail. It was terrifying."

"Did you give them anything?"

"No. I…no."

"I think it's all a bluff. They may know that you and Julie faked your credentials, but that's not proof of a crime. Just shut up, and keep out of sight."

"I don't know. They know so much. I don't want to go to jail."

"Don't think like that. They're trying to stampede you into a confession. If they had rock-solid evidence, we'd all be in jail right now. There is no proof of anything unless someone confesses, so relax. He's probably coming after me as well. I'll let you know how it goes."

"You've got to get me out of this."

Max was not one to announce his presence. He just showed up at Dana's house the next morning and rang the bell. Dana was sober and expecting him.

"I'm Max Moon with the Pugh Western Insurance Company. Do you mind talking to me about a matter at the MacKenna Company?"

"All I know about MacKenna is my husband used to work there."

"It does involve Scott, and it's serious."

"Come in. What's this about?"

"As you know, your husband was fired for having an affair with a woman named Julie Wilson. What do you know about that? Who was involved, etc.?"

"What do you mean, who was involved? He coerced the poor woman into having sex with him, and he got fired. That's why I divorced him. It's not complicated."

"Actually, the H.R. director has been fired, and the person who made the harassment claim has disappeared. I believe they conspired to commit a fraud."

"How? What fraud?"

"I think her relationship with your husband was probably consensual, but she coerced and manipulated him. She filmed them having sex and then made a harassment claim. The question is whether your husband is a victim or coconspirator?"

"I don't know anything about that, but I can believe my husband was a clueless dupe, that's his usual mode."

"I also wondered about any connection this might have with your relationship with Fiona Dalton. Don't you think it's more than a little odd that he would wind up being fired by the woman having an affair with his wife?"

"Look, I'm romantically interested in women. I met her at the spa. It's pure coincidence. What's my motive in having him fired? I need the alimony and I need him working. It doesn't make sense."

"You're having an affair with both Fiona and a fellow named Lance Tavidian. Do you mind telling me about it?"

"Look, Mr. Moon. I like men and women. It's called bisexuality. Look it up. At any rate, it's no business of yours."

"One more question. Do you know where Julie Wilson is?"

"No. I think we're done."

Max dropped his card on a table.

"Just in case you think of something."

CHAPTER

23

cott stood by his car in the Rose Bowl parking lot, stretching before his run, when he spotted Amy's blue Bug driving slowly into the parking lot.

She got out of her car and waved to him.

"Ready?"

"Let's go. Take it easy on an old man."

Scott checked his phone and selected Cream for his musical motivation. Amy took the lead and kept it. An exhausted Scott leaned on his car when they returned.

"Boy, I'm out of shape."

"I thought you did pretty good. I'd say your running style is ambulatory."

"There's a fine line between smart aleck and wiseass, and I think you just crossed it. How about breakfast at Masterson's?"

It was a beautiful morning, so they sat outside and ordered French toast, bacon, and coffee.

Amy examined Scott's plate with interest. "I don't think the run will offset the calories in that French toast."

"I am rewarding myself for being healthy."

"That's not rational."

"How are things going? Is Lance behaving himself?"

"It's okay. Mom seems quite edgy lately, and she snaps at old Lance a lot."

"Been there and done that. What's she got to worry about?"

"I'm only catching part of the conversation. Some guy came to visit her, asked a lot of questions, and got her very upset."

"Probably Max Moon. He's an insurance investigator."

"What's he got to do with Mom?"

"He's looking for an angle to claw back the money Julie got from the insurance company. He's just sniffing around to find out if she knows anything because we were married."

"I can't believe Julie was such a faker. I thought she was so nice."

"Well, she fooled me. Do you know what a psychopath is?"

"Someone who's crazy?"

"Close. It's someone who knows right from wrong, but they just don't give a damn. I think she just uses people."

Dana had just screwed Lance into exhaustion. He lay on the tangled sheets starting to doze off.

"Hey, wake up!"

"What? Let me alone, I'm exhausted."

"Listen to me. This is serious."

Lance recognized "that tone" in Dana's voice and perked up.

"How much money did you make last year?"

A little sensitive about his modest financial success as a sleuth, he dodged the question.

"Enough. Why do you want to know?"

"I'm guessing you made just enough to live on. Do you want to bump along making chump change or make some real money? I mean, really big money?"

"I'm listening."

"Big money comes with big risk. Are you willing to do whatever it takes?"

"What are you driving at?"

"I need to know that you have what it takes to stick your neck out for what you want."

"What kind of money are we talking about?"

"Millions."

"Of course, I'm in."

"You're sure?"

Lance was annoyed. "I said yes, didn't I?"

"Then I need you to do something for me today, right now."

The following day, Dana called Fiona late in the afternoon. Fiona was drunk again, and Dana thought she sounded depressed.

"How are you doing?"

"I'm sorry I got involved in this crazy thing. We don't have the money, and now we're probably going to jail."

"Listen to me. That's not going to happen. They have nothing but circumstantial evidence, and we're safe unless someone talks. They can think anything they want, but they can't do anything. That's why you need to keep your mouth shut and just ride it out."

Fiona was unconvinced. "I understand. I understand that everything you promised me has not come true."

Dana made up her mind and settled on a path to resolve the Fiona problem.

"I have great news. We found Julie. We need to go see her and get our money. When you get your share, you can just disappear, and you'll never see Max Moon or anyone else again."

"Really?"

"Yes. She's been hiding close by, where no one would think to look for her."

"Why would she stay around here?"

"I think she must really like Scott. She's probably waiting for the dust to settle, so she can rejoin him without arousing suspicion."

"She's close?"

"Yes. I'll pick you up at eight tonight. We'll go over there and make her give us the money."

"Thank God."

"You need to stop drinking. We have to be on the top of our game for this."

"Okay."

Later that evening, Dana picked up Fiona on a street corner near her apartment. She could smell the alcohol on her when she got in the car.

"Are you sober?"

"Enough."

Dana drove and told Fiona where Julie had been hiding. She explained the plan to her.

They drove into a motel parking lot.

"What's she doing in this dump?"

"It's the last place anyone would look for someone with six million dollars."

They walked to a room. Dana tried the door. It was unlocked.

Dana pushed Fiona into the room. Fiona looked around, and shock registered on her face.

"You!"

Fiona felt a sharp stab at the back of her neck. She turned.

Fiona frantically cried, "What did you do!"

Even as she spoke, she was fading; her words stayed in her mind and couldn't find their way out. Her vision dimmed, and she started to collapse. Someone caught her as she fell. Fiona finally understood the plan.

CHAPTER

24

ene was in his office with Linda, discussing a recent creative lane change that precipitated the murder of one motorist by another, when Detective Rodriguez called.

"King, I got something on the motel sleeper."

"All ears."

"Fiona Dalton. She was the H.R. director at MacKenna Company; lived in Glendale. No family, locally anyway. MacKenna's office is downtown on Brand. Her boss's name is Jack Bowman." Rodriguez gave Gene the contact information.

"Thanks, brother. Say hello to Lupe. Uh, you're still married, right? Yeah. Okay."

Gene turned on the speakerphone and called the county morgue, asking for Dr. Kevin Kilmeade.

"Killer, you pie-faced Irish fuck, are you sober enough to give me something on the motel sleeper we sent to you?"

"Hi, King. Are you still dressing like a bus-station pimp?"

"And looking damned good. What have you got?"

"We're busy, so I haven't cracked her open yet, but I got you a couple things because I knew you'd be crawling up my ass. The tox screen showed that she had an elevated blood alcohol level of 2.7. She also had enough Ketamine in her to put the brakes on a buffalo stampede. There was a puncture wound in her neck just above the hairline. She probably died quickly. By the time they got done mucking around posing her and hooking her up to the bottle, she was probably done breathing. They should have put a bararm hold on her and put her to sleep her before they did her. Pretty sloppy."

"Thanks, Doc. I had it figured for a murder. What do you say we catch a Dodger game when this is over?"

"You're buying."

Gene hung up, looked at Linda, and shrugged. "I told you. Let's go see Jack Bowman."

Linda shook her head. "On the way you can explain the arcane rituals of male bonding to me."

Linda and Gene showed up at the MacKenna Company offices, asking for Bowman, but they were directed to the Legal office. Todd rose from his chair to shake hands and took their business cards. "What can I do for you officers?"

Linda asked, "We want to see Jack Bowman."

"No problem. He's in today. Anything else?"

"What can you tell us about Fiona Dalton?"

"She no longer works here."

Linda asked, "Why's that?"

"That's a confidential personnel issue. Let's just say that she was removed from her job, and we wouldn't hire her again under any circumstances."

"I think we have a workaround on the confidentiality issue. She's dead."

"My God! What happened?"

"Actually, it appears to be suicide, so maybe we should talk about why she left."

"She killed herself?"

"That's what we're investigating. Why was she fired?"

"It's complicated. We recently suffered a huge loss due to a sexual harassment claim arising from the bad conduct of one of our managers. He was fired for sexually abusing his subordinate. The victim secretly videoed some sexual encounters that occurred in our offices after work hours. She got a lawyer, and we got our asses handed to us. Our insurance carrier and MacKenna each kicked in three million for 'go away' money."

Gene's jaw dropped. "That's a hell of a lot of money for that kind of settlement."

"There was some physical abuse of the employee as well as other complicating circumstances. The organization wanted to put it to sleep and have her sign off on a confidentiality agreement."

Linda asked. "What complicating circumstances?"

"The employee apparently miscarried because of the physical abuse. Her partner, if you can call him that, was determined to be the father. It was feared that publicity with all the attendant ugliness would damage the company's image at a sensitive time. We're in takeover negotiations. And then there's the stock valuation to consider."

"Sounds like they had your butt in a crack."

"No kidding. Technically, Fiona was fired for falsifying her job application, but we suspected that she was really a coconspirator in a scheme to rip off the company. She hired Julie Wilson, the supposed victim in the harassment incidents. She had also falsified her credentials and job application. We weren't able to prove that the harassment itself was staged, but the whole thing stank. Jack was Fiona's boss, and he's still working here only because it appears that he was duped as well. We fired Scott Milner, Julie's supervisor, and gave him two hundred grand to keep his mouth shut."

"Quite a soap opera you have going."

"It's been a strange business. Fiona was having an affair with Dana Milner, the wife of Scott Milner, the harasser she eventually fired."

"You're serious? How does that figure into a scam?"

"I don't know. We pressed Fiona, but she got on her homophobe hobbyhorse, so we just backed off. We didn't need to make her a victim and give her cause for a lawsuit."

Linda nodded her understanding. "Where are you at on Scott Milner?"

"We couldn't figure out if he was a coconspirator or just someone else who got used. Ms. Wilson has since disappeared with the money." Todd smiled. "Milner is the one who really got hosed in all this. He was double-crossed, fired, and divorced all in the same week."

Gene gathered his thoughts for a moment. "Why again is Bowman still working here?"

"He's a good manager, and it looked like he was fooled by an elaborate plan to validate Fiona's fake résumé. As for Julie, he just accepted a recommendation to hire her that came from a trusted H.R. manager."

"Any thoughts on Dana Milner's relationship with Fiona?"

"Anyone's guess. Dana's a special piece of work. She appears to be bisexual, and the relationship could have been a coincidence, if you believe in coincidences."

"Ballbuster?"

"More like an anaconda; she just squeezes until they drop off."

169

"Do you have the videos?"

Todd reached in his desk drawer, extracted a business card, and gave it to Linda. "Maxwell Moon, Pugh Western's insurance investigator. He can give you a set."

"We want to talk to Bowman."

Todd asked, "Do you want me there?"

Linda thought for a second. "That's actually good. It might keep him from trying to blow smoke."

"As you wish." Todd picked up his phone.

Gene said to Linda, "Doesn't 'Ann Anaconda' sound like a great stripper name?"

Linda shook her head. "Not this again."

"Can't you see her in a snakeskin body thing?"

Jack Bowman knocked on Todd's door, interrupting Gene's fantasy.

"Enter."

Todd handled the introductions while Jack found his seat. He looked grave. Gene and Linda watched him intently for a "tell" that he was lying.

Gene began. "Fiona Dalton's dead."

"Oh my God, what happened?"

"Looks like suicide, maybe. We're awaiting the autopsy."

"I can't believe it. She was here just last week."

"Todd told us all about the suspected scam and her possible role in it. What do you know about that?"

"Nothing. She conned me and got the job, but oddly enough, she was good at it. I don't know if she researched the job or was just lucky, but she was very credible. Actually, she was a little too credible. Some of the employees thought she was a bit strident."

"Do you know anyone who hated her or might want to harm her?"

"Scott Milner. Fiona had investigated him on a prior harassment issue, and she was with me in the meeting when I fired him. There was also an unpleasant scene when he picked up his severance check."

"Why did you pay him to screw up like that?"

"It was a Management decision to shut him up. He could have run his mouth and possibly caused us problems with our buyout. It cost two hundred grand to get his name on a nondisclosure agreement."

Gene shook his head. "Sexual harassment pays very well."

Jack continued. "Fiona was also having an affair with his wife. Considering that these events imploded his marriage, and his wife's romantic interest in women, I suppose he could have developed some enmity for Fiona. Seems like a stretch though. If your wife decides she likes women, what can you do but move on? You can't compete, right?"

Linda gave Jack a card. "If you think of anything else, call us."

"You bet."

Gene caught him going out the door. "Just one more thing. When did you find out that you were going to be laid off if there was a takeover?"

"Rumors started six months ago. I don't think I knew for sure until about three months ago. Why?"

"Nothing."

When Jack left, Gene said to Todd, "We'd like to see Fiona's office and whatever's left of her things."

"No problem."

Security brought up the boxed contents of Fiona's office. Gene and Linda looked through the various photos and personal items. Nothing seemed to shed light on her behavior.

Driving away, Linda asked. "What's your take?"

"I think something is wrong there. With Jack, I mean. There's something hinky about his story. How about you?"

"They could all be in on it. Either someone wanted to cut Fiona out of the money, or she maybe became a threat. She could've gotten greedy. Also, Jack knowing about the buyout early on means he had time to plan something and act against the company."

CHAPTER

25

The MacKenna case continued to bother Max. He was annoyed with himself for his inability to find Julie. She wasn't using her phone or credit cards. Her car was abandoned in her apartment parking lot, with a note stating the manager's intention to tow it away when her rent expired at the end of the week.

He was looking at social media for Julie and found nothing useful. Then he looked up her parents and sister. He scrolled through all their postings and found a couple of references to "the cabin."

"Interesting."

Max got dressed and drove to MacKenna's offices. He dropped in on Todd unannounced.

"Hi, Todd, I need a favor."

Todd was just hanging up on his caller. "Name it."

"Did Julie leave anything here when she left?"

"She didn't bother to clean out her office, so Security boxed up everything and put it in storage, just in case."

"I'd like to see it."

"Why?"

"A super sleuth isn't obliged to give up his trade secrets. It is written."

"Funny you." Todd called Security, and within ten minutes Julie's office remains were spread out on Todd's conference table.

Max picked through the various items until he saw a framed picture. It was an old faded photograph of Julie with her parents in a mountain setting with a beautiful blue lake in the background. Max went to the window to put some extra light on the photograph.

"Ha! There it is. A sign in the photograph that says the dock in the background is part of Arrowhead Bait and Rentals. I bet her family has a cabin in Arrowhead. I need to use your computer." Max sat down at Todd's desk without permission. He looked up the San Bernardino County Assessor's office, clicked on a link to their website, and began a search for properties in Julie's family name, Townsend. In five minutes, he found the address for the family vacation cabin.

"It's just a hunch, but I may have found a place where she could stay off the grid. Buck's got me very busy, but I'll get up there in a couple of days and see what's going on. I can't force her to do anything, but maybe I can talk some sense into her."

"You're going to talk a young, beautiful, unattached woman into giving up six million tax-free dollars out of the goodness of her heart?"

"Well, when you say it like that...maybe."

At that moment Jack came into the office with some paperwork for Todd.

"Hi, Max. How's it going?"

Todd blurted out. "Max has a slim lead on Julie, and he's going to check it out."

Max visibly cringed at Todd's revelation. Jack said, "Well, good luck." He dropped the papers into Todd's in-basket and left.

Max was irritated. "That was a mistake. Don't tell anyone else what we're doing. We don't know who may have been involved."

Lance was angry when he returned to the house. Dana was at home drinking as usual when he confronted her. "I understand you have been carrying on with a woman while you've been with me."

"So, what?"

"So, what in the hell do you want?"

"Look, it was a small thing. I got drunk at the spa, and she seduced me. I guess I always wondered about making love to a woman, and now I know. It's not for me. Don't be threatened by that. I still love you."

Lance was rapidly deflating. "It's over?"

"Definitely, and you're still here, are you not?"

Lance paced. "What did you want with that Ketamine? You're not taking that crap are you?"

"No. I gave it to her, sort of a going-away present."

"You'd better. I don't want anyone in my life who's screwed up on drugs."

"Have you had any luck finding Julie?"

"Not yet, she's just disappeared."

"Do you have one of those GPS tracking things you see on TV shows?"

"They're cheap. I can easily get one. Why?"

"That investigator Max Moon's pretty sharp, and he seems to have a lot of information. I'm thinking he may be able to find her. I want you to start following him as soon as possible."

"If I can find him, all I have to do is attach the sending device to his car and track him. Could be boring if he doesn't know anything, but it's worth a try. Where's his card?"

Gene and Linda had agreed that they should find out what Max Moon knew before confronting Scott. He agreed to meet them for dinner at an Italian restaurant in Montrose. Max was there early as usual and watched them come in. He signaled, and they came over to the table.

"Hi, Max Moon. Please sit."

"I'm Officer Linda Garcia, and this is Detective Gene Perkins. As we said on the phone, we're investigating the murder of Fiona Dalton. Todd filled us in on the possible harassment fraud angle, and we thought we should get your perspective."

"Anything I can do, it'll be my pleasure. Todd told me to expect you. He also told me about Fiona. What happened there?"

"She was murdered. She caught an involuntary overdose, and we think someone tried to fake her suicide. Do you have any ideas on that?"

"I have a hard time figuring anyone I've met on this case so far caring enough to murder her, except maybe for Scott Milner. Even at that, I just don't see him having the guts to do it. I was with LAPD for twenty years, and I don't get 'killer' off of him. His wife is interesting. She was having an affair with Fiona Dalton. I didn't see anything going on there that rose to homicidal motivation, but you know how it is, people do crazy things."

"What happened with LAPD?"

"Disability forced me off. It was a car accident that killed my partner and messed me up pretty good."

"That's tough. How's the insurance career working out?"

"It's a living, and hardly anyone ever shoots at me."

"What about the Wilson woman? What's going on there?"

"In the wind with the money. Assuming the harassment was real, there's nothing unusual about someone going off with a financial windfall to have some fun. I'm still looking for her. I'd like to talk to her face-to-face, just to get a fresh read on this thing if nothing else."

They gave Max their cards and shook hands. "If you find her, let us know. We'd like to check her out as well."

"Sure, do me the same, okay?"

"You got it. By the way, do you know where Milner's living now?"

Max got out his phone and looked up a note. He wrote down the information on the back of one of his cards and gave it to Linda.

"One more thing, we'd like to see those videos."

"I figured that, so I copied them." Max handed over a thumb drive to Gene.

Linda and Gene stood on Scott's porch looking around.

"Doesn't look like the six-million-dollar man, does he?"

Linda sniffed. "At least there's no odor."

Scott answered the ring. "Can I help you?"

Gene and Linda showed him their ID.

"Glendale Police. We'd like to talk to you."

Scott hesitated. "Sure, come in."

Linda and Gene walked into the living room looking around.

"Sit anywhere. What's this about? I'm getting a beer. Want one?"

"No thanks. You knew Fiona Dalton, correct?"

Scott returned from the fridge with a cold bottle of Dirty Old Man Ale and poured it into a tall glass. It looked so good that Gene caught himself staring at it.

"I have the feeling you already know the answer to that…and a lot more."

"She was found dead a couple days ago in an apparent suicide."

"Interesting. Fiona didn't seem like someone with enough self-awareness to know that she was depressed."

"You don't seem upset by that news."

"I don't wish anyone dead, but I'd be lying if I said I was saddened by her death. She didn't like me and went after me. She was mean, vindictive, and sleeping with my wife. Want me to go on?"

"Actually, it turns out she was murdered, and everyone seems to think you're a likely suspect."

"That's more like it. I could see her pissing someone off enough to put her in a box. However, in order for me to have anything to do with her death, I'd have to give a damn. What's done is done. I've got a daughter to raise, and I'm looking forward, not back."

"Where were you last Friday night from five p.m. to midnight?"

"I took my daughter to the movies and a dinner. I dropped her off at my house about eleven, that is, my former house."

"Was your wife home?"

"Yes."

"We'd like to talk to your daughter."

"Go see my wife. I'm sure she'll arrange for you to talk to Amy. Well, maybe. Call me if she pisses backwards on you. Her cooperation will depend on how drunk she is."

"Who do you think might have killed Fiona?"

"Well, to get up that kind of passion, someone would have to be well motivated. That might include my wife, seeing as how she was sleeping with Fiona and a private detective named Lance Tavidian at the same time. Maybe someone objected to sharing."

"How do we contact this Tavidian guy?"

"Go see Dana. He's usually lurking around the house somewhere."

"Do you know where we can find Julie Wilson?"

"She used me to rip off six million dollars and screwed up my life, or at least the part I haven't screwed on my own. We aren't communicating."

"Some people think you and she teamed up for the fraud."

"Look around. Crime pays, doesn't it?"

"Maybe she double-crossed you?"

"We had a consensual relationship between two adults. She said she wanted to do it in the office and play rough. I went along. She secretly filmed us and used it for her scam. The sex on company property was real, and the rough sex play was elective. The idea that I was complicit in a fraud is not factual. She ripped up my life, stomped on it, and hit the road. I don't know where she is, but I hope she stays gone. Are we done?"

Gene and Linda drove off to see Dana and Lance.

Gene asked, "What's your take?"

"Not a murderer. Something went down for sure, but if he killed Fiona, he's a pretty sly customer. I just think he got fucked over and he's moving on."

"Yeah. I don't see it either. I think it's likely they did a scam, and she screwed him out of his part of the money. Good luck proving it without a confession from both of them. Nothing he said in there comes close to the proof we would need."

26

cott called Amy. "Hi, how are you doing?"

"Okay, there's an odd feeling around here. I can't put my finger on it."

"Keep your head on a swivel. You're always welcome here. How'd you like to run tomorrow?"

"I'd love to. Okay if I bring a friend?"

Scott did mind, but he put a good face on it. "Sure. Nine o'clock. Better park at the north end of the golf course; there's a swap meet at the Bowl on Saturday."

Linda drove to the Milner house and saw it as a well-maintained sixties rancher in a pleasant cul-de-sac, not too far from a little green park with scattered maple trees.

Gene rang the doorbell. Dana answered quickly.

They held out their identification. "Ms. Dana Milner?"

"Yes."

"We're Glendale Police. We'd like to come in to talk with you for a minute."

"What's this about?"

"Fiona Dalton's death."

Dana opened the screen door without comment, allowing them to enter.

"Take a seat if you wish." Linda and Gene sat in adjacent barrel chairs.

"Fiona's dead?"

"Yes. We're investigating, and it looks like murder."

"That's terrible."

Dana struggled to make her concern sound believable.

"You had a sexual relationship with Fiona, correct?"

"Briefly, but it ended a while ago."

"Why was that?"

"Look, I don't like people prying into my private life. Is there a crime here?"

"We don't enjoy this either, but this is necessary. The sooner you answer our questions, the sooner we'll be gone."

"It was a fling. I decided I wasn't gay. I was curious, and now I'm not curious anymore."

Just then Lance walked into the room.

Gene stood up. "Who are you?"

"Lance Tavidian. I'm Dana's...boyfriend."

Gene introduced Linda and himself. "You live here?"

181

"Sometimes. I have an apartment downtown. What's this about?"

"We were about to explain that Fiona Dalton's death wasn't a suicide. She was drugged and murdered."

Lance started pacing, obviously unhappy. "That's too bad, but I didn't know her. Never met her. What do you mean by drugged?"

"Someone gave her a full load of Ketamine, and a chaser. They tried to fake a suicide."

Dana turned on the crocodile tears. "I'm so sorry. She was a good person. I liked and respected her. She was so gracious, even with our parting."

Lance looked like he'd swallowed a razor blade.

"Where were you last Friday night between six and midnight, Ms. Milner?"

"Here with Lance. My daughter was off with her father for the evening."

"Is that right, Lance?"

Lance stammered. "Uh, yeah. We made dinner and watched a movie."

"What did you watch?"

Lance thought a moment. "An old movie, *The Man Who Would Be King*."

"Good one. Who did you like better, Sean Connery or Michael Caine?"

"Caine, he was hilarious, but they couldn't make that movie the same way today with all the political correctness."

"Who did Christopher Plummer play?"

"Rudyard Kipling."

"It's an old movie, you could have seen it at any time."

"We watched the movie on my computer. Get a subpoena and you can check out the time it was on, but I'm not going to help you snoop on my life.

"What can you tell me about Fiona's alleged participation in a fraud perpetrated on the MacKenna Company?"

Dana feigned ignorance. "What fraud? I didn't hear anything about that."

Lance shrugged.

"There is some speculation that Fiona, Julie Wilson, and possibly your husband participated in a conspiracy to defraud the company with a fake sexual harassment claim. What do you know about that?"

"She never said anything like that to me. Neither did Scott. How much did they get?"

Linda spoke. "Six million."

"Wow! Well, he's not living like he has any of that money. I'm worried he won't be able to come up with his end of the divorce settlement."

"Do you know anyone who might have wanted to harm Fiona?"

Lance and Dana looked at each other. "No, not really."

"Fiona fired your husband. How about that?"

"Just business. He got himself into all that sex trouble. Why blame Fiona for doing her job?"

Gene looked around. "Is your daughter home?"

"No. She's at a friend's house. What do you want with her?"

"Just a routine check."

Gene and Linda dropped their cards. "Call us if you remember anything."

Lance watched them drive away and then turned on Fiona.

"You killed her! You used the Ketamine I got for you! What in the hell is going on?"

"Calm down. It was an accident. She was panicking. She was about to give us all up. I tried to calm her down, but I gave her too much. What was I supposed to do?"

"How about not making me an accomplice to a murder? I can't believe this!"

"Don't go crazy on me. No one will find out."

"Fuck you!"

"Probably not tonight. Don't forget, you're tailing Moon tomorrow."

Lance grabbed his keys and stomped out of the house.

Lance drove aimlessly for a while, and then he decided to go to the club and get wasted.

He looked around the bar. It was nearly empty in the afternoon, and that suited him just fine. He ordered a margarita. He was on his third when they came in. Lance tried to ignore them, but they came right up to him.

"Hey, what's up, Kojak?"

Gor and Armen were dressed in black, wearing gold knock off designer wristwatches and expensive athletic shoes. Just looking at them made you want to get a tetanus shot. After the Soviet Union cratered in the eighties, their relatives immigrated to the U.S. Five years ago they got family visas on their uncle's coattails and stayed. Coming from a family involved in the black market in Russia, they found a more promising environment for a criminal enterprise in America. In particular, they liked the fact that police wouldn't hook your sweetbreads up to a field telephone, and crank it until you screamed like a smoke alarm.

Gor looked around, making sure no one was within earshot. "You like our K? You want some more? I give you frequent-flyer price now."

"No thanks. That was a one-time deal."

"Going straight, eh? That's bad for my business."

"It wasn't for me."

"What's the big deal you got going, your big-money deal? You remember bragging how you were going to come into some real money?"

"No."

"You were plenty drunk, but you said it."

"I was lying. I wanted to impress a couple big-time gangsters like you two."

Armen stuck a hard thumb into Lance's left kidney. He felt the stab of pain and flinched as it shot up his back.

"Hey, be nice. It's not good for your health to fuck with us."

"What was that for? I told you, I don't know anything about money. I was drunk and telling stories, okay?"

Lance pushed the stool away, brushed past them, walking out the back door to the parking lot.

Gor and Armen looked at each other. "Bullshit, yes?" Gor nodded his affirmation.

Bob got in his car and drove away, thinking he must have been out of his mind to brag to those two cretins about the money. Armen and Gor watched Lance go, got into an older black Cadillac sedan, and followed him.

Scott was warming up at the north end of Lakeside golf course watching for Amy's car to appear, when an older Nissan Murano parked near him. Amy got out of the passenger side, and a young man exited the driver's side, locking up the SUV.

"Dad, this is Jordan. The guy I told you about from my English class."

Scott shook hands with him. Jordan's handshake was firm, dry, and strong. Jordan was an athletic young man with even features, bright blue eyes, and a buzz haircut. Scott noticed that there didn't appear to be any ink on him.

"Hi, Mr. Milner, Amy told me a lot about you. I'm glad to finally meet you."

"Same here. Let's go?"

They spontaneously began their jog around the Bowl. Scott dropped a little behind them. He was glad that his immediate impression was positive. The kid looked like a beast and could probably kick his ass if it came down to it.

They got halfway around the jogging loop, with Scott bringing up the tail end of the trio. As they approached the entrance to the swap meet, Scott was feeling a bit tired. "Hey, hold up." Amy and Jordan ran in place while Scott caught up.

"Have you ever gone to the swap meet? It goes all around the Bowl."

Jordan looked at Amy and shrugged. "Why not?"

Scott checked his jogging wallet to make sure he had some cash.

Amy got the spirit immediately. "This is amazing. Look at all this stuff!"

They walked past a variety of vendors, jewelers, clothing makers, artists, photographers, and people selling all manner of handmade personal items that you never knew you needed until you went to the swap meet.

Scott trailed behind the kids, allowing them some privacy. He saw Jordan pull out some money and buy Amy a small trinket. He figured the kid must be smitten if he was cutting loose with his hard-earned beer money.

They wound up among the food vendors. Scott bought a box of tacos and some drinks. They ate on a picnic table shaded by a huge oak tree.

"Jordan, tell me about yourself."

"Not much to tell. I go to school with Amy. I have a part-time job working for a local car dealership. I shuttle cars around, wash, and polish them. I like playing sports and reading. I can't afford the cost of a four-year college, so I'll probably go into one of the officer training programs in the military and let the government educate me. When my obligation is done, I guess I'll figure out my life from there. At least I won't be saddled with a lot of college debt."

"What about your family?"

"My parents are divorced, and my mother's a librarian working for the City of Pasadena. She's still friendly with my dad, but he wants to be on his own. He's no financial help, so that's that. I have a sister in the eighth grade."

"You seem to have a plan for your life."

"I'm looking to take every advantage I can. My mother can't afford to pay my way through school, so it's up to me to make my own breaks. I don't pretend to have it all worked out, but I work hard, and I figure that's a good start."

"How about poetry? Amy said you are a big fan."

"It's okay."

"So, you pretended to like poetry to get Amy's attention?"

"Well, yeah, but I had good intentions."

Scott saw Amy's indignant expression and started to laugh.

"I told Amy that you were just blowing smoke on the poetry."

"I'm a fan of poetry, but I'm a bigger fan of Amy."

Scott stopped laughing long enough to say. "Nice save."

All Amy could think to say was, "Men."

When they walked back to the parking lot, Jordan shook hands with Scott and hugged Amy. She decided to drive home with her dad. They drove up San Rafael past the beautiful homes and got on the freeway towards Glendale.

"What do you think of Jordan?"

"I think he's a solid kid with his head screwed on right. Anyone who's willing to work hard, take responsibility and some calculated risks that early in life will always land on his feet. I like him."

"I think he's cute."

"There is just one rule we need to talk about."

Amy was wary. "What's that?"

"No sex until I'm dead."

"You better check that life insurance policy again."

27

That afternoon Lance sat in his car watching the Pugh Western Insurance administrative offices. He couldn't believe his good luck. Max left the building at noon and got into a nondescript blue Ford Explorer.

Max drove away with Lance on his tail. When he stopped at a convenience store, Lance parked three spaces away. When Max went inside, he walked to his car, dropped down, and attached a GPS tracking transmitter. He immediately scuttled away and fired up the tracking application on his phone. When Max came out with a cup of coffee, Lance began to track his car. It was working!

Max drove east for over an hour and then turned onto a two-lane road leading up to the mountains and Lake Arrowhead. The road rose in elevation through thousands of pine trees, the village of Crestline, and finally the lake itself. Max admired the deep blue water and crisp air as he drove around the lake consulting his GPS, eventually stopping at an old-style log cabin tucked away on one of the side streets. Following far behind, Lance lost Max when he dropped off his screen. Rebooting his program, he tried to reestablish contact.

Max checked out the place from two cabins away. It was a brown vacation-size cabin with white trim and a green shingle roof. A half flight of stairs led up to the front door. The lot rose from the street on a gradual slope up to a detached garage at the rear of the property. A small silver car, maybe a Toyota, was parked in the driveway by the garage. Max walked to the front of the cabin, up the stairs, and knocked on the door. Julie answered.

"Can I help you?"

"Please don't close the door. I'm Max Moon, and I just want to talk about the MacKenna Company."

Julie started to close the door. Max stuck his foot in to keep it open.

"Please. I promise I have no wish to harm you. I just want to talk."

Julie quickly retreated to a table and picked up a canister of pepper spray.

"You won't need that. Look, I'm an investigator working with the Pugh Western Insurance Company. I have seen the videos, I know all about the settlement, and I want to make a proposal. The insurance company thinks it's been defrauded, and it intends to pursue that avenue of investigation. If fraud can be proven, you'll be a criminal on the run. All they want is the money back. If you return the money, they'll pay you a ten percent finder's fee. That's three hundred thousand dollars, and they won't pursue criminal charges. The smart move is to take the three hundred grand and walk away free and clear, knowing that you won't have to look over your shoulder for the rest your life. If you want to consider the deal, I'll try to broker the same fee with MacKenna. That would give you six hundred thousand tax-free dollars and no legal entanglements. What do you say?"

"Thanks for doing the math for me. I've been treated very badly, and I've done nothing illegal. I deserve to keep what's mine, and I want you to leave."

"Okay, I've said my bit. I'm leaving as promised. One last thing: Fiona was murdered on Friday. This thing is getting serious, and I wouldn't be surprised if someone wasn't coming after you right now. If they find you, things could get real gangster in a hurry."

"Please leave."

Max dropped two cards on the table.

"In case you change your mind, there's my card and Eric Kim's card. He's an investigator and a partner of mine, ex-Green Beret, very honest, and very good at his job. You may want to spend some of that money on personal protection until Fiona's death settles out."

As soon as Max left, Julie quickly packed her travel bag, went out the back door, and put it in the trunk of her car. She returned to the house to have one last look around.

Lance was watching the house from down the block. He saw Max get into his car and leave. Lance strolled by the house, noting the license plate number of the car in the driveway. He walked up the front steps and rang the bell.

Julie answered the door, thinking it was Max returning to make another pitch. When she saw Lance, she froze for an instant.

"Julie? Dana wants me to talk to you about the money."

Julie charged, knocking the astonished Lance backwards down the stairs. He hit every stair on the way down and landed with a crunch. Julie blew out the back door and leaped into her car. She floored it down the driveway, narrowly missing Lance as he staggered toward the car in a failed attempt to stop her.

Lance limped to his car, but he was in no shape for a pursuit. Something was wrong with his left hand, and his knee was killing him. By the time he got over his shock, Julie was out of sight. He sat there, stunned and in pain, thinking he might pass out. A thin ribbon of blood trickled into his eye.

Scott had finally concluded that Julie and Fiona were probably in a conspiracy, and he didn't like the circumstances of Fiona's death. He figured if someone had come after Fiona for the money in lieu of the missing Julie, the same people might come after him. Amy was spending a lot of time at his apartment, and he was concerned for her safety.

Amy had been restless lately, so he thought of something useful for them to do. He bookmarked the State of California DOJ Firearms Safety Manual in his computer. He figured it was time to teach her about firearm safety when she got home from school.

An hour later she breezed through the front door. "Hi, what did you do today?"

"I updated my résumé and did some more job searching."

"Are those people at your old job going to cause you problems because of Julie?"

"No. I made sure the nondisclosure contract cut both ways. I also made them give me my personnel records. Even if they get a signed release from some employer, there's nothing to look at. I think I'm okay, as long as I refer any inquiries to Todd in Legal. I've got something for us to do tomorrow."

"Great. What's up?"

"Firearms safety."

"You're kidding, right?"

"There are guns in the house, and I'd be negligent if I didn't educate you on how to handle them. It's a matter of your personal safety. Also, with Jordan talking about going into the military, he might be impressed if you knew a thing or two about shooting."

"I'm in."

"You need to read the state firearms safety manual." Amy sat down at his computer, Scott looked up the California Department of Justice website, and he opened the PDF file for the manual. "Check it out, I'm cooking dinner. You read this stuff, and then we'll talk."

After cleaning up from dinner, Scott checked on Amy's progress.

"I finished reading and aced the practice test, but I have questions."

"That's what old dad's here for." They went over the material a couple times.

Amy looked a little confused. You can only do so much on paper.

Scott unlocked his guns, unloaded them, and showed her what she needed to learn about working the safety on the .45, loading, unloading, and aiming the guns.

"They're a lot heavier than I imagined."

"A couple things you need to know about guns. This is very serious, and you need to listen. If you're ever at a friend's home and someone takes out a gun, you must leave immediately. That situation is a bad accident waiting to happen. Second, for everyone's safety, you need to think of every gun as loaded all the time, even if you just checked it ten minutes ago. Every time you pick one up, you must check it to verify that it's unloaded. If you don't know how to check the status of a particular gun, don't pick it up. Lastly, do not point a gun at anything you don't want to shoot."

"The manual mentioned a test. Can I take it?"

"Sure. It's pretty simple. As usual, the state does it all wrong. They allow you to miss thirty percent of the questions and still pass. That's moronic. If you are supposed to know all the information, you should be required to get them all right. If education is the goal, we'd be better off if they let people take the test an unlimited number of times, but in the end, everyone should get all the questions right."

"That makes sense."

"Consider this. Over thirty thousand Americans die in automobile accidents every year. The drivers are presumably all tested and licensed, and the cars are registered, insured, and approved by the federal government and the state as safe to operate. Yet due to stupidity, negligence, substance abuse, and willful lawbreaking, those thirty thousand people die every year. The same logic applies to firearms. Ultimately, it falls upon the owner to use them responsibly and safely."

"Is this where the Marine Corps anthem starts playing?"

Julie drove like a demon and didn't stop until she was off the mountain. She checked and double-checked her mirrors to make sure she wasn't being followed. She pulled into the first place she found with parking hidden from the street, and called Eric Kim.

Second ring. "Kim."

"Hello, Mr. Kim. My name is Julie Wilson. Max Moon referred me to you. I believe I need your services."

"Max is an old friend and an associate. How can I help you?"

"I just came into a lot of money, and some people are following me. I'm worried about my personal safety."

"Where are you now?"

Julie gave him her location.

"I'm an hour away. I want you to turn your phone off, just in case they're tracking it. Turn it on again exactly one hour from now, just in case we miss our meeting, and park your car out of sight."

"Got it. Please hurry."

The next day Scott and Amy took their guns to an outdoor gun range near the Angeles National Forest. They checked in, and Scott bought Amy some hearing and eye protection, and some targets. They walked out to the pistol range and waited for a cease-fire. It was a slow day, and there were only about a half-dozen shooters on the pistol line. Scott explained that the standard self-defense target setup was seven yards away because the FBI had determined it was likely that most self-defense shooting events would happen twenty-one feet or closer. He explained that she couldn't handle guns or ammunition during a cease-fire because people would be out on the range setting up targets. When people are out there, he told her, you're supposed to keep behind the white line painted on the ground. They put their guns and ammunition on the bench and stepped back behind the line. The cease-fire was soon announced, and Scott went forward to mount their cardboard target.

When he returned, he cautioned Amy. "Wait for the announcement."

A few minutes later the speaker by their station blared. "The line is hot and open. Wear your eye and ear protection at all times."

Scott took the old .22-caliber Ruger revolver out of his briefcase and again showed Amy how to load and unload it. With Scott's help, she fired several cylinders of six rounds each. She eventually figured out the sights and consistently hit the bull's-eye using both hands to hold the gun.

Amy then stepped up to the .38 Smith & Wesson. Scott put her in a knees-bent shooting stance, leaning forward with her free hand supporting her hand gripping the gun. The extra recoil and muzzle blast from the short-barreled revolver set her back a bit and broke her concentration. Eventually she adjusted to it, hitting the center part of a silhouette target consistently.

"Well, what do you think?"

"It's fun. Nothing I'd do every day, but something new to learn."

"Want to try the .45?"

"Sure."

Once again Scott demonstrated loading and unloading, and fired a full magazine to show her what to expect in recoil.

Amy picked up the big old Colt, slightly bent her knees again, and leaned forward holding the gun in a two-handed grip. She touched off the first shot and looked at Scott in surprise.

"That's not so bad."

Then she fired the remaining six rounds, reloaded, and shot another seven.

"Are we about done?"

"I think I've got it. I like that Colt. Guys make such a big deal out of things. It's not really that hard. I'm a girl, and I can shoot the forty-five just fine."

"That's the spirit. Jordan will be impressed."

Scott packed up everything, smiling the whole time.

They went to a nearby coffee shop owned by an Ethiopian couple. A side menu offered several Ethiopian specials, and Amy tried one.

Lunch came, and Amy dug in.

"Wow. That's spicy. Healthy food, but a little warm."

"You did good today. You don't seem to be afraid of the guns."

"Once I understood how to handle and control them safely, I was fine. Kind of like my car."

"A couple more pointers for you to consider, if someone ever accosts you, always watch their hands. Their mouth won't kill you, but what's in their hands will. Shoot for center mass, nothing fancy. Those stupid TV show scenes where two people point guns at each other and make speeches? That's a lot of Hollywood fake drama. If you see a gun or a knife in an aggressor's hand, you immediately shoot to kill, and you don't talk to them. Once you are convinced you are in mortal danger, hesitating to shoot can easily cost you your life. Just make sure you see a weapon and not their cell phone."

"I understand, but I don't want to ever make that choice."

"That's up to the people who would harm you isn't it?"

"I guess so."

"I don't want to frighten you, but there is a reason for all this. Do you remember Fiona Dalton?"

"Sure, the H.R. person at your work. I met her."

"She was murdered last week."

"No! What happened?"

"Someone drugged her and then tried to make it look like a suicide. I don't know if that has anything to do with Julie or me, but I want you to be able to protect yourself if something happens and I'm not there. Just don't shoot me when I come home late."

"Maybe it's time to renegotiate your no-sex for me until you die rule?"

"Not funny."

28

ax called Buck concerning his encounter with Julie.

"Sorry, Buck. I made the offer, and she turned it down with an attitude. I don't know what else to do."

"We wait. You never know. If it looks like more money will make a difference, we can negotiate a new number."

"Fiona Dalton, the H.R. director at MacKenna, was murdered last week."

"That's interesting. Sounds like someone was unhappy with the deal."

"People get killed for a lot less than six million."

Max called Todd to brief him.

"Hi Todd, just to bring you up to date, I found Julie and talked to her about giving up the money for a fee. No dice. She wants to keep it all.

Considering Fiona's death, I told her to think about hiring Eric Kim, an associate of mine, just in case she wanted some personal protection. She's got to be alive to give back the money if it ever goes that way."

"That's too bad. I was hoping we could claw back some of the loss."

"Of course. What I don't know is why she's still hanging around here."

Eric Kim pulled up in front of a restaurant and texted Julie. It came back "Inside." Eric was fairly short and built out wide from lifting weights. His bald head rested on a thick muscular neck and shone in the sun. He checked around the outside of the restaurant, inspecting a few cars before entering. Julie signaled him, and he went to where she was seated in a back booth.

"Julie? I'm Eric."

"Thank you for coming out on short notice. I need some personal security, and I'm hoping you can help."

"That's what I do. I came because Max wouldn't have referred you unless he thought you needed me. I trust his judgment. What's going on?"

"I recently came into a lot of money, and I've attracted some people who want part of it. I want to keep them away from me."

"Tell me more. I don't want to get involved in anything that is legally questionable."

Julie put her copies of the Pugh Western and MacKenna agreements on the table.

"I was sexually harassed and attacked at work by my supervisor. Those documents tell what happened with my settlements."

Eric read the documents, pausing to order a coffee when a waitress came to the table.

"Pretty clear-cut. Who's trying horn in?"

"Max came to talk to me where I was hiding out. He was professional and offered me a deal with the insurance company. When I turned it down, he gave me your card. Shortly after he left, another man came to the door and said he wanted to talk about the money. He mentioned the wife of the guy who sexually harassed me, Dana Milner."

"How do they fit in?"

"She divorced Scott shortly after the events that led to my settlement. They signed off on the divorce agreement, but he tricked her into excluding some settlement money that he was getting from the company. It was a lot, two hundred thousand dollars. Maybe she's nuts, thinks I'm responsible, and wants some money from me? I don't know. It seems bizarre."

"Did you know the guy who came the second time?"

"Never saw him before."

"First things first. I can shelter you in a safe place, and then I'll go talk to this woman and see what her problem is. Let's talk about my fees."

"We can do that later; I'm sure it will be fine. How about we get going?"

"This is short notice, but I do have a large home with guest facilities that could easily accommodate you. The house is registered to a private corporation. No one will trace you there. Okay?"

"Perfect. Let's get to hell out of here."

Eric carefully checked the underside of Julie's car for any tracking devices and found one in the front fender well. Lance had apparently slipped one under her car before going to her door. Eric attached it to another car in the parking lot. They started out for his home in the upper part of Altadena, Julie going first, with Eric following close behind in a common-looking white Dodge Durango R/T with tinted windows. After a ninety-minute, nerve-racking drive, with Eric constantly checking for a tail, they arrived at his home. Julie unpacked, and Eric drove her car out of sight into the garage. Eric's home was set away from other homes on a private drive. It was secluded but close enough for easy access to the outside. Eric showed Julie to the guest quarters and gave her a tour of the house.

"I may be able to clean this up sufficiently so you can get back to normal living soon. I'll go see this woman you talked about and give her something to think about besides following you. I'll also try to identify whoever visited you and talk to him about tracking your car."

"Good luck. I don't think they'll quit anytime soon."

"I can be persuasive. I offer other services. I can get you to another geographic area for a fresh start and hide your identity. It's too soon for such drastic measures; changing people's minds is a lot more efficient."

Eric went outside and called to update Max.

Dana drove to the Urgent Care facility after Lance called. She parked, noting his car in the lot, and went in to fetch him. He was sitting in the waiting room with a large bandage on his forehead, two fingers in a splint, and a brace on his knee.

"What happened?"

"I found her by following Max. When I tried to talk to her, she charged into me and knocked me down a flight of stairs. I'm lucky I didn't break my neck."

"Where is she now?"

"Could be anywhere."

"How badly are you hurt?"

"Sprained knee, two broken fingers, and a mild concussion."

"Come on. Get in the car. We'll pick yours up tomorrow."

They arrived home, and Dana helped him into the house, entering through the garage.

"Are you taking painkillers?"

"Yes."

"No wine for you."

"Where's Amy?"

"With Scott."

"That's probably best for tonight. What's for dinner?"

"What do you think about Chinese?"

Max was thinking again, and he called Scott.

"Scott, Max Moon. Do you remember me?"

"Vividly. What do you want?"

"I just wanted to talk a bit about money."

"What money?"

"I've been authorized to offer a ten percent reward of three hundred thousand dollars for the return of the three million Pugh Western settlement. I also can pledge that the MacKenna Company will match it for a total of six hundred thousand dollars. I know the money went to Julie, at least on paper, but just in case you still have some sway with her, I'm offering. The offer comes with indemnification from Pugh or MacKenna legally pursuing you."

"I don't know anything about that money, and I haven't seen Julie since we worked together. Are we done?"

"Just to let you know, I was able to contact Julie. She wasn't interested in the deal either. Something unusual happened. Someone accosted her, wanting to talk to her about the money. I don't know who it was, but there was a physical confrontation, and she's now in protective hiding. It sounds like there are some unintended consequences from this incident. I thought you might like to know."

"Could be Lance, Dana's boyfriend. Where is she?"

"Uh-uh. Can't divulge that. Confidential information. Call me if you change your mind. I'll try to broker a deal."

Max hung up without waiting for a response.

Scott went to his briefcase, got out his contact phone, and called Julie. Still no answer.

CHAPTER

·········· *29* ··········

or and Armen parked across the street from the Milner home. They watched the house intently, but no one seemed to be home. A pair of headlights appeared and slowly approached from up the street. They ducked down as the headlights swept their car. The garage door opened, the car drove in, and the door closed behind.

They took out their pistols, checked them one last time, and tested the dog collar.

"DAMN!" Armen accidentally shocked himself.

"Shut up, moron. You'll wake up the whole neighborhood."

"You think it's fun getting shocked? You want to try it?"

They waited a half-hour and walked across the street, looking for any possible witnesses. They didn't see any people or cameras, so they climbed the steps and knocked. Dana opened the door, and they pushed their way in. Dana struck at them, and Armen hit her full in the face, breaking her nose. Lance heard the battle and limped into the room. Gor slammed him to the ground and taped his hands behind his back, kicking him for good measure. Dana lay groaning on the floor.

Lance tried to manage the situation. "What do you want?"

"You know what. The money."

"Take my wallet. Her purse is in the kitchen."

"Don't be stupid. We want the big money you were talking about."

"I told you there was no money. I was drunk and bragging."

"We don't believe you. Has she got the money?" Gor pointed to Dana on the floor.

Lance yelled, "There's nothing here!"

Gor and Armen picked up Dana, taped her arms to the chair, and put the dog collar around her neck. She was bleeding profusely from her nose.

"Tell us about the money, now!"

"I don't know…"

Gor pressed his remote control, shocking Dana. She screamed, and Armen stuffed a cloth in her mouth.

"You scream and we hit you some more."

Lance yelled, "Let her alone. She doesn't have any money."

Gor walked over to him and viciously kicked him again.

"Shut up. You don't know anything, right? Shut up."

Gor shocked her again, and she screamed into the cloth.

"Where is it?"

Gor and Armen looked at each other in frustration. They shocked her again. Her head hung down, and they got no response.

"Let's go look."

They began a search of the house, tearing into desks, closets, any-place they thought might hide something of value. One of them always stayed within sight of Lance while they searched. Eventually they found the safe in the study.

They went at Dana again. "What's the combination?"

They took out the rag. Dana opened her eyes and muttered, "Five, two, eight, nine."

Gor and Armen both ran into the study, thinking they had found the big money.

Lance struggled to his feet and limped to the sliding glass door open-ing to the back yard. With his hands tied behind him, he turned his back to the lock, unlocked the door, and slid it open. He ran limping through the backyard. Just then, Gor came into the room with some cash in his hands and spotted Lance disappearing into the night. He ran to the door, took aim with his gun, but held fire when he saw the neighbors behind the Milner house. The whole family was watching TV in a rear room directly in his line of sight. He dropped the money and ran after Lance. Just as Gor got close, Lance flipped himself over the rear fence and disappeared into the night. With no time for a pursuit, Gor ran back to the house.

Lance hid in some bushes until he was sure no one was following. He freed his hands by rubbing the duct tape on the corner of a cinder block wall, scraping his hands in the process. Lance saw a man walking his dog and ran up to him. He begged the startled man to borrow his cell phone. The shocked dog-walker gave it to him, and he anxiously dialed.

"Scott, you have to come to the house now. They have Dana!"

"Who is this?"

"Lance. Come now. She needs our help!"

"Why? What's happening?"

"They tied her up. Please come now!"

"Call the police."

Lance disconnected and called 911, screaming for the police to come immediately.

Scott got dressed and drove to the house. By the time he arrived, the first patrol unit was parked in front of the house with its lights blazing. He ran up the steps and pushed his way past a cop who tried to stop him. He saw Dana tied to a chair. She wasn't moving.

The cop grabbed him from behind and forced him out of the room.

"That's my wife! Help my wife!"

Two cops held him in the study, along with Lance, who'd returned after the police arrived.

Lance's bandage had torn loose, and he was bloody from his forehead wound. The dive into the rosebushes had scraped him up, and his hands were bleeding.

Scott looked him over, "What happened?"

Lance stopped crying and spoke with his head down.

"They broke into the house and tied her up, then they tied me up and kicked me. They were beating and shocking her. They wanted to know where our money was. They wouldn't believe that there wasn't any money."

"Who was it? How did you get away?"

"They came into this room thinking there was money in the safe, and I ran out the back door into the next yard."

Scott glanced over to the safe, now open and empty.

"Was there anything in the safe?"

"Fifteen thousand. The money you gave her."

Ten minutes after the first cop had shown up, Gene arrived. Linda followed five minutes later while Gene was talking to the first officer on the scene.

"What happened?"

"Home invasion. I caught the call and entered the house through the open front door. Someone had tossed the place, the safe in the study was open and empty. This woman was tied to the chair like you see her. I took off the shock collar and checked for a pulse, but she was long gone. That's about it. Those two in the study showed up right after I got here. The guy with the wound on his head says he called it in. The other guy says he's her husband."

"Okay, thanks. I'll see if I can make any sense out of it."

Gene and Linda walked into the den. Gene had Scott stand up, and he took him into the kitchen.

Gene questioned him. "Do you remember me?"

"Of course."

"What happened here?"

"I don't know. I was home when I got a frantic call from Lance, the other guy."

"I know who he is. And?"

"I ran up the stairs. The front door was open, and I found Dana in the chair like that. Lance came shortly after and was very distraught. The house was wrecked, as you can see."

"What happened here?"

"I have no idea. It looks like a robbery, but you had better ask Lance. Apparently, he was here when it happened."

"I'm thinking you had something to do with this, and somehow it's all mixed up with that MacKenna business."

"Listen, Sherlock. I got the divorce, and that's all I wanted from Dana. Now I have to go home and tell my daughter that her mother was murdered. How about do your job and look at the video from my security system."

"Calm down. Where is it?"

"It's uploaded daily to an off-site server. If you're lucky and they didn't spot the cameras, you might get their pictures."

Gene looked at him for a moment.

"Don't go anywhere."

Gene joined Linda in the study. Lance was still tearful but getting himself under control.

Linda took the lead. "Lance, come on, focus. What happened here?"

"We were just ordering some food for dinner when these two guys broke in. They taped my hands together and beat me. They put Dana in the chair and kept asking her about money. They seemed to think there was a lot of money here. They put a collar on her neck, shocked her, and hit her. She gave them the safe combination, and when both of them went into the den, I took off through the backyard. I found a guy walking his dog on the next street. He let me use his cell phone, and I called Scott and the police."

"What was in the safe?"

"Some cash. She got some cash from her divorce settlement and kept about fifteen thousand in there. I told her to bank it, but she wouldn't listen. She never listened."

"How did you get injured? Did they do this to you?"

"Some of it. I fell down some stairs and got this on my head. Broke these fingers." He held up his two filthy, bandaged fingers.

"Describe the intruders."

"I don't know. Two Russian guys, I think; they had guns."

"Give me some more."

"It's hard to remember, Medium height, black hair. Black clothes. Just two guys."

"Could you identify them if you saw them again?"

Lance wasn't sure he wanted the Ketamine dealers found, "Maybe."

"Did Scott have anything to do with it?"

"No. He came to help."

Gene went back to Scott.

"How can we get the security tape?"

"Get my laptop from my car. I can log in and download the video."

Gene sent a uniformed cop to retrieve the computer.

"Where's your daughter? Amy, wasn't it?"

"She's at my place. How am I going to tell her?"

"You can go as soon as you get us the video."

Scott turned on his computer and logged into his security account. He put a thumb drive into the side of the computer and downloaded the day's security video.

Gene watched the video. It plainly showed two men climbing the stairs and entering the house. Luckily, Scott had mounted one security camera low and partially obscured by vegetation just off the porch. They had missed seeing it, and that mistake gave Gene and Linda a clear picture of their faces.

"Look at that. Got those two cold."

Gene told Scott he could leave. He packed up his laptop and went home to tell Amy the tragic news.

Linda looked at Lance. "I know you've had a rough night, but you can't leave until our forensic team gets here and checks to see if you can offer up any forensic evidence. Are you okay?"

"I could use a drink."

"I'll see what I can do." Gene went into the kitchen, opened the fridge, and found a half-drunk bottle of wine. He poured some into a water glass and brought it to Lance.

Scott sat in his car looking at the lighted window in his apartment. He dreaded going inside and telling Amy the bad news.

Sergeant Ari D. Onassian had a combination of language skills that made him uniquely suited to run the gang unit for the Glendale Police Department. He spoke Armenian, Spanish, Russian, Korean, and English.

Gene pulled out his phone and called Ari's number.

"Ari, how would you like to come down and ID a couple of guys who just did a home invasion?"

"Can't it wait until tomorrow?"

"I have a video and an eyeball wit. I really can't wait for prints. Someone died, and these clowns are dangerous."

"I'm liking pastrami, been a while since I had a nice pastrami sandwich."

"Really? You're holding me up for a sandwich?"

"It's called leverage. You pick it. Langer's, Canter's, or Brent's. I'm just pastrami horny."

"Deal. This thing with the deli food, are you sure you're not part Jewish?"

"I could be for the right sandwich."

"I'll be waiting."

Twenty minutes later Ari ambled into the police station. He was a medium-height, athletic-looking man in his late twenties, with a shaved head, a short black beard, and a gold cross on a heavy chain around his neck. He wore athletic shoes, black skinny jeans, and a black leather jacket. He looked like a volunteer preacher in a high-security correctional facility.

Going into his office, Gene passed him a paper cup of black watch coffee.

"It's getting hard to tell you from the assholes."

"That's the idea, right?"

"I've been wanting to ask, what the 'D' stands for in your name."

"Don't ask."

Ari inserted the drive and watched the video.

"Slam dunk. Armen and Gor, the fuck up twins. These idiots have turned up in a half-dozen small-potatoes crimes over the last couple years. Too stupid to be trusted by the serious players, they do piecework for cheap, and whatever harebrained schemes they can come up with on their own. Gor's under the delusion that he's a criminal mastermind, and Armen has the attention span of a bipolar humming bird on crank."

"Do you have a location on them?"

Ari looked up their file and printed it out for Gene.

"That's what I have. Good luck, and I'll be around to collect my pastrami."

"How about coming along and earning it?"

"Sure. Wait one."

Ari called in, getting permission to change assignment, and finished his coffee.

"Let's do it."

Gene drove north as they took the 2 and then the 210 freeway to the Los Angeles border, got off at Lowell in Tujunga, and drove up into the hills. He shut off their headlights as they slowly cruised down a darkened street. There were no sidewalks, and the road was illuminated only by an occasional streetlight that the kids hadn't shot out. They parked a couple doors down from the house. Ari looked at the surrounding houses to pin the location.

"Yeah, this is it. I don't want to be identified with police, so how about I wait here? You can send me a picture of anyone you want me to check out, okay?"

Neighborhood dogs barked as they passed. A dim light shone behind stained bedsheets hung up for curtains in the front room of the house. They separated, standing on either side of the door, and knocked. Linda had her hand on her gun. A young woman with dirty blonde hair, tattoos, and a cigarette in her mouth opened the door. She looked like she was high. Gene held out his ID. "Police. We're looking for Gor and Armen. Are they here?" The woman didn't seem surprised or troubled by the appearance of the police at her door so late in the evening.

"No. I don't know where they are."

"Do you know when they'll return?"

"Don't know."

"Do you mind if we look inside?"

Linda took her picture and sent it to Ari.

"What are you doing? Stop that!"

The text came right back. "Nobody."

"Piss off." She slammed the door.

They looked at each other.

"Her pipe must be getting cold." Linda said.

They joined Ari in the car.

"Where to, boss?"

Ari scratched his cheek, "I've got a snitch we could try."

Gor and Armen slouched in their car at the top of the hill watching the police leave.

CHAPTER

30

ene drove to a tobacco shop. The sign was written in Armenian and English, and there were hookahs for sale in the display window. Ari went inside. Gene and Linda waited impatiently, watching Ari talk to a middle-aged guy with a potbelly who was adamantly shaking his head. Ari entered a room at the back of the store, came out a few moments later, returned to the car, and shrugged.

"He says he doesn't know anything, and he's going to call me if he hears anything."

"You believe him?"

"It's a definite maybe. We had him under surveillance for a while last year when we thought he might be involved in something. All we found out was that he has a Turkish girlfriend on the side in South Pasadena. I own this guy. If his brothers-in-law ever find out about the girlfriend, he'll be in deep shit."

Scott paused at the front door of his apartment before entering, dreading what he had to do. He put his key in the lock and entered the living room. Amy was watching TV. He took the remote from her and turned off the TV.

"We need to talk."

"Why? What happened?" Amy sensed Scott's mood.

"There was a home invasion robbery at our house tonight. Unfortunately, Dana was attacked, and she died."

"Mom? Someone killed Mom?"

"Yes. I'm sorry."

"There must be some mistake! Who told you this?"

"I saw her. It's true."

Amy threw herself into Scott's arms and cried with the sorrow of a breaking heart.

Eventually, Amy emptied out and gathered herself.

"It just can't be true. Who'd want to harm her?"

"I don't know. The robbers were looking for money, and they also attacked Lance. He was beaten, and he narrowly escaped with his life. I actually felt sorry for him. I think he really loved her."

"Why didn't he do something?"

"They had guns. It was all he could do to escape and call the police."

"What happened to her?"

"I don't know. We need to wait for the police to tell us. They'll be around later to talk to you."

"It can't be true."

"This is awful, but you still have me. I love you, and I'll take care of you. We're together."

Amy cried off and on the rest of the evening. She was emotionally spent and eventually went to bed. Scott sat drinking a beer with the day's events swirling around in his head. He picked up his phone and dialed.

"Max? Hi. I'm sorry for the late call, but I need to tell you something. If you still know how to contact Julie, please tell her that Dana was murdered tonight."

"What happened?"

"Home invasion by a couple of guys who thought she had the money. If you can pass it along, she needs to be very careful until the police find out where this thing came from."

"How are you and Amy doing?"

"She took it hard. I am still trying to process it. Even though our marriage turned bad this year, we were married a long time, and there are lots of good memories from long before these troubles came along. I'm confused, and I don't really know what to think or feel."

"Don't try to think yourself out of this. Just ride it out. The only thing that helps is putting time between today and finding a new path that you can live with. Keep focused on Amy and the future."

"Thanks, and please tell Julie."

"I think I may be able to get that message to her. You take care while they're still out there."

Gene was still at the station when he got a call from Dr. Kilmeade at the coroner's office.

"King? You still at work?"

"Justice never sleeps. What have you got for me?"

"Thought you might be interested. Dana Milner died of a heart attack."

"Really?"

"Yeah. Apparently, the stress of the beating and the shocking kicked her into cardiac arrest."

"I'll be damned. That might mitigate murder one. Thanks for calling, man. I owe you a beer and a dog when we catch that Dodger game."

"And peanuts."

"Yeah, and peanuts."

Linda overheard the conversation.

"What's up?"

"Kilmeade says Dana Milner died of a heart attack."

"No shit?"

It was after midnight when Gene dragged himself through his front door. He was thankful that Ari had taken the duty in case anything came up over the weekend. Doris met him in her robe. Exhausted, Gene hugged and kissed her.

"What's that for?"

"Do I need a reason?"

The following morning Scott got Jordan's phone number from Amy's phone contact list and called him.

"Hi, Jordan. This is Scott, Amy's father. I know it's the weekend, but I was wondering if I could ask for a favor."

"Sure, Mr. Milner. What can I do?"

"Call me Scott. The only people calling me Mr. Milner lately are the police. A couple burglars trashed our home last night, and it's a mess. Could you help me straighten it out? I don't want Amy to see it messed up, and I could use a hand."

"Sure. When?"

"Meet you at ten?"

"I'll be there."

Jordan was sitting in his Murano when Scott drove up. They greeted each other and climbed the front steps. Scott tore the police crime scene tape apart and went in. Jordan followed but stopped short when he saw the mess.

"Wow. They really trashed the place."

"Yeah, they did. That's not all. Amy's mom was killed during the attack, and her new boyfriend was badly beaten."

"Oh my God! That's horrible. I texted Amy, but she didn't say anything about it."

"Well, I think she's still in shock."

They worked for several hours putting the house back together. Luckily, the murderers only had limited time to toss the house, and they quit when they found the safe.

Jordan stopped in his tracks and stared at the floor, calling, "Mr. Milner?"

Jordan pointed to a dried spill of blood on the hardwood floor.

"Leave it. I'll take care of it. Why don't you go upstairs and finish up?"

Scott got some cleaner and paper towels from the kitchen, got down on his hands and knees, and cleaned the dried blood. Three hours later they had the house back in presentable condition, and the refuse bin was full. They locked up the house, and Scott took down all the crime scene tape.

"Won't the cops get pissed?"

"I guess they can write me a citation if they want. How about lunch?"

Scott and Jordan sat in a small restaurant dining on excellent burgers and onion rings, neither of them felt like conversing.

"Thanks for helping me. I didn't want Amy to see the house in total chaos. I think we may be moving back there soon."

"I'm glad to help. I wish I could do more. How's she coping?"

"Taking it rather well. Still, I expect more grief as the reality sets in."

He took a hundred-dollar bill from his wallet. "I'd like to pay you for your time."

"Absolutely not. I wouldn't take a dime for this job."

"Then lunch is on me."

They finished their lunch in near silence. Scott was amazed to find thoughts about sons-in-laws creeping into his head for the first time. He didn't know if Amy and Jordan would last, but he now had new confidence in her ability to pick a good, decent guy.

Scott excused himself and went outside to call Jeff.

"Well, look who surfaced. You must be staying out of trouble."

"I tried, the problem is, more trouble found me. Two thugs broke into our home last night and killed Dana. They trashed the place, looking for money."

"My God. What happened?"

"Well, that's about it. They got some cash and beat Dana and her boyfriend. I've been cleaning up the house today."

"I'm so sorry to hear that. How's Amy?"

"That's what I want to talk to you about. The crooks who trashed our house and killed Dana are still on the loose, and I don't like the idea of Amy being at my place alone. I was wondering if you could take her in for a while."

"Absolutely. Just bring her over any time this weekend. My girlfriend will love it."

"I appreciate that. I have the feeling this thing's not over yet. Not by a long shot."

Scott walked Jordan to his car and thanked him again. He drove back to his apartment, stopping off at an electronics store on the way.

31

cott got out the toolbox he'd salvaged from the old house. He enlisted Amy's help installing a smart front doorbell with a camera and then put another camera near the kitchen door. He also installed extra stick-up, battery-operated cameras front and back. All these devices were electronically linked to his computer and mobile phone. He figured the security system might give them an edge in the face of bad company.

Amy suggested they do some running. They drove to Griffith Park and jogged the trails until the light faded and Scott tired. Running around the flat Rose Bowl loop was one thing, but jogging up and down dirt trails in the park was quite another. When the run was over, they went to another small, family-run Mexican restaurant for dinner, found a table, and waited for service.

Amy's face was flush from the run. "I was hoping we would meet P-22."

"What's P-22?"

"The mountain lion who lives in Griffith Park. People see him all the time."

"Easy for you to say. You could run away and he'd be on me in a minute."

"You're too old and tough."

"You didn't invite Jordan to run with us."

"I know. I just wanted the two of us to be together."

Scott reached out and squeezed her hand. At that moment a large friendly waitress dropped off some utensils, chips, salsa, and menus.

"Are you having some issues with Jordan."

"Kind of. I like him a lot, but I just don't know."

"Don't know what? Is he bothering you?"

"No, not at all. He's a perfect gentleman."

"Seems like a nice enough guy."

"It's just that he has all these plans, and well, they are not my plans. He's going into the military, and that means moving away. If he stays in the military that means we would be moving even more. He wants a lot of kids. That also means if I eventually married him, I'd be a housewife and raising kids for twenty years. I'd carry a lot of that responsibility all by myself when he was gone. There is nothing wrong with that; it's just not what I thought about for my life."

"If it doesn't work, keep trying. That old saying about there is only one person for you is nonsense. Mostly, the person you fall in love with is pure chance, and a matter of having a fairly limited choice of people if you think about it. Even if you date online, you may look at hundreds of guys, but you only really get to personally know a couple of people, if that. Often people fall in love with someone at work, church, or school, someone close so they get to know them well. The bottom line is, most of the time the right person comes along if you're receptive."

"How will I know what to do?"

"You're asking me about romance advice with my recent history?"

"Give me a serious answer, please."

"Okay. I'll give you a dad's point of view. Find someone who's intelligent and has a good sense of humor. Also, find someone who's not addicted to anything, because an addict will always love their addiction more than you. Find someone who's curious, ambitious, confident, and responsible. Make sure whatever their personal quirks are, that you can live with them, because in the long run, they'll probably get worse. Don't take on someone thinking you can change them; you might change ten percent if you are lucky."

"Is that what you did?"

"Not exactly. I married your mother because she was hot."

"Seriously?"

"What do older people say when their spouse dies? 'I lost my best friend.' You need to find your best friend. Someone you can talk to about anything, and someone who enjoys being with you above all others. Find someone who respects you and will forgive you. You can't control who you fall in love with, but you can control who you marry."

"Maybe I'll never marry."

"Lighten up. You're sixteen, and you're thinking way too far ahead of yourself. Someone will be there. You'll have a pretty good idea when it happens."

The food arrived. They ate in silence with Amy deep in thought.

Scott paid the bill. "That was great chili verde. Home, sweetheart."

"Dad?"

"Yeah?"

"That helped, I think."

"Anytime. Do you think that maybe I could adopt Jordan?"

Amy just stared at him.

The weekend at home brought some stress relief to Gene. The simple case of alleged suicide in a dive motel had spiraled into a convoluted mess. Doris went to shop a big special sale, and Gene retreated to his room with a beer, pinned up more documents from the case. He turned on the stereo and slipped in a CD. In a moment the room was filled with the soothing voice of Andrea Marcovicci. Gene looked at the liner notes for a moment and then looked back at the board.

"What am I missing? Something's screwy about this case. All the players haven't made themselves known. What did Dana and Fiona's relationship have to do with anything? And what about Lance, the oddball?"

Later, Gene went to the kitchen for another beer and found Doris returning with some shopping bags.

"I want to hear some live music tonight." Gene said.

Linda woke early on Saturday, anxious to get started on the Dart.

Uncle Rudy was an engineer on the Southern Pacific and had been working a lot of overtime in the past month, but now he had some spare time for Jesse. She heard his truck pull up in front of the house, so she went out the back door and opened the garage, while Rudy backed his truck up the driveway.

Rudy was a small, wiry man in his mid-fifties. He wore a salt-and-pepper goatee and a Dodgers cap. He had workingman's hands, and his skin was a deep bronze color from a life of working in the sun.

"Hey, good score on the Dart. How about it Jesse, are you ready to get your hands dirty?"

"You bet. Just tell me what to do."

Rudy laughed, dropped the tailgate, and removed a toolbox, some jack stands, a floor jack, some rags, and a washing pan for parts. Just as it looked like he was done, out came a case of motor oil, some brake cleaner spray, a new battery, and various other cleaners and lubricants. Rudy looked the car over.

"Let's see if it turns over."

He cleaned the battery cable clamps, hooked up the new battery and checked the oil level. The engine cranked over and it coughed through the carburetor.

"Not frozen up. That's a good start." He removed the air cleaner to see how much gunk was in the carb and sprayed in some cleaner.

He held the dipstick for Linda and Jesse. "Smell that? The oil's shot, black, old, and sour. We need to change it."

He pulled off the valve cover, and the rockers were clean, no sludge. "Looking better."

He pulled off the gas cap and smelled the gas in the tank. "Old but not too bad.

We'll leave it for now. The first lesson is you need compression, fuel and spark to light off an engine. The gas is okay, so now we need to check the spark."

Rudy pulled off a plug wire, stuck a screwdriver in the end, and handed it to Linda. "See if it sparks."

Rudy cranked the engine. Linda jumped at the electrical jolt, dropping the tool and the wire.

Rudy and Jesse laughed. "Oldest trick in the book. We have fire."

Linda rubbed her hand. "Looks like someone doesn't want lunch."

Rudy sprayed some starter fluid into the carburetor and cranked the engine. The old six fired up in a couple revolutions. Jesse jumped up and down with joy.

Max wasn't letting go of the MacKenna case. The circumstances and known facts swirled in his investigator's mind, giving him no rest. He called Bruce.

"Got another job for you. Meet you at noon at the coffee shop?"

Bruce walked in, looking left and right, radiating guilt as usual.

"What's up, man?"

"Been to the track lately?"

"Don't mock me. What do you need?"

"I want you to take up where you left off on those four people, but I want the phone records since we last met. There's a grand in it for you."

"I need five hundred a head."

"Fifteen all in. My employer is tired of throwing good money after bad. I'm on a tight leash."

"Yeah. Okay."

"I'm worried about you. How about starting a 401K this time?"

"Piss off."

Gor and Armen sat on an old cracked leather sofa in the Tujunga house, getting high on some coke they'd scored with Dana's money. They were grim in spite of the mood elevators. At the rate they were going, they could Hoover up the entire fifteen grand by the end of the week.

Gor was glassy-eyed and manic. "What about that guy she gave up, Scott? Maybe he's got the money."

"Her husband? I don't know about him, but someone's got it. How about that clown, Tavidian? We should have squeezed him some more when we had the chance."

"We could have done it, if you hadn't fucked up and left him alone. You screwed up the whole thing."

"Shut up. You left him to look in the safe. Maybe you have a bad memory."

"I say we go find out what her husband knows. Where's that address, or did you lose it?"

CHAPTER

32

or and Armen parked a couple doors down from Scott's apart-ment. They looked around, saw no threats, checked their guns, and waited in the dark.

"Armen, you go around and see if there's a back door. Signal me if you find one. I'll go in the front, and when you hear me kick in the door, you do the same from the back. Okay?"

"Yeah. I got it."

Gor stood in the shadows waiting for Armen and looking around for any witnesses. He noted that the apartment next to Scott's was dark. No one home, a lucky sign. Shortly, Armen appeared around the corner of the building and gave Gor a thumbs-up sign by grabbing his crotch.

Gor thought. "Something's wrong with him. I need a better partner." He walked up to Scott's front door, running the last ten feet and planting his boot near the door lock.

Scott was working on his computer, searching for sales jobs, when his security system sent an alert. He answered the prompt and saw Gor walking up to the porch with his hood up over his head and a gun in his hand. Scott looked for Amy. She was still in the bedroom. No time. He opened his briefcase, pulled out the Colt .45, and racked the slide just as Gor kicked in the front door.

Gor looked surprised when Scott shot him the first time. It wasn't supposed to go that way. He was struggling to raise his gun when a second heavy bullet slammed into his chest. He fell like a piano off a balcony, convulsed once, and died.

Scott's ears were still ringing as he covered Gor's body, watching for any movement. Hearing a crash behind him, he swung around, firing twice into the partially open back door. He thought he heard a human noise, then silence. Amy ran out of her room.

"What happened?" Then she saw the body on the floor and ran to Scott.

"Get back in your room and call 911. I need to deal with this. I don't know if someone's still out there." Amy went back to her room and locked the door. Scott picked up Gor's gun, dropped the magazine, and jacked a round out of the chamber. He put the magazine and the round in his pocket. He put Gor's gun on a table and stepped over the body. Out the front door, he carefully moved around the side of the house to the kitchen door. The back yard was empty. He heard a car start and drive away. Checking the back door, he saw the splintered frame and a heel mark on the door. He saw some blood drops on the rear steps. He went inside and called Amy out from her room. She looked around cautiously, then ran to Scott, hugging him. "What happened?"

"I think this is one of the guys who killed your mother."

Scott held Amy while waiting for the police.

When Scott heard the sirens coming up his street, he told Amy to go in his room and hide the .38 and .22 pistols so the police wouldn't confiscate them. He unloaded his gun and placed it on the table alongside Gor's pistol. He walked onto the front porch and held his hands up as the police came out of their patrol car with guns drawn.

Scott was sitting in his kitchen with one of the uniformed officers when Linda and Ari walked through the front door. They stepped over Gor's body and talked to the uniformed sergeant, discussing the situation. Ari knelt down and quickly examining the body. Wiping his hands off, and he headed for the kitchen.

Linda paused at the door and pulled out a small notebook and a pen.

Scott squinted at her. "You again."

"This is what I live for. Who's the dead guy?"

"I was working there at that table, when I got a ping on my computer. I looked at the camera and saw a stranger armed with a gun charging onto my porch. I concluded that he intended to harm my daughter and me. In fear for my life, I picked up my gun and armed it. He kicked in the door and pointed his gun at me, but I was faster. I shot him once, but he didn't go down. I felt my life and that of my daughter were still in mortal danger, so I shot him again. Just then, someone kicked in the kitchen door, and I shot at him. That one got away, but he left some blood on the stairs. End of story."

"Your daughter?"

"Amy!'"

Amy came out of the back bedroom and went to her father.

"Amy, this is Officer Linda Garcia and another detective. They're investigating the death of your mother."

Ari smiled and shook her hand. "Sergeant Ari Onassian. I'm pleased to meet you, Amy. I'm sorry about your mother. We're doing everything we can. What were you doing while all this was going on?"

"I was in my room. I locked the door when I heard the shooting."

"You didn't see anything?"

"No. My dad called me when it was safe."

"Okay, you can go back to your room if you want to."

Amy stayed by Scott and closely watched Ari, thinking he was pretty cute.

"Do you recognize the shooter, Mr. Milner?"

"He looks like one of the guys on the security video from when my wife was killed."

Ari went back into the living room lifting Gor's head to the light.

"Huh."

Ari returned to Scott. "Good catch, but why's he here?"

"I think Dana gave me up to them hoping they would leave her alone."

"That's not nice."

"Did I say I was divorced? There's a reason."

The forensics and crime scene people spent an hour gathering what they needed, then the body snatchers hauled Gor's body to the county morgue. Scott and Amy were sitting on the sofa, Amy resting her head on Scott's shoulder.

Linda looked around. "We're done here. Looks like a clean shooting. You were lucky. This guy's a local punk, been arrested several times. Somehow, he and his partner got it in their heads that your family has a lot of money. I'm betting the other one was a guy named Armen. Be careful until we sweep him up. Your gun has to stay in evidence until the DA looks at the shooting and makes a finding."

"Okay. No offense, but I hope I don't see you anytime soon."

"Ditto."

When the police left, Scott called his landlord.

"Hi, Arbi, I apologize for the late call."

"It's okay. What do you want?"

"Some robbers tried to break into the apartment tonight. The police just left. The bad news is, they wrecked the front and back doors. Do you know anyone in construction?"

"Sure. My son-in-law. I'll call him."

"If he can come here tonight and put some plywood over the doors, it would be good. We're going to move back to our other house until the repairs are done. Just send me the invoice, and I'll pay for it. Okay?"

"Sure. You're safe, and the little girl?"

"We're fine. I guess we're going to need a new living room rug as well."

"No problem. I've got an extra from another unit."

Scott told Amy to pack her things, got Lance's number from Amy's phone, and called him.

"Lance, It's Scott. I'm sorry for the hour, but those two guys who killed Dana just came after Amy and me. I killed one of them. Armen, the other one, is still out there. If they're going after everyone they think has the money, you're probably in danger. I think I winged Armen, but I have no idea how badly he's hit."

"Thanks for the heads up, but I've been half expecting them. I'll be careful."

"Where are you?"

"Back at my apartment." Scott thought he sounded drunk and was going to say something, but Lance quickly hung up.

While Scott and Amy were packing their things, Arbi's son-in-law showed up with two guys and some plywood. Scott thanked him and left the crew with a six-pack of craft beer.

231

They moved back to their old house that evening. It felt strange, like he'd lived another life there.

Scott looked at Amy. "Are you okay with this? I can get a hotel suite until the doors are fixed."

"I'm fine. It'll be good to get back in my old bed."

Scott was glad that Jordan and he had cleaned up the house. He dropped his travel bag and went into the kitchen looking for something to drink.

CHAPTER

·················· *33* ··················

Armen was angry and frightened. The attack on Milner's apartment was a disaster. Gor was probably dead, and he had a wounded shoulder that hurt like hell. He drove his car into an all-night gas station. The men's room entrance was on the outside, he tried the door, and it opened. He peeled back his jacket and shirt to look at his shoulder. Not bad. The bullet had grazed the outside of his right arm and left an open wound. It missed the bone and most of the muscle. Just some blood and torn flesh, but it burned like crazy and his hand was stiff. He stuffed the inside of his jacket with paper towels, got his phone out, and called his cousin Daniel.

"Daniel? It's cousin Armen. I need help."

He drove to Daniel's house and pulled into the driveway. Blood loss and shock had made him so weak that he couldn't get out of the car. Daniel heard the horn and came out to investigate. He pulled Armen out of the car and helped him into the house. He got him into the kitchen and sat him down. Daniel was a distant cousin of Armen's. He had been a medic in the army, and since then had found a lucrative career in auto recycling.

"What happened?"

"A fight. I was shot."

"What do you mean, a fight?"

"Me and Gor were going to get the money some guy owed us, but he had a gun."

"What do you want?"

"Fix my arm, and I need a place to stay for a while."

"Five hundred a day because you're family."

"Five hundred! Some family."

"Take it or leave it. I heard about the shooting on the news. Gor's very dead, and they're looking for you. I don't need to go to jail."

"Okay, but get my car out of sight."

Daniel disappeared into the bathroom and returned with his old army medic bag. Armen had dumped a mound of coke on top of the kitchen table.

"You want a taste?"

"Save it for yourself, I'm going to have to sew that up."

Scott rose early from a night of disturbed sleep. He showered, dressed, and went to the study to look at his home financing information. He went online to check his loan balances and searched the net to see what their home might be worth, then he went to the kitchen to see if there was anything to eat. Amy joined him, looking quite sleepy.

"Let's see. We have cereal and sour milk or eggs that might hatch any moment. How about frozen waffles?"

"Fine."

Scott put four frozen waffles in the toaster oven, dug out the maple syrup, and after a sniff test, set out the butter. He poured them coffee, and they ate in silence. Scott finally spoke.

"How are you doing?"

"Okay."

"Good."

"Do you think that guy last night really killed Mom?"

"The detectives think so. Linda told me that Dana died of a heart attack. Apparently, the stress was too much."

"Does it matter? She's gone. What about the other one?"

"He's still out there, but he'll get caught."

"I'd like to see him dead, too."

Scott let that comment pass, figuring she'd earned it.

"I got up early and looked at the home loan information on the house. Between the variable loan and the second mortgage we took out on the house, we owe a lot and don't have much equity. There's no way to support the house payments now that I'm unemployed. It's also a lot more square footage than the two us need. I think it's best if we call a Realtor and sell it before any more payments are due. We can cover the Realtor fees and maybe clear a little money for your college fund."

"I don't really want to live here now because of what happened."

"Okay. I'll get the ball rolling. Let's go for a run to clear our heads out. How about it?"

"Okay."

Amy was sluggish and depressed. They finished breakfast and dressed for a run.

Before they left, Scott sifted through all the mail that had accumulated since Dana's death. He found four Realtor advertisements. He liked a woman's picture and called her.

"Ms. Matthews? My name is Scott Milner, and I'm thinking about listing my house."

Scott set up a meeting with her for later in the afternoon, and while he was at it, he called Jeff.

"Hi, Jeff. I have a quick question. Who owns the house now that Dana is dead? I bought it before we married, so it's actually in my name."

"Dana and you made out wills, remember? Amy and you now own the house."

"There is no hassle if we sell it?'

"No. In fact, I'll go to the court today and kill the divorce proceedings."

"Thanks. That's what I need to hear. We have to sell the house. Can't afford to keep it, not to mention bad memories it has for us. I'll bring Amy by to read the will. She's a party, and I want her to get some closure on all this."

"I saw on the news that you shot a home invader last night. That wasn't Lance, was it?"

"No, not him. Long story that requires a drink. How about meeting me after work? It's been too long since we tipped one."

"Five-thirty at The Cat."

Amy and Scott pulled into the Rose Bowl parking lot, stretched, and began their run. They always enjoyed watching the golfers as they jogged. There was something peaceful and inviting about all the greenery.

"Come on, Dad. You're daydreaming again."

"A guy has to dream."

On the backside of the loop, Scott stopped in front the clubhouse.

"Come with me."

"Why?"

Amy followed Scott to the pro shop. They approached an older guy in a bright-green golf shirt working behind the counter.

"Hi. How does one get some golf lessons?"

"We have group lessons, and there are a couple of pros who'll give private lessons."

Scott picked up a business card from the counter. "Thanks."

Once they were outside Amy looked puzzled.

"You're taking up golf?"

"We're taking up golf."

"Not now, Dad. Please, not now."

Lance wasn't doing well. He was depressed, anxious, and drinking far too much. His sleep was disturbed, and his appetite for anything but vodka was nonexistent. Dana's death was an ever-present misery. He kept going over the night of the robbery in his head, thinking there must have been something more he could have done. Then there was the undeniable fact that his drunken bragging had brought the killers to the house. His only relief was washing down painkillers with a bottle of Skyy.

Lance finally medicated himself into a fitful sleep. Upon waking, he put away the vodka, took a shower, got dressed, and went out for some breakfast. He wanted to do something about Armen. Over coffee, oatmeal, and bacon, Lance figured it out. He needed to find Armen and even the score. He also didn't need Armen cutting a deal with the police and giving him up as the Ketamine supplier in Fiona's death.

He went home and got his guns. A compact Springfield Armory 9mm went into the slim waistband holster, and its twin went into an ankle holster just in case. In his time as a private investigator, Lance had met some shady characters and had a pretty good grip on the local criminal class. Maybe he could make that pay off. He would have to go to the bank and get some money. Information cost money.

Bruce called Max to set up a meeting. They sat in their customary spot and tried to look inconspicuous. Bruce handed Max the information folded into a supermarket ad, and Max slid some money to him folded in a napkin. Max was a little annoyed.

"I'm fed up with this cloak-and-dagger stuff."

"Well, it's my butt if we get busted. Live with it."

Bruce got up to leave. Max threw in. "Don't forget that 401K."

Bruce flipped him the bird on his way out.

Scott waited in his den for the Realtor. He'd spent several hours mowing the lawn and tidying up. He thought the house looked as good as ever. He was looking forward to leaving the house and the bad memories associated with it. The ringing doorbell brought him out of his reverie. He opened the door to find a pleasant, sharply dressed woman in her thirties.

"Mr. Milner?"

"Please come in."

They shook hands.

"Please call me Debbie. What a nice home. Is there somewhere we can work?"

Scott led her to the kitchen table.

"I looked up your property; it was built in 1966. I checked, and there were no outstanding liens other than your loans. I also did a valuation study. Is there anything I should know? Did you make some additions or major modifications without getting a building permit? Are there any hidden problems like a leaking roof or termite damage?"

"No, the house is sound. We just did the usual painting, a new roof five years ago, and appliance replacement. There's one thing, we had a home invasion robbery here a week ago. My wife had a heart attack and died during the robbery."

"Oh dear, I'm so sorry. I understand how hard that can be. My husband was killed in a car accident two years ago. I think it would be best to declare that to the buyer, just so they can't come back on you later. In an active market with little inventory like we have now, most people don't even blink at that kind of thing. It's sort of viewed like a lightning strike. A crazy neighbor is something else."

"On this street, I think that's us."

She had a nice laugh. "Would you show me around?"

After a tour of the property, she got down to business. She showed him the valuations, estimated a likely listing price, and explained her fees and the process.

"Based on the market now and what you owe, I think you'll net out a minimum of fifty thousand cash when it's all done. That could go higher if we get in a bidding war. Lately, half of our sales have been bid over the asking price."

"That all sounds fine. I just need a quick sale. No contingencies. Anyone with a preapproved loan goes to the head of the line. I want to do this as fast as possible."

"That's not a problem. Here's my card and my personal mobile number if you need anything."

Scott signed the contract, and they shook hands. She went out front, marked where the sign should go in the yard, and marched off to list Scott's house. He looked at her card, wondering if she was flirting with him?

He muttered, "Don't be an idiot."

Scott dialed his phone. "Arbi, how are the repairs going?"

"They're working now. I got you a new carpet. You didn't say someone got shot. It's hard to find people who want to clean up blood, and they charge plenty."

"Look on the positive side. I'm a good shot, so there aren't any bullet holes in the walls. When do you think it'll be done?"

"Tomorrow sometime. They need to get back to their other job."

"Good, I'll cut you a check when it's finished, plus extra for your inconvenience. Are we good?"

"Sure, sure. Do you have any more enemies that shoot?"

"One, but I think I've seen the last of him."

CHAPTER

.... *34* ....

Max checked his watch and called Eric Kim.

"Eric, how's the babysitting going?"

"Fine. She's getting a little squirrely, but that close call at the cabin got her attention. It's harder on me. I'm think I'm falling in love. She's just amazing. What a woman."

"Down, boy. People are dying all around her. Two guys did a home invasion and killed Scott Milner's wife. Milner's the guy Julie filed her complaint against. A couple days later, the same two guys attempted an armed break-in at Milner's home when his daughter was home. Milner chilled out one of them, but the other one got away with some kind of wound."

"Do you think they were looking for Julie?"

"I think they were looking for her money. I thought you'd like a heads-up. These guys are dangerous; you can't be too careful."

241

"Should I tell her?"

"I would. It's her neck, and it's her money that seems to be generating these incidents."

"That's what I was thinking. I'll keep an eye out."

Max went to the fridge, opened a dark beer, and poured it into a tall glass. He kicked back in his easy chair and studied the enhanced phone records. The beer was almost gone when he realized what he was looking at.

"I'll be damned!"

It was still early, so he gathered up some photographs, and drove to the 8 Ball Lodge.

Cliff was half asleep and nodding over his biology textbook when Max came in the office. "I'm working with the Glendale Police to solve the murder that happened here a while back."

Cliff awoke with a start. "Uh, you need to be more specific. We've had a couple."

Max showed him a picture of Fiona. "I'm interested in the fake suicide with the gas bottle."

"That's what she looked like before?"

"That's her."

"Not bad. What about it?"

Max put two photographs on the counter.

"Do you remember either of these two people being here that evening?"

Cliff looked at both pictures for a long time.

"You're not a cop, are you?"

"Insurance investigator."

"What's in it for me?"

"Depends on whether you're jerking me around."

"A Franklin would jog my memory."

"I can do fifty, you get the rest if you have some good stuff and you're not bullshitting me." Max slid a fifty across the counter, and Cliff snagged it like an eagle diving on a salmon.

"I saw both of them. This woman was in the car with the dead one when she came here. The other one drove in an hour before."

"You're sure? You would testify to that?"

"Yeah, sure. I would have told the cops, but they didn't have any pictures. I never forget a face."

Max opened his wallet and put five twenties on the table. He overpaid but wanted Cliff's memory to stay intact. Max liked happy witnesses.

"Cool, I can use some book money. I think the college book store is running a criminal enterprise."

Lance racked his brain thinking how he could locate Armen. The first night, he drove around the Glendale area looking in all the bars and clubs that might be a hangout for him. Finally, he went to the club where he first met Gor and Armen. Luckily, the same bartender was pouring.

"Remember me?"

"Yeah, why?"

"How about Gor and Armen?"

"They used to come in here all the time. Not lately."

"I'm looking for Armen."

"Better look somewhere else."

"Gor's dead, and Armen is wanted in connection with a murder. Might be some reward money if you have anything worthwhile?"

"Talk's cheap. What's it worth in my pocket?"

Lance slipped a hundred-dollar bill onto the bar. The bartender reached for it, and Lance pulled it back.

"Might not be worth a hundred. Let's hear something."

"They've been trying to intimidate small businesses, a protection thing. Scaring some little fish."

"Who?"

"One guy owns a deli on Colorado, 'Best Shish Kabob.' He was in here drinking a couple days ago. He's pissed off about getting ripped. Maybe he knows something."

"Anything else?"

"You can try Raffi's Smoke Shop. He keeps his nose in the wind and knows a lot of what's going on. People get drunk, come in for a smoke, and talk too much."

Bob let go of the bill.

"I was never here."

"Man, I don't even know who you are."

Lance entered the small deli near closing time, ordered a chicken kabob, mutabbal, rice, some pita, and asked to speak to the owner. They sat at a small table while Lance ate his dinner.

"This is great. I'll be back for sure."

"Thank you. We use only the best ingredients."

"Someone told me that a couple guys named Armen and Gor are holding you up for protection money. I'd like to find Armen."

The owner stood up and made a gesture like washing his hands.

"I don't want any trouble. I got nothing to tell you. Enjoy your chicken."

"Wait! Armen's wanted by the police in connection with a murder. I can get him off your back."

"Good luck. I don't know anything."

The owner walked into the kitchen. Lance finished his dinner, put the remains in the trash, and yelled. "The chicken was too dry!".

As Amy's depression over her mother's death deepened, she avoided reality by sleeping late and staying in her room. Scott thought she might do better with more activity, doing something to help put it behind her. At almost ten in the morning, he knocked on her bedroom door.

"Amy, are you up?"

"No."

"Sounds like it to me. I'm coming in."

"No."

Scott entered the room to find Amy buried in covers.

"Too late. Time to get up."

"I'm tired."

"You've been in bed for eleven hours. You're feeling bad because of your mom, but you have to get out of bed. You can feel bad while we run."

Scott pulled the covers off, and Amy got out of bed, but she wasn't happy about it.

"Go away. I'm going to take a shower."

"Okay, but don't go back to bed."

Scott went to his bedroom and dressed for running. He checked his emails.

Scott shouted, "Are you getting ready?"

"Yes. Quit pushing me."

Amy came out after ten minutes looking puffy.

"Want some breakfast? I've got some energy bars."

"I'm okay."

Amy slowly walked out to the car. Scott drove them to the Bowl, parked in the shade, and they got ready to run. No music this time. Scott wanted to keep his mind on Amy. They kicked it off and ran at a moderate pace. After a lap around the Bowl and the golf course, they quit for lunch. A short drive found them at a restaurant that specialized in salads and lighter food.

"Feel any better?"

Amy grunted.

"I know things are bad right now, but try to stay engaged so we can keep moving through this."

"It doesn't feel like it. I just can't understand why someone would harm her."

"It was one of the random cruelties that exist in the world. A couple greedy criminals wanted money, and didn't care who they hurt to get it. Unfortunately, those people exist."

Their salads came, and they ate in silence. Amy started to perk up with some food and an iced tea fueling her system.

"We need to do some things. Your mom had a will. I think it would be good for us to go see Jeff and get that taken care of. I know it seems like an unpleasant task, but I think doing these things will help us put this behind us."

"Umm, okay."

"The house will be sold soon. What do you say we go home and look through our things? We should take what we will want for the sake of the memories. Unless you want some of the furniture now, I plan to put it all in storage. I think you might like to look through your mom's clothes and jewelry?"

"Yes, I think I'd like that."

Scott paid the bill, and they went to their car. He dialed his phone.

"Jeff, please. It's Scott Milner."

"Hi, Scott. What's up?"

"Can we come over and check out the will? Amy's with me."

"Ah, sure. I'll change an appointment and get it ready."

They arrived at Jeff's office and were ushered in. Jeff hugged Amy.

"Hi, Amy. I'm so sorry about your mother."

"Thanks. It's been hard."

"Well, this doesn't need to take a lot of time. Here's the will."

He handed copies to Scott and Amy.

"As you can see, she left everything to you two. No relatives, charities, or whatever. It's really very simple and clean. Scott's the executor."

Scott looked at Jeff with raised eyebrows. He had expected Dana to leave him nothing. It seems she hadn't got around to excluding him before she died.

"I'll handle the proper notifications and paperwork. Do you have any questions?"

Scott stood, and Amy followed.

"Thanks again, Jeff. You have been a rock through all this. See you for dinner."

Amy brushed away some tears, hugged Jeff, and they left.

35

Lance drove past the tobacco shop several times. It didn't look very busy; a few people came and went with their purchases. Some customers went back into the smoking lounge. He assumed that some customers would hang out in the lounge having a bowl or two from a hookah, then they would move on for other evening activities. He parked nearby and checked his guns once more. He wore a light denim jacket to conceal the holstered gun. He walked into the shop, looking around. He gazed into the floor-to-ceiling cigar humidor while also watching activities reflected in the glass. Eventually, he stepped into the humidor, selected a cigar, and took it to the cash register.

Raffi smiled, "Ten ninety-five. That's a good one."

"Yeah? I'm just getting started. I liked the way it smelled."

Lance paid him for the cigar.

"You're Raffi?"

The man nodded yes.

"I understand you are a well-informed man."

Raffi became reserved and tight lipped.

"Who says?"

"Just a thing I heard."

Lance laid a hundred-dollar bill on the counter.

"I'd like to find a small time crook named Armen."

Raffi started fiddling with a cigar clipper on the counter.

"Do you know where to find him? He's a suspect in a murder. Anyone helping him might be considered an accomplice. Got any idea where he is?"

Raffi became very nervous. "I don't want any trouble."

Rafi wasn't much of a poker player. He glanced at the door to the lounge.

Lance looked at the back door.

"He's in there, isn't he? In back?"

"Please, no trouble."

Lance drew his pistol, held his bandaged fingers to his lips for Raffi's silence, and turned toward the lounge at the back of the store. He had only taken a step when the curtain parted, and Armen came into the shop. The instant Armen saw Lance he went for his pistol.

Lance yelled, "Freeze. You're under arrest."

In one swift movement, Armen drew his gun from his belt and pointed it at Lance. Caught off guard by Armen's speed, Lance quickly fired, taking a chunk out of Armen's ear. Armen reeled, grabbed his ear, and fired twice, hitting Lance square in the chest and again in his left thigh. Lance fell to the floor, firing three more times, hitting Armen in the upper chest and head. Lance felt like a horse had kicked him in the chest. He tore at his shirt in spite of the pain. His body armor had stopped the bullet to his heart, but his leg felt paralyzed and on fire. He struggled to stop the bleeding in his leg and was near passing out, when he thought he heard someone talking in the distance.

A uniformed patrol cop arrived with his gun out. He carefully entered, checked the store, and picked up the guns. By then, everyone had emptied out except for Lance and Raffi, who was kneeling next to Lance and holding a bloody towel compressed on his leg. The cop called for an ambulance and checked Armen's body; nothing to do there but wait for the coroner. The paramedics arrived and took over from Raffi. Lance was in shock and near cardiac arrest as he was transported to the closest hospital for medical treatment.

Raffi slyly pocketed the hundred off the counter, figuring he had it coming.

Scott sat with Jeff in what had become "their" booth. Two festive-looking drinks with colored umbrellas cheered up the table.

"How's Amy doing?"

"Better now. She's adjusting. Thanks for going over the will with her."

"What are you going to do about Dana?"

"Dana's body is going to the mortuary when the county releases her. I think she wanted to be cremated. Considering the circumstances, I don't think there will be much of a service. I'll probably include Lance if there is one."

Jeff wondered, "Where do you think you'll scatter the ashes?"

"Do you need any cat litter?"

"Let's not speak ill of the deceased, no matter how tempting."

"I would be more forgiving of Dana if she hadn't given up my address to the goons knowing Amy was staying with me. Endangering Amy's life was unforgivable."

"Don't you think it's about time I heard the whole story?"

Scott relented, "Yeah, okay. Julie and I had a plan to scam some money from MacKenna with a fake sexual harassment claim after we discovered they were going to lay us off and screw us out of our bonus compensation. The plan worked. Trouble is, I didn't realize that she and Fiona were in a scheme to use me and take off with the proceeds. Fiona's dead, Julie is in hiding with the money, and I'm strung out. Somehow, I think my wife figured into the plot, but I have no proof. I don't know where the killers came from, but when they came after Amy and me, I had to shoot one of them."

"I knew something was going on. You really screwed the pooch this time. Where does Julie fall in this? Did she ever feel anything for you?"

"Hell, I don't know. She sure made it sound believable. All I know is she's not here now, and it doesn't look like she's coming back."

"Time for a fresh start. Got any ideas?"

"So much stuff has been happening, I haven't had time to think about it. All I know is I'm going to bust a gut to make sure Amy gets through college and gets a decent start in life."

Scott's phone rang. "Yes, Arbi, what's going on? Excellent. See you tomorrow."

"My apartment's been repaired. We can go back now."

They ordered more drinks and some dinner, and the conversation lapsed during the demolition of their New York steaks, fries, and salads.

Scott and Amy combed the house and carefully assessed all of their belongings, looking for things to keep. Amy picked some of her mother's jewelry, packed up the rest of her own clothes, and also took two photo albums. Scott picked up the remains of his personal possessions, packed up his clothes, and took a couple photos.

Scott and Amy took one last look at the house and left without any tears. It was time to move on, and too many bad memories had poisoned their home. They drove to Scott's apartment. Entering through the new door, they put their belongings away and checked out the repairs. Arbi had upgraded to solid wood doors with some serious hardware and dead bolts. The new rug looked like some kind of sci-fi test pattern, but it was thick and soft. It was all good, and strangely enough, it was starting to feel like home. Amy looked relieved.

Scott smiled, "Funny how this stupid place has grown on me."

"Yeah, it's weird."

There was a knock at the door. Arbi stood there with a bowl in his hands.

"Arbi, come in, and I'll get you the check. How much?

"Twelve hundred. I got you a deal."

Scott wrote out a check for two thousand and put it in Arbi's shirt pocket.

"What do you have there?"

"Is your little girl home?"

Amy had heard the voices and came from the bedroom.

Arbi held out the bowl for her.

"I'm sorry about your mother. My wife made this for you."

Amy smiled and took the bowl.

"What is it?"

She took the lid off a bowl of chicken salad, roasted chicken, peas and other greens, yogurt, and spices. The aroma was wonderful.

"Thank you so much. It looks delicious. Please thank your wife for me."

She gave him a kiss on the cheek. Arbi touched his cheek, a little embarrassed, and nodded his head in appreciation.

Scott shook his hand. "Thanks for everything."

Arbi made a sign as if to say "No big deal" and left them.

Scott's phone rang. Lances' number came up.

Scott listened for a while. "I'm coming."

"Lance's in the hospital. It looks like he found Armen, the other guy who killed Dana. I'm going to go see him."

"Can I come along?"

"Next time. Sounds like he's in bad shape. I'll be back soon."

Scott drove to the hospital and was directed to Lances' room. Gene and Linda were already there, interviewing him. Lance was hooked up to several tubes, and his leg was heavily bandaged and elevated.

Scott looked around the room, "Officers. Nice to see you again."

Gene looked Scott over. "Milner again."

Scott looked at Gene, "Now that we have a relationship, is it okay if I call you King?"

Gene glared at him. "Now you're a comedian?"

Linda stood by the bed, "Mr. Tavidian, tell us about the shooting last night."

"Not much to tell. I wanted to find Armen and bring him in on a citizen's arrest for killing Dana. I tracked him down, and after I announced my intention to arrest him, he drew and shot me. I fired to protect myself and killed him."

"How did you find him?"

"I did some detecting. It is my job."

"We talked to the store owner and whatever witnesses we could find; lucky for you, they back up your story. It was a legal citizen's arrest attempt, so the whole incident is basically a push. I don't anticipate any further action from the DA, but they're going to have to sprinkle some holy water on the case."

Going out the door, Gene gave Scott a dirty look.

Scott was relieved once the police were gone.

"How do you feel?"

"Okay, considering."

"What happened?"

"You heard most of it. Armen shot me in the chest and leg. Luckily, I was wearing my body armor. He took a bite out of my leg, but he missed the femoral artery. That bastard had a ten-millimeter. I've got two cracked ribs where it hit me. It felt like I stopped a cannon ball. The doctor says I should be okay after rehab."

"That's a big gun."

"Yeah. It was close: the son of a bitch surprised me and almost did me first. That round you put on him must have slowed him down a bit."

"Is there anything I can do for you?"

"Yeah, keep as far away from me as humanly possible. Ever since I've come in contact with your family, I've been threatened, beaten, shot, and kicked in the nuts. I just can't take any more."

Scott laughed, but one look at Lance's eyes told him he wasn't entirely joking.

"It's over now. Do you want to tell me what you know about this whole thing? I think I might have that coming."

Lance thought about it for a minute.

"Close the door."

Scott looked down the hall both ways and closed the door.

Lance took a deep breath. "Jack and Dana had been having an affair for about a year. When Jack found out about the takeover, the two of them cooked up this whole scheme. Jack hired Fiona, Dana seduced her at Jack's direction and proposed the scam to her. Fiona hired Julie, and Julie seduced you. Their affair was over by the time I came along, but the plan was well on the way. Fiona thought she had a deal with Dana and Julie and didn't know Jack was in on it. Julie thought she had a deal with Fiona but didn't know about Jack and Dana. You thought you had a deal with Julie and didn't know about the rest of them. The whole thing was convoluted as hell, and then Julie stuck it to everyone by taking off with the money."

Scott stood there with his mouth open.

"Who killed Fiona?"

"Dana and Jack. She became a liability."

"I can't believe it."

Lance looked at the ceiling. "In spite of it all, I loved Dana, and now I understand things better."

"What do you mean?"

"If God wants to fuck with you, he gives you what you wish for."

36

Armen's death lifted a dreadful weight from Scott. He thought about Jack's involvement in the insurance scam, and decided that he had no choice but to let it go because Jack could implicate him in the scam. He would tell Amy what happened in the tobacco shop. She would remain unaware of her mother's involvement in the MacKenna fraud. There wasn't any point in giving her more bad news.

Over a take-out Thai dinner, Scott told Amy about Lance. "I talked to Lance in the hospital. He went after the other man who attacked your mother and found him. He tried to make a citizen's arrest, but the guy was armed and resisted. There was a gunfight, and he was shot in the leg, but he killed Armen, the second robber. Lance's going to be okay eventually, but he's not in good shape right now."

"I'm sorry Lance got hurt. I never thought I'd be glad for someone's death, but I am. Armen deserved it."

"No one is coming after us now. We're free to start fresh, begin a new life."

"What are we going to do about Mom? Are we having a funeral?"

"I don't remember her ever saying anything about funeral plans. I guess it's up to us to figure out what she would have wanted."

On Monday, Max walked into the Glendale Police detective bureau looking for Gene and Linda. He found them eating deli sandwiches at their desks.

"I came all the way down here to help you out, and I find you've turned the detective bureau into a cafeteria."

Gene looked up from his tuna sub. "After all those years at LAPD, you'd think you'd know what a real dick's bureau looks like."

Linda patted Max on the back. "Don't listen to him. I believe you were a real detective a long, long time ago in the last century."

"There's some fish on your necktie, but let's not squabble. I come with information."

Max put two pictures on Linda's desk while Gene dabbed at his tie.

"I showed these pictures to Cliff, the ever-vigilant night clerk at the Lodge, and he identified them. This woman was in the car with Fiona when they came to the motel on the night of the murder, and this man came to the motel about an hour earlier. I also went through their phone records, and there's a pattern of communication that indicates collusion at critical dates and times. It implies a conspiracy related to Fiona's death."

Gene gave Max a disapproving look. "That's great, but I shouldn't have to tell you that those phone records are not public records and must have been illegally obtained, right?"

"The MacKenna phone information was legally obtained from Todd Betts with company permission. You could use that information for probable cause to get a subpoena and then access their private accounts. Back in ancient times, we used to call that investigating."

Jack waited until Todd went to lunch and quietly entered his office. He opened Todd's desk and quickly found Max Moon's business card with "Eric Kim" scrawled on the back. He photographed both sides with his phone, returned the card to its place, and returned to his office. Jack closed his office door and called his attorney.

"Hi, Dave, got time for lunch today? Marty's? See you there."

David Franklin Rees, Esq., met with Jack over lunch and drinks in a local restaurant.

"Thanks for meeting me on short notice. I have a job that needs to get done discreetly. I want to find a guy who stiffed me out of a lot of money on a shaley investment deal. Do you have someone who can do that?"

"Of course, who is it?"

Jack showed Dave the picture on his phone and then emailed the pictures of the business card to him. "He's a private investigator, and we need to find him to serve him. He's in partnership with the other guy on that card, a P.I. named Maxwell Moon. I thought you might be able to pull Kim's P.I. application with the State of California to get an address, or maybe do a court records search. There must be legal records from when they were witnesses. Maybe you could get lucky and pull Kim's address from the courts."

"I'll see what I can do. Got any more information?"

"Moon is an investigator for the Pugh Western Insurance Company."

"Okay. I'll give it a shot. This seems highly unusual; it's all legal, right?"

"Sure. Kim's just a clever flake. Once we locate him, I'll see if he's willing to fix my problem. If not, I'll be back at you for some legal persuasion."

Scott got a call from the Funeral Home people. Dana's ashes were ready to be picked up. He went to Amy's room, found her reading and, thankfully, not sleeping. He took that as a positive sign. They had earlier agreed that they would cremate her remains and not hold a service.

"Your mom's ashes are ready. Want to go with me to pick them up?"

She hesitated.

Scott said, "Closure? Growing up means we have to do the things we need to do."

"Okay. I'll go."

They sat in the waiting room until called by a mortuary representative. Egon F. Decker was in his middle fifties, with silver-gray hair that swept around his head and over his ears. He wore a shiny charcoal-gray suit and a black-and-white striped tie over a white shirt. When Scott shook hands with him, he noticed the polished fingernails, a heavy gold chain bracelet, and Egon's initials carved on a large gold ring. More than anything, Egon looked like a Vegas pit boss.

Egon addressed Amy as "Little Lady." Scott thought he could see Amy wince, but she held her composure. Egon ushered them into his office; his desk was immaculately clean except for a bronze urn placed precisely in the center.

"We have your beloved's remains prepared for you."

He officiously moved the vessel towards them. There was no sales pitch or play to sentiment. Scott had pointedly told him what he wanted over the phone, and Egon wisely picked up on his no-nonsense demeanor. He took Scott's credit card, ran it, and Scott signed off on the charge.

Amy lifted the urn.

"It's heavy."

Egon explained, "The remains weigh about six pounds."

Scott asked, "Are there any regulations limiting where and how to spread them?"

"Yes. However, you are not in the mortuary business, so just use your head. Do it privately, away from anyone who might be offended, and no one will be the wiser. Obviously, you can consult with your spiritual advisor for suggestions if you wish."

Scott said, "We haven't made up our minds yet. No rush, I guess."

"I wish you and your loved ones a peaceful and loving experience."

They shook Egon's hand and left with the urn. Amy hugged it all the way home, like she was afraid she might drop it. She carefully set it on the coffee table.

Amy gazed at the urn. "She can't stay there forever; what are we going to do?"

"Let's find some appropriate place to spread them."

Amy paused, already pondering the problem. "I'm working on it. Let's get out of here and go for a run."

CHAPTER

37

ene, Linda, and Max were going over the phone records and matching dates to events. Gene went to the evidence locker and found a box of security videos from the 8 Ball Lodge murder investigation. He brought them back to the office while Linda was checking with the DMV to nail down Jack's car registration.

Gene asked, "What did you find out?"

"We're looking for a 2016 red Dodge Challenger or maybe his wife's 2011 gray Lexus 350RX SUV."

They each got a cup of strong coffee, sat down at three different computers, and began scanning the security videos. An hour later, Linda hit pay dirt.

"Got it!" Linda exclaimed.

They huddled around her computer and watched Jack's car come and go twice from the Lodge and once from a pizzeria. They even got a clean shot of the license plate.

"Looks like we need to have a talk with boss man Jack." Linda said.

"We have to put him in the motel room to get a conviction." Gene observed.

Linda called Todd Betts and told him about the video results.

"Todd, we would like you to get us something that has Jack's DNA on it. If we can genetically link him to the motel room, we have a chance of nailing him for Fiona's murder."

"I'll see what I can do."

"This is your chance to be a hero and solve this, so I wouldn't rule out sex."

"Aren't you funny. I'll see what I can do short of sleeping with him."

Scott and Amy jogged along the Los Angeles River Walk. It wasn't as charming as a park with all its greenery, but there was an open feeling of Spartan freedom jogging down the massive winding concrete ribbon. They ran from Atwater Village south to Frogtown and Dodger Stadium and back again, smiling at the cat faces painted on the large hinged sewer covers feeding the river during high-water events. They exited the river walk at Los Feliz Boulevard near Griffith Park and walked to a little nearby pitch-and-putt golf course. They ate lunch in the attached café: burgers, fries, and strawberry milkshakes. The golf course and café had been there at least seventy-five years, defying the condo-crazy, omnivorous developers.

Amy spoke first. "That was fun. There's a lot of concrete in that riverbed."

"You can take it all the way down to the ocean. It was a massive public works project. Before they built it, winter rains used to flood parts of L.A. In your granddad's day kids would cut the fence, go down there when the bed was dry, and drag race on the river bottom. LAPD cops would sit up on the bridges with their coffee and donuts and bet on the racers. Eventually, the City Council ordered them to shut it down.

There's a guy up the street here who rents bikes. Maybe someday we could take a bicycle trip down the river to the ocean; we could rent a tandem."

"So, I'd have to ride behind with you wearing bicycle shorts?"

"Humiliation is endemic to parenthood. Have you thought about your mom's ashes?"

"We could try to spread them at her favorite clothing store, but it would be hard to explain if we got busted."

"I think I have an idea about that."

"What?"

"I have to make a call first, then I'll tell you about it."

Jack's lawyer called him.

"I have the information you wanted. I sent you an email."

Jack checked his phone. "I got it."

Dave continued, "Eric Kim is former military. He's been a P.I. for ten years, with no complaints filed against him at the state level. He works for various insurance companies along with some private clients. The address we were able to pull is 520 Stony Canyon Road, Altadena, 91005."

Gene, Linda, and Todd entered Jack Bowman's office unannounced. He looked up from his computer, obviously startled.

Gene spoke first. "Jack, we've got a couple more questions for you."

"Okay. What can I tell you?" Helpful Jack.

"We've been looking at your phone records and matching your calls to Fiona; they coincide with the events relating to the harassment fraud and

Fiona's murder. We also found calls you made to Dana Milner. Why were you calling these people on your personal phone at all hours of the night?"

"We're a hard-charging operation here. Fiona was a manager on salary, and she was on duty 24/7 as far as I was concerned; all of our managers are."

"Dana too?"

"So, you found out about our affair. Yes, Scott had neglected her, and we hit it off. That relationship ended several months ago, but I don't see that it's any of your business. Even with our relationship ending, I still liked Dana, and we had a good, amicable friendship. We often chatted as friends, particularly when she and Scott were having relationship issues. I don't see that as a problem."

"You had several calls to Dana on the evening of Fiona's death. Got an explanation for that?"

"I just use my phone when I need it. I had nothing to do with that unfortunate event."

Linda bored in. "We have your car filmed by security cameras at the 8 Ball Lodge and the liquor store in the neighborhood on the night Fiona was murdered. There's also a video of you picking up a pizza a half-mile from the motel on the night of the murder. A box from the same pizzeria was in the room with Fiona's body. You want to explain that?"

"Am I under arrest?"

"Not yet."

Jack stood, put on his jacket and walked straight for the door.

"Any further contact will be with my lawyer."

"Before you go, you should know that we're having our technicians check your DNA against some trace evidence gathered at the crime scene when you slobbered on your pepperoni. If we can put you in the room with Fiona, you will be a prime candidate for the needle," Gene said.

Jack looked at them, then angrily stared at Todd, having guessed where the DNA sample came from. He turned and walked away.

"That went well."

Scott arrived at their old house early the next morning, met the movers, and confirmed where they were to store the contents of the house. He also gave them instructions so they could deliver Amy's bed to their apartment, thinking she would like that. Moving the furniture and taking down pictures uncovered some more cleaning to do. Shortly after the movers left, a cleaning crew showed up to make the house look presentable again. Scott met the movers at his storage space, supervised the unloading of the household goods, and locked the storage space up tight. He supervised the delivery of Amy's bed to the apartment and returned to the house. The cleaning crew was still working when he got a phone call.

"Scott? It's Debbie Matthews. We have an offer on your house."

"How much?"

"Enough to pay for Realtor fees and net you about sixty-eight thousand dollars cash after your loans are paid off. I told them the house was sold 'as is.' They're okay with that as long as you buy a two-year home maintenance insurance policy for them, something that I think is entirely reasonable. What do you think?"

"What are the chances of a better offer?"

"I think this is about it. We actually had five people bidding, and all are very close on their offers. In that kind of situation, we tend to quickly find what the real fair value is in today's market. I think it's a good deal, considering they didn't hesitate at the death-in-the-house issue."

"I accept the offer. Just make sure their financing is solid. I don't want to get down the road and have them blink out on me in escrow."

"I'm looking into that right now; they seem very solid. I'll get back to you when I'm positive. We'll build in a healthy reneging penalty to discourage any flaky behavior. Congratulations. Looks like we've sold your house."

"Great job, Debbie. This is exactly how I wanted it to go."

CHAPTER

38

ack drove to Kim's Altadena address, hoping Julie was still hiding there. He drove up and down the block, looking for something to use to his advantage. It was a difficult layout; all he could see was a gated driveway that trailed off into the trees and some dense foliage. He thought he caught a glimpse of a house deep into the property. He was sure Kim had security devices, so the trick was, how to approach the house undetected? He parked on the street several doors down and watched from a vantage point that didn't make him seem too obvious. He was settling in when an earsplitting screech pierced the air. He sat up straight with the hair on his neck erect. He looked around and saw a peacock strutting by the side of his car. Another screech tore at his ears.

"Damned peacocks."

Jack had forgotten about the free-ranging peacocks that roam some Altadena neighborhoods. They looked beautiful, but they made a mess on everything, and their screeching call could be heard all day long coming from one bird or another. The peacocks would raise a risk of discovery during the day, so he would have to make an assault on the house at night. He started his car and tried to run over the offending peacock, but the bird nimbly hopped out of the way with an indignant squawk.

Driving away, Jack thought about the situation and decided he needed some extra leverage for what he had planned.

Scott got up early and spent some time working on his job search. So far, he had a couple of job nibbles. He was cheering up, thinking that he might actually snag another job soon. Amy was dressed and looked like she wanted to do something, but she wasn't sure exactly what. Scott stood and stretched.

"Come on. I have something for us to do."

"What?"

"It's a secret for now."

They drove to the clubhouse at Lakeside Golf Course and mounted the steps. Scott led Amy through the building to the grassy area in back, where a practice tee and a big putting green had been installed.

"We're going to learn how to golf today."

"I don't think this is for me. All I see are a lot of old people here. No offense."

"Keep an open mind. A lot of young, eligible guys play golf. I took golf for a PE class in community college. They still have PE, don't they?"

"Your lack of adolescent social skills isn't the point. It looks boring."

"It's exciting relaxation. If you take it too seriously, it'll aggravate you, but if you just take it for a walk in the park, you can relax and enjoy the atmosphere."

They met Carl in back of the pro shop. He was a dandy, immaculately attired in a white outfit, tall, slim, with rangy blond hair cut a little too long. He had a nicely bleached toothy smile and sympathetic soft brown eyes. He was born to comfort golfing divorcées.

Scott noticed Amy quit complaining and started showing some interest in the lessons. He definitely liked it better when Amy hated boys. Carl got them outfitted with a set of rental clubs: seven and nine irons, a three wood, and a putter, all in the correct lengths. They moved out to a practice tee. Carl gave Amy directions on the basics and helped her get her swing coordinated.

"Keep your feet spread the width of your shoulders and align your feet with the pin, head down, check your grip. Draw the club back smoothly, put your energy into the down stroke, follow through with your club flowing naturally over your other shoulder, and keep turning until you're facing the pin. That's good. Do that again."

Scott relinquished his time to Amy and sat down on a bench with a Diet Cola to watch the lessons. Eventually the big moment came when she swung on a real ball, but her first hit dribbled off the tee.

"Remember to keep your head down. Your club goes where your head goes, that's why you topped the ball."

Amy was the picture of concentration. On the second swing, she connected solidly with the ball, and it flew straight for about seventy yards. Amy flashed Scott a big grin and then hit another. After a dozen balls, Carl switched her to a three wood and let her get the feel of the different swing. Later they followed up with some putting on the green, with Scott joining in.

Scott took Amy to the club restaurant for lunch. They ordered two "Hole in One" salads and iced teas.

"Well, is it as bad as you thought?"

"I liked it. I can see how people would really get involved in the game. I'd like to try it some more, but maybe with a different teacher."

"Why?"

"Carl's kind of slimy, and his breath almost knocked me over."

Scott laughed. "Boy, you're getting tough."

"They're your rules."

Scott and Amy spent the rest of the day wandering through Pasadena's Old Town and caught a movie.

When they were finally tired out, Scott drove Amy back to their apartment.

"I need to check on the house, make sure the cleaners finished, and I have a dinner engagement with Jeff."

Soon after Scott left, the doorbell rang. Amy answered to find Jack standing on the porch.

"Hello Amy, is Scott home?"

"Hi, Mr. Bowman, Dad's not here right now."

"That's what I wanted to hear."

Jack pushed his way in and reached for Amy.

Scott was going through the house checking everything when he got a call from Debbie Matthews.

"Hi, Scott. The deal is done, and all I need is your signature on the paperwork."

"That's excellent. How long is escrow?"

"Could be a week or a month; it depends on how busy they are. Is it okay for me to come over to get final signatures on the paperwork?"

"Now?"

"Yes, let's put this deal to bed before the buyer changes his mind."

"I'm at the house."

Fifteen minutes later, Scott answered Debbie's knock and showed her in.

"That was fast."

"There's always a chance the buyer will get squishy on you, so I like to lock them in as soon as possible. Tell you what, this calls for a celebration. I'd like to take you and Amy out to dinner soon. Someplace nice."

Scott smiled, "I think I'd like that."

CHAPTER

.... *39* ....

When scouting Eric's property, Jack discovered that the house behind him was for sale and vacant. Dressed in dark clothes, he skipped over the fence bordering Eric's property and slowly made his way through the trees, hoping not to set off warning sensors before he had the advantage. He slow-crawled along a wall from the trees to the house, thinking the motion detectors probably wouldn't pick him up if he moved at a snail's pace. He stood up at the last moment, his back against the rear deck, then crept around to the front of the house. As he was approaching the front door, he saw a shadow move.

"Freeze, or I'll shoot."

Eric Kim stepped out of the shadows with his gun trained on Jack.

"Who are you, and what are you doing here."

Kim didn't notice the black object in Jack's hand, but he felt the shock like a lightning strike. He lost control of his body and fell to the ground. Jack dropped his Taser and was on him in a second using large nylon ties to bind his hands and feet. Jack put a strip of duct tape over his mouth and picked up Eric's gun.

"Stay put and keep quiet. If I see you again, I'll have to kill you."

Jack went to the front door and knocked. Julie answered.

"We have to quit meeting like this!"

Jack shoved his way in before Julie could close the door.

Scott and Jeff were out celebrating Scott's "go away" money. Dinner, heavy drinks, and Uber rides home was the plan. Just as the meal arrived, Scott's phone rang.

Before he could say anything, "Hi, Scott, it's Julie."

"What is this, a bad joke?"

"No. It's really me. I've been wanting to call you. I thought about how badly things turned out, and I wanted to hear your voice."

"You are hearing it. What do you want?"

"I'd like to meet with you tonight. We have some unfinished financial business, and I'm leaving the country."

"What are you talking about?"

"Half the money is yours, and I'd like to talk to you about that."

Scott hesitated, thinking it was all wrong, but he couldn't help himself.

"Where are you?"

"I'm staying at Eric Kim's house in Altadena, hiding from the people who wanted to harm me. He's been a gracious host, and I feel protected here. I'm sorry I didn't have the confidence to contact you sooner, but I just didn't understand everything that was going on. That's all changed with the deaths of Dana's killers."

"What do you want with me?"

"I want to finish off our business as I promised."

"I think we're done now."

"I've got your half of the money, and I want to know if you still have feelings for me."

"I don't want back in at any level."

"Think about Amy. What kind of life could you two have with the money? I'm not greedy. It's here for you and Amy."

Scott waited, thinking about everything.

"Scott?"

"Where are you exactly?"

Julie gave him the address. "Can you please come tonight? I'm leaving early tomorrow."

Scott told himself not to go, but he had to see her one last time.

"Give me an hour."

"That's wonderful, the main gate will be open. Just drive in and come to the front door."

Scott made his apologies to Jeff and promised to do the dinner again on another evening.

"You're really not going to meet her after all that's happened?" Jeff asked.

"I need to put a coda on this thing and if that means seeing her once more, I'll have to do it. I know it's not the smartest thing, but then, why should I start making good decisions at this late date?"

Scott wanted to see Julie again, but something bothered him. It was too convenient, and why now? She'd had plenty of time to contact him. Given the recent events, he had begun to carry a gun in his car. Something told him to be cautious, so he took the Smith and Wesson from his briefcase, checked to make sure it was loaded, holstered it, and put it into his right front pocket. He also loaded the little .22 pistol and stuck it in his belt. Who in the hell was this Kim guy anyway? He felt better with something to protect himself against another ominous uncertainty.

Scott found Eric's house without difficulty and checked out the neighborhood, looking for anything that seemed to be suspicious. He saw nothing that raised an alarm, but he still had a bad feeling. He parked by the front gate and walked up the driveway with his gun in hand, looking for anything that might be a threat. Eventually he returned to his car and drove up to the house. He walked to the front door and knocked.

Julie answered the front door and invited him inside. Once in the living room, he saw Amy standing frozen in place, with Jack standing behind her holding a gun to her head.

"Welcome to the party, Scott. The first thing you're going to do is take that gun out of your belt and throw it to me on the floor. Nice and easy. Don't screw up."

Scott carefully picked the gun out of his belt with two fingers and tossed it onto the rug.

"I'm tired of playing games. I'm leaving with the money or everyone here dies."

"Let Amy go. I'll give you what I have, but I never did get any of the insurance settlement money."

"Not until I get what I came for. Julie wasn't very cooperative, so Amy here is my leverage. You and Julie are going to tell me how I get that money, or you get to watch her die first."

Scott turned to Julie, "Give him the damned money. You know I don't have it."

"He won't listen to reason. I can't get it until the banks open. Who carries that kind of money around?"

Jack was sweating and shifting from one foot to another. Scott thought he looked a little crazy.

"Someone better come up with something pretty soon, or this is going to get nasty. I won't do this quickly, it's going to be unpleasant, and people are going to suffer."

Then, Jack heard a sound that cocked his head, something dark, moving fast in the corner of his eye, nails clicking on the hardwood floor, and a blood-chilling snarl. Against all his instincts, Jack had to turn around. In that same instant, a large black dog launched at him from behind, ferociously sinking its teeth into the back of his leg, powerful jaws tearing at his flesh. Jack screamed in pain and turned to shoot the dog. Amy felt his grip relax and spun away from him, running for cover. Jack realized his mistake and tried to bring his gun back around to shoot Scott. He turned in time to see Scott draw the .38 from his front pocket and fire. He felt the paralytic shock of the hollow-point bullet expanding in his chest, burning like a hot dagger. He staggered backward, his nervous system convulsed in shock. He was struggling to stay on his feet, when a second bullet exploded his heart. Jack dropped his gun and fell backwards across the dog.

Eric shouted, "Merkki! Merkki!" The dog let go of Jack's leg and returned to Eric's side.

A shocked veil of silence fell upon the room. Amy ran to Scott and hugged him. Eric held his Belgian Malinois back from having another go at Jack's body, and Julie sat frozen in her chair speechless, her eyes bulging.

Eric put the dog in the kitchen, collected Jack's gun, and checked him for any signs of life. He was dead, and Eric was relieved that he didn't have to give the asshole any CPR.

There was banging at the door.

"Police! Open the door, now!"

Scott put his gun down and raised his hands. Eric unlocked the door and stood with his hands spread open, obviously not armed.

Gene and Linda came into the room, saw there was no threat, and put their guns away. Linda went to the body, checked it, and called for backup, paramedics, and the coroner.

Gene took in the whole scene.

"What in the hell is going on here?"

"Hi, King. Good to see you again."

Gene glared at him. "Milner, once again I find you in the eye of a shit storm. What happened here?"

"Jack found out that Julie was staying here under Eric Kim's protection. He got the drop on Eric, shot him with a Taser, and hogtied him in the bushes outside. Jack had gone to my apartment earlier, kidnapped Amy, and brought her here to extort us. He forced Julie to call and lure me here. I guess the idea was, he was going to get Julie's money at any cost and extort it from us by threatening our lives.

"I was leery about the call I got from Julie, so I walked up to the driveway checking for an ambush before I drove up. I heard something in the bushes, and found Eric tied up. I released him, and then I went into the house, where I found Amy and Julie. Eric couldn't get to his guns with Jack in the house, so he got his dog out of its run, came in through the kitchen door, turning her loose on Jack. While the dog was trying to turn Jack into a Happy Snack, he aimed at me, and I got a chance to shoot him before he could harm anyone. He pointed to Julie. That's Julie Wilson. The dog is now locked in the kitchen."

Gene shook his head, "Man, it's never easy with you."

Gene and Linda interviewed people individually, inspected the whole house, trying to preserve the crime scene for the technicians. Scott, Julie, Eric, and Amy all sat in the den while police matters were attended to. Julie got up to go to the bathroom. Now that Eric's dog was calmed down, he brought her out of the kitchen. She sat at Eric's feet, and Amy moved to pet her.

"Is it okay to touch her?"

"Sure. She loves it."

"What's her name?"

"Reko. It means 'watchful' in Finnish. Her trainer was a Finn."

Amy let the dog sniff her and then began to pet her.

"Good girl. What did you say to make her stop biting Jack?"

"Merkki. It's Finnish for 'stop.' 'Kayde' means 'go' or 'attack.' She only responds to commands in Finnish."

"That's weird."

"Not really. If she attacks a criminal, you don't want her to stop or get confused if the criminal yells 'stop' in a language she recognizes. We don't get too many Finnish crooks around here. When we're doing business, other languages means nothing to her."

Scott asked Linda, "How come you two came out here all the way from Glendale?"

"Max Moon called Eric earlier in the evening to check on Julie. Just then, Eric got the security alert on his surveillance equipment and told Max to call the police."

Gene finished talking to Eric and went into the living room.

"Where's Ms. Wilson?"

Everyone reflexively looked around. She had slipped out and was nowhere to be found.

CHAPTER

 *40*

cott answered a knock at the door. A messenger stood with an envelope requiring a signature. Scott signed, thinking it was paperwork related to the house sale, opened the envelope, found a note, an address, and a bank deposit box key. He put them on the table shaking his head in disbelief.

Scott pulled into the parking lot of Glendale Community Bank and Trust just after opening. He asked to see his safety deposit box. After signing in and showing proper identification, he was led to the secure room. They removed the box, and the bank employee left him alone.

Scott slowly opened the box and found an envelope. Inside was a statement from a bank in the Cayman Islands and a password. He closed the box, returned it to its spot, and drove home.

With trembling hands, Scott got on his computer and accessed the bank account specified in the note. He entered the password and waited for the computer. The account opened, showing a balance of $3,000,000.00 in his name. He read the note again.

"Dearest Scott, I know I've put you through a lot, and here is your reward. I wish I could see us having a life together, but we both know that wouldn't work. I'm sorry for any pain I caused you. Enjoy the money and have a great life. Say goodbye to Amy for me. Love, Julie."

Scott went to the kitchen and opened a beer. He drank half and looked at the computer again. The screen timed out as he finished his beer. Scott called Jeff, and they had a conversation about the money. They agreed on a plan and hung up.

Amy came home a couple hours later. Scott told her to sit down because he had some great news.

"I have something interesting to tell you. Today someone sent me a note and password to a Cayman Island bank account. There is three million dollars in the account for us."

"That's incredible! Where did it come from? Are you a secret drug lord?"

Scott smiled. "Not even close. It came from Julie. It's exactly half of the money she got from her harassment claim."

"But that's like stolen money. She faked the whole thing."

"Well, it's her money now, and she's given half of it to us."

"That's not the point. It's dirty money."

"You could look at it that way, but it's a gift from her."

"I don't care. It's not honest. Give it back!"

"Really? Three million dollars?"

"Yes. All of it. My mother was killed for that money!"

"I don't know. It's a lot of money."

"I don't care! It's blood money. I don't think anything good could come from it."

"Actually, I did give it back. This morning I had Jeff give it to the insurance company."

"What are you doing, testing me?"

"I think I did a good job raising you. I was just checking my work."

"You can be an ass sometimes."

"You know, you don't find all of this father stuff in a self-help book."

"The insurance company was so happy to have the money back, they gave me a reward. Is that okay with you? I think I earned it because without me, they would never have gotten it back."

Amy frowned and bored in on Scott with narrowed eyes.

"This sounds like a trap question. I guess I'm okay with it as long as they volunteered a reward."

"That's the way I see it, considering that I was prepared to give it all back regardless of the reward. There's enough money to pay for your college and seed money for a new start. I think we should accept it, considering everything that happened."

Earlier that day:

Jeff sat paging through an old magazine while waiting to see Buck Preston. Buck emerged from a warren of offices and greeted him.

"Mr. Teller. What's the nature of your business?"

"It involves your MacKenna harassment liability, and I think we should conduct our business in private."

"Very well, this way."

They walked down a hallway and entered an elegantly appointed office with deep brown leather chairs and Remington prints on the walls. Jeff took a seat. Buck sat opposite him behind his polished desk, wearing his usual poker face.

"Mr. Teller?"

"You're offering a ten percent reward for the return of the three million dollars lost in the MacKenna sexual harassment case, are you not?"

"And what do you have to do with that?"

"Do you want the money back or not?"

"Of course, we do. How are you involved in this?"

"I'm authorized to return the money to you in consideration of a reasonable finder's fee and certain guarantees for the individual I represent. I came here first, but I could also offer the same deal to MacKenna Company if you're not interested."

"I'm skeptical, but tell me more."

"I represent someone who will return the money for the right fee, say twenty percent."

"How do I know this isn't some kind of scam?"

"I am prepared to transfer the money to you here and now, less the finder's fee, provided you give me certain protections. You need to sign my hold-harmless documents contingent upon the return of the money. You give me the signed documents, I transfer the money to you, and we all go on our merry way."

"Show me the documents."

Jeff handed over the documents, and Buck read them without expression.

"I don't object to the documents. I'm amenable to the deal, provided you can hold your end to fifteen percent. I think $450,000 and immunity from any further legal action by Pugh Western is a generous proposition."

"I'll take the fifteen. Sign the papers, and I'll transfer the money while we are sitting here."

"Just a minute. Please wait."

Buck disappeared down the hall and returned in ten minutes. He looked over the paperwork once more.

"Here you are. Signed by our president and notarized, contingent upon the receipt of $2,550,000.00 today."

Jeff checked the notarized signatures and carefully placed the paperwork in his briefcase. He took out his laptop, logged into the Cayman Islands bank account, and transferred the money to the proper Pugh Western account indicated by Buck. Buck double-checked the account balance and called his CFO.

"Mr. Avery, it's delivered. The transfer went through."

Buck and Jeff stood and shook hands.

Buck smiled. "I'm curious to know how this came about."

"Curiosity about this money has already killed several cats, Mr. Preston."

CHAPTER

. . . . *41* . . . .

The following evening, Scott looked through his clothes and picked something suitable for his evening out with Debbie. It wasn't particularly easy, what with the recent packing and moving around. He went to the living room and presented himself to Amy.

"What do you think?"

"Very handsome. Are you sure this date is all business?"

"It's not a date. Realtors customarily do something nice for their clients after a sale, like a bottle of champagne, ballgame tickets, or whatever. It's customary. In this case, I'm getting wined and dined."

"It's the whatever that I'm wondering about. I want you in by ten."

"Don't wait up."

There was the knock. Scott opened the door, and Debbie came into their living room looking very pretty. She saw Amy and went to her.

"Hi, I'm Debbie, you must be Amy. Your dad has said so many good things about you; I'm pleased to meet you."

"Thanks. He's a bit biased."

"Probably so. I think my kids are the greatest too. I hope you won't miss the house?"

"No chance. We need something new."

"Scott said that you won't be joining us for dinner, so I got you this for you." Debbie handed her a greeting card with a hundred-dollar gift card inside.

"Great! Just what I needed. Thank you!"

Scott picked up a bottle of wine, and they left for dinner.

They drove to a quiet, elegant restaurant located in an old Craftsman-style house in Pasadena. Scott was nervous. Debbie was relaxed and looked very elegant. The waiter opened the wine while they sat for a while in an awkward silence.

Debbie kicked it off by holding up her glass.

"Here's to a successful sale, and may you find a lovely new home."

Scott clicked her glass, and they sipped the wine.

"Depending on how things go, maybe you can help me with that one too."

"This is a very good Pinot. Do you have any immediate plans?"

"Not really. I'm sending out my résumé, but my heart isn't in it. Too much disturbing stuff has gone on for me to pretend everything is normal. I guess eventually I'll settle down and get a new life going for us."

"I'm curious as to what happened, but please don't go into it if it's too painful."

Scott paused and drank deeply from his red wine.

"It's pretty embarrassing and not something I'm proud of, because I had a part in everything that happened."

"Well, if you think it will help to talk about it, I'm a good listener. Just so you know, you're not alone. I can tell you about the embarrassing mess I wound up in. Tell me yours, and I'll tell you mine."

"Here's the short version. My marriage was failing, so I had an affair. At the same time my boss and my wife were also having an affair. They conspired to hire an employee to seduce me. She subsequently used our relationship to get a big settlement for sexual harassment. It was a scam. I got divorced and was fired in short order. She ran off with the money. Somehow, a couple of local thugs got the idea that my wife had a lot of money, and that resulted in a home invasion robbery, during which, she had a heart attack and died. That's most of it. It sounds like some soap opera, but it was deadly serious. The robbers are now deceased, and Amy and I are starting fresh."

"Oh my God! I'm sorry. That must have been hard on Amy. She seems like such a nice young woman."

"She's been my touchstone throughout this mess. I figure if I can do right by her, maybe I'll salvage some karma."

Debbie drained her glass, and Scott poured another.

"I got married to my true love in college. We finished school, and he wanted to go on to law school. I worked my tail off, and he eventually passed the bar. We married and had two boys. He worked as a public defender for several years, and everything was fine for a while. Then he went into private practice as a criminal defense attorney. Eventually he wound up with one big client, a Colombia-based drug gang. He never told me about this, or the fact that they were paying him off in cash with drug money and high-grade cocaine. It all lasted for a couple years, and then things fell apart. He became more and more erratic, and it was obvious that he was addicted to something. He was abusive and lying so badly he couldn't fool a child. One night, local police and the DEA showed up at our door. It turned out he was loaded out of his mind and getting a hand job from his girlfriend when he drove his car into a bridge abutment at

286

two in the morning, killing them both. There was a kilo of cocaine in the trunk. BATF wasn't far behind, and our bank accounts, house, and cars were all confiscated. I was out on the street with my sons. I just kept working, and the boys stuck it out, getting part-time jobs. It's been almost three years now. We have a nice apartment, the kids will be going to Community College soon, and life has moved on."

Scott sat looking at her for an unblinking moment, then he raised his hand to attract the waiter.

"I think we're going to need another bottle of wine here."

Debbie smiled warmly at Scott.

"We're quite a pair, aren't we?" she said.

"That must have been a terrible experience for you, but in a weird way, it made me feel better."

They laughed, toasted again, and ordered dinner. It was a long, enjoyable evening.

Scott parked in front of Debbie's apartment.

"I'd invite you in for coffee, but it looks like the boys are still up."

"I understand. I had a wonderful time tonight. Do you think we could do this again some time?"

Debbie kissed him softly on the cheek.

"Anytime."

Scott arrived home in a state of euphoria.

Amy was watching a late-night TV show. "How did it go?"

"Very nice. It was good to have a normal night out and relax. I needed it."

"How'd that lipstick get your cheek?"

CHAPTER

42

cott and Amy settled in for a pleasant drive out from Glendale and then north along the coast. Amy drove all the way.

"I get to pick the music this time."

"Okay, what am I in for?"

"Pink"

"Pink Floyd?"

"That's her name, Pink."

"Oh, okay."

They drove up the 101 until they found the turnoff for their destination. Los Olivos was a very small, pretty, wine-tourist town north of Santa Barbara. The main street was all of three blocks long, so calling it a village might be a better description. It boasted one nice hotel, a couple of restaurants, and some shops for the tourists. A sports car club was making

288

a day trip to the wine country, so parking was a challenge. Scott and Amy sat on the patio of a pleasant restaurant and wine shop across the street from the hotel.

"This is nice, such a pretty little place," Amy said.

"Did you ever wonder what it is like to live in a really small place like this?"

Amy looked around, "I think it's okay as long as a bigger place like Santa Barbara's not too far away."

"As I get older, I think a little differently. A half-hour drive in an ambulance is a long time when you are having a heart attack."

"Really? That's all you can think about in this nice little town?"

"Sad, isn't it? The hotel across the street used to be owned by a Hollywood actor. He played a cowboy in an old 'fifties TV series. He moved up here and got into the hotel and wine business. I think I'd prefer this to Hollywood myself. He died a while back."

"That's way out of my frame of reference."

"Are you ready to go?"

"I'm ready."

Scott took over driving the last couple miles on Highway 54 and turned onto a dirt road that ran through a vineyard. They pulled up in front of a huge metal barn and were greeted by a large man in work clothes. Scott's old friend Mark was a tall, robust guy, dressed in jeans and a flannel shirt. His face was browned by the sun, he had a bushy beard, and he wore a straw cowboy hat.

"Hey, Scott. Haven't seen you in an age!"

He held out a large calloused hand and smiled at Amy.

"Hi, Mark. This is my daughter, Amy."

"Nice to meet you Amy."

"Hi."

Amy couldn't help but smile at his infectious good will.

Scott asked, "Any place in particular?"

"Nah. Just pick any of these dirt roads and find your spot."

"You don't mind?"

"Absolutely not. Where do you think I'm going to wind up?" Mark laughed.

Scott and Amy got back into their car, drove down a maintenance road and up a small hill that overlooked the countryside planted with vines as far as they could see. Amy took out the urn and looked a little lost as to what to do next.

Scott said, "Do you want to say anything?"

"Not really. She knew I loved her. I like the idea of spreading her ashes in a vineyard. She did love her wine."

Scott thought for a minute. "I want to remember early on when we were happy. The good times, your birth, raising you, our laughter, and the love we had. I don't want to let the stuff that happened later on poison the good memories. Most importantly, she gave me you."

Amy looked at Scott and took the lid off the urn. She gently spread the ashes over the ground.

"I want to say goodbye, but I feel stupid talking to a pile of ashes."

"Don't worry, she would have appreciated this."

Amy's tears started to run, and Scott was ready with a pack of tissues.

They drove back to the winery and found Mark.

"Thank you so much, Mark. This was a nice thing for you to do. How was the harvest this year?"

"Come on into the tasting room and judge for yourself."

Mark looked Amy and said, "Amy, how old are you?"

"Sixteen."

"What? Twenty-one? That's what I thought. Have you ever had any late-harvest dessert wine?"

They tasted Mark's excellent wines and spent an hour chatting. Mark suddenly got serious and looked at Scott as if he'd made up his mind.

"I have had trouble getting more than local distribution for my wines. I'd like to start a nationwide campaign, expand my customer base, and maybe even rope in some of the big-box stores. How would you like to work for me and take that job on?"

Scott was stunned.

"That sounds like something I'd really enjoy."

Amy looked at Scott. "Do I get a vote?"

Exhaustion had set in; it had been a very long, emotionally draining day. They stopped at a coffee place and got some lattes to perk them up on the way home.

Back on the road, Scott looked over and saw that Amy was awake.

"What do you think about Mark's offer? I could do most of the work from home, but there would also be some business trips. We could stay in Glendale, and you could keep your friends."

"I really like it. I think you'd do a great job."

"I want to ask you about something else. The other night when I was out with Debbie, we really clicked, had a lot in common. She impressed me."

"I could tell."

"It seems so soon after Dana's death, but I'd like to see her again. What do you think about that?"

Amy smiled at him. "Go for it."

"That's my girl."

"You can stop saying that any time you want."

ACKNOWLEDGEMENTS

I would like to thank everyone who has helped me with my writing and generously contributing their suggestions and support in the writing of this novel.

Carol and Ron Brusha, Barbara Nicoll, Peggy Constantine, Leslie Elmore, Marie Fish, Nello Iacono, John Peter Kousakis, Margie Manos, Rosemary Montana, Kerry Morford, Laurel Patric, Lee Roberts, Russ Siverling, Randy Shaughter, Dottie and Rob Sharkey and Greg Wessels.